Cruel Charade

by

Alana Lorens

Cover Art by *Kristian Norris*

The Wild Rose Press, Inc.
PO Box 708
Adams Basin, NY 14410-0708
Visit us at www.thewildrosepress.com

Publishing History
First Edition, 2024
Trade Paperback ISBN 978-1-5092-5639-6
Digital ISBN 978-1-5092-5640-2

Published in the United States of America

Dedication

This book is dedicated to women with chronic illness, who often go years without proper diagnosis, with doctors who don't believe them, and their ongoing fight to educate themselves and those around them. May they have their best lives in the end.

Acknowledgments

Special thanks to Greg A. Agosti of Agosti Emergency Preparedness Solutions, LLC, and Steve Marshall, firefighter extraordinaire, for information about arson investigations and connected police work. Also the staff at the Everglades National Park who conferred with me on location of trail cameras and the like.

Thanks to the crowd-sourced suggestion, from WAX-West Asheville Exchange, for Richard's snooty drink at the 94th Aero Squadron—David Harris, Jeremiah Jackson and James Brennan agreed on Pappy van Winkle 23. Bravo!

A thank-you to the judge who sent me home the day I went into labor in court, just like Bet. Even if the shouting, "Get out! Get out!" was a little disturbing.

Always a pleasure working with my editor, Ally Robertson. Here's to another successful collaboration.

Finally, thank you, thank you, thank you!!! to the Area One Pennwriters critique groups, both Fellowship of the Quill and Meadville Vicinity Pennwriters, who regularly review my work, provide thoughtful commentary and support one another as we all work along the path to our chosen avocation of writing. I couldn't do this without you.

Prologue

Head spinning. Heart racing.

Wet. I'm WET. Mud on my hands and face. They hurt.

She pushed herself, sitting upright. *Dark. Dizzy.* Nothing looked familiar. Her breaths came faster and faster and she thought she'd pass out.

Can't have a panic attack now…

Hyacinth's voice whispered from that safe place inside Bet's mind. "Calm down, Bet. Five things you can see."

Tall grass. Moon overhead. A silhouetted car some ten feet away. A pool of water in the other direction. Large birds flying overhead.

"Four things you can touch."

Sucking mud, both hands covered with it. My hair, sticky with something. Reeds. She pulled up her hand as something squiggled past it. *Whatever that was.*

"Three things you can hear."

Keening of insects. A lot of them. Bird calls. A deep bass sound like a growl.

"Two things you can smell."

Brackish smell of standing water. Smoke, like something's been burnt.

"One thing you can taste."

Coppery taste, sharp. Blood.

She gradually realized she was thoroughly soaked.

I've got to move. The water wasn't deep, halfway up her legs. Warm. Full of living things that swam and crawled around her. A snake slithered past, its scales scraping her naked calf. With a scream, she was on her feet.

The moonlight illuminated her surroundings. Grass. Water. More grass. Her feet squished slowly into the swamp.

"Fuck. I'm in the Everglades."

How did I even get here? Where's my... The car. Was it hers? She reoriented herself and sloshed her way through six inches of water to the silhouette. The closer she got, the stronger the burnt smell became. When she was close enough to touch the sedan, she found the passenger door radiated heat. Using the hem of her skirt to protect her hand, she wrenched it open.

The smell of burnt flesh gagged her, and she turned away to vomit into the nearest shock of tall grass. *Who is that? Why are they in my car? And why are they dead?*

My flashlight's in the glove box. I need it.

She took several deep, shuddering breaths, envisioning Hyacinth's quiet office, feeling that good Spanish leather under her hand, the scent of diffused lavender in the air. *I can do this.*

Pinching her nose closed with her left hand, she inched into the open doorway, staring up at the stars, right hand questing for the latch. The glove box popped open and she reached in. The only thing inside was a gun. She snatched her hand back.

This isn't my car.

What the hell is happening?

The sight of her outstretched hand in the moonlight caught her attention. It was bubbly and red. Gaze following her arm upward, it, too, was burnt, the shadows melting into her skin. *How can I not feel that? It looks—*

And then she could feel it. As her shock wore off, she felt the destruction of her hand and her arm and her leg and her body. She screamed into the night.

I was in the car I was in the car I was in the car

Someone tried to kill me.

Her thoughts spiraled out of control. She stumbled away from the sedan, reaching desperately for that mental picture of her therapist's room, her chair, that comfort. She couldn't find it. She tripped over a mangrove root and fell with a splash. Reeling and unsteady, she shoved herself up against one of the vertical shafts of the mangrove, her back to the trunk, bark digging into her skin, then closed her eyes.

She fought to control her shuddering breath, knowing she would not rein in her thoughts until she could. "Five things…" she began again, but she couldn't concentrate through the pain.

Maybe it's just my time to die.

No. No, I can't accept that. Won't.

But her breathing cycled faster and faster until at last the blackness around her became the blackness within.

Chapter One

May 16, 1996

"Hey, lady."

Fuzzy, half-awake. *Am I in heaven or hell?*

"Hey. What happened here?" Someone shook her injured shoulder.

The sharp pain brought her around fast. "Ow! Don't touch me!"

"Sorry. I thought you were dead!"

So did I.

She opened her eyes. Still in the Everglades. Light now. It must be morning. She examined her limbs and found them raw and blistered. Her skirt was ruined, torn and full of mud. Her expensive matching jacket—where had it gone? She tried to put it all out of her mind. *At least for now.*

Someone spoke. "Chet, there's a body in here, man. It's dead! Gross."

The young man in front of her, presumably Chet, looked over at his blue-jeaned friend standing by the blackened hulk, where the driver's door stood open. Chet's eyes widened. "Holy crap, lady, were you in there? You look terrible."

She took in the scene. The two young men, who appeared just older than her daughter Jane, *maybe seventeen?* dressed casually in jeans and sleeveless shirts. Two fishing poles lay on the ground nearby. The sun was halfway up in the sky. A dirt trail headed off from the rear of the car to the…east, she guessed by the position of the sun.

"Should we call 911?" Chet asked. His tanned face wrinkled with concern.

She started to say yes, then wondered if someone—*that* someone—would hear the emergency radio call and realize they'd failed.

"No! Can you take me home?" Her voice rasped. Maybe she'd breathed in the smoke. *Of course I did.* She tried to avoid looking at the car.

"Uh." Chet looked at his friend. "We were gonna catch some fish, but…" The friend nodded. "Okay. Can you pay for gas, though? Cause we just had enough to get here and back."

"Where's 'here'?"

Chet frowned. "Sisal Pond."

"And that is?" She winced as sunlight fell on the burns. It stung like hell.

Chet's friend said, "Well, you musta drove here. In the car, right? Driver's seat is empty, and you're here."

Her jaw set in irritation. "I did not. It's not my car."

"Huh," he said.

She looked to Chet. "Where's your car?"

"Down the path five minutes. It's a pickup."

I need a hospital, is what I need. But I can't. Right now I just have to get out of the sun. And away from here. Away from…death.

Chet's friend said, "Wait. If you weren't driving, then you didn't set the fire? Were you in the car? Who did, then? Why?" He glanced around nervously. "Are they still around?"

She rubbed her teeth together, trying not to cry out. The pain chased thought out. "Chet, I need to leave. Now. I can pay you for gas when I get home and something else for the trouble. Are you interested or not?"

He stepped back, clearly having second thoughts, but finally held out a hand.

"Ah, sure. Come on."

Chet's friend had already started down the dirt road, muttering. Bet took Chet's hand and let him pull her to a standing position. Sometime in the night she'd lost a shoe. *I've never been this vulnerable in my life. I just want it all to go away.*

Wondering if any of her belongings were left in the car, she stopped and looked inside, avoiding the sight of the dead body. Neither her phone nor her purse were in evidence. Or her shoe. *Damn it.*

She blanked her mind to as much as she could, leaning on Chet's shoulder to limp along. Before too long, she slid onto the passenger seat of a beat-up F150, and then they were driving. It seemed to take forever to leave the river of grass, but they came to the Park's Main Gate and headed out.

Chet dropped his friend and the poles in Homestead, just off Krome Avenue, where a design of decorative cement flowers had been set into the street in the very center of town. Bet half-noticed as Chet drove past.

He asked, "Where we goin', anyway?"

"Coral Gables. By the University."

"You sure you wouldn't rather go to the hospital? James Archer is up the road a couple blocks. Or another up the road, if you don't want to stay close to…ah, you know."

"No." She huddled near the door, shivering. It wasn't cold. She must be going into shock again. *I've got to get far enough away that They can't find me. Whoever They are.*

"Okay, whatever you say." He turned up the next cross street and took the Turnpike Extension north.

A terrible itching started. Small red bumps over what wasn't charred… *Definitely torn up by mosquitoes. Damn. Damn.*

But how am I not dead? I must have, what, got out the door somehow, not in time to keep me safe, but better than…and who was that?

I've got to quit thinking about it for now. It will drive me mad.

Bet drowsed, leaning against the door. The car came to a stop. She eyed the terra-cotta building in front of her. "This isn't Coral Gables."

"No, it's not." Chet didn't look a bit perturbed. "It's Baptist Hospital in Kendall. My mom's a nurse, and you need to be here." He ripped a piece of paper and wrote something on it, and handed it to her. "Here's my address. Mail me gas money."

An orderly knocked on the window. "You need help?"

"She does," Chet said. "Take her in, now. Goodbye, mystery lady."

The orderly opened the door, his eyes widening as he took in her appearance. He grabbed a wheelchair and helped her sit in it. Then he took her inside.

She eyed the others waiting in the lobby with a full-on suspicion. No reason to believe they were Them, but she didn't hold out much charity for anyone right now. *Maybe Chet. If I can get out of here safely.*

The triage worker at the window didn't reassure her.

"What are we…oh." The middle-aged Latina's hand went to her mouth as she took in the extent of the blisters. "How long ago did—this—happen?" She waved a manicured pink nail in the direction of the wheelchair.

She squirmed in the chair, her wounded leg still burning. "Last night. I think."

One eyebrow went up. "You think?" She started typing on her keyboard. When she got no reply, she shrugged slightly and went on. "Name?"

Bet was caught off guard for only a moment. "Josephine…March." *Does anyone read* Little Women *anymore? Let's hope not.*

"Address?"

She gave the number and street of the branch courthouse in Coconut Grove.

"Insurance card?"

"I don't have it. I—I lost my purse."

"In the accident?"

Nothing accidental about it, goddamn it. "Uh, yeah."

"We can call the police for you, if you'd like to make a report."

"No, thank you."

"Your pain level now? On a scale of 1 to 10?"

Bet laughed dryly. "It's worse than usual, if that's what you mean." She took a moment to consider her chronic muscle and joint pain with the new pain from the burns. Opening up to it washed her in a wave of hurt. "About 8, I guess."

The woman stared, then shrugged. She took a quick temperature, blood pressure, and pulse ox, and notated her findings in her electronic file. "Take her to the burn room. I'll call the plastics man on duty."

Plastics… surgery? Was it that bad? She hadn't let herself move down that path yet. All her effort so far had been to get herself safe. That involved holding on tightly to her mental state. Definitely no dwelling on implications, not yet. Once she opened the door to her fear, it would run rampant over all her carefully controlled emotions. But just thinking about not thinking about it, of course, brought it to the forefront.

The orderly pushed the wheelchair to a treatment room, waiting lackadaisically while she moved onto the white paper sheets of the ER bed, then he strolled off through the plastic curtain.

Who tried to kill me? Did they do it themselves? Send someone else with dirty hands?

The steady beep from the next curtained area grabbed her wandering attention, and she held onto it like a lifeline as her suppositions spiraled out over the next half hour. Two years she'd worked as a criminal defense attorney now, two years' worth of "innocent until proven guilty." The "proven" part haunted her sometimes. She'd won the freedom of numerous accused who she believed fairly strongly had deserved their anticipated punishment.

Those ones you never asked the question: Did you do it? It was better not to know.

Someone unhappy with their representation? Maybe.

Someone unhappy because her representation got someone off? Maybe.

Someone from the Metro-Dade police department, where a client of Bet's had testified against two officers and had them fired for misconduct. *At my urging. And*

I'm sure they know it. And they don't forget things like that.

And whose was that charred body?

The curtain was shoved back and a Black woman in blue blazer and slacks came in, clipboard in hand. She stared at Bet first, dark eyes piercing over the top of her cheaters, then she sniffed, cleared her throat, and looked at her paperwork.

"I'm Tasha, from Social Services, here to make sure your care proceeds smoothly, Miss…ah, March." Her eyes narrowed. "Jo March? Really?"

Bet tried like hell to keep a straight face. "My mother was a reader."

"Mmm-hmm." *Said in that snarkily judgmental way that only a Black woman can.* She paused, obviously waiting for something more. Bet didn't give it.

"Well then. Our records show you haven't been at this hospital before, so I'll need to go over the demographics. You also declared no insurance. Who will be covering the bill for this treatment?"

"I'll handle it."

"I can offer financial assistance through the hospital if… You'll have to qualify through our income scales."

"Not necessary." Bet squirmed, the pain solidifying. "What I need… Is there a doctor in our near future? Or at least some water?"

Tasha tapped a pen on her clipboard. "Let me see if you're allowed to have water." She pursed her lips and stepped out.

Bet took a deep breath. Tasha's once-over look had reminded her she'd been lying in a swamp half the night. She slid off the bed, kicked off her remaining shoe, and went to the small sink. Taking a handful of paper towels, she soaked them in warm water and painfully washed the smears of mud off her legs and arms. A tear ran down her cheek, and it burned.

"My face, too?" she muttered. A mirrored medicine cabinet hung opposite. She steeled herself, then took a peek. Her right cheek was pocked with red blisters. "Damn it to hell." Even her hair hung with a ragged, blackened edge where it must have come in contact with the flames. The rest was a tangled red-gold rats' nest. She wished for a comb. *No, what I want is my purse. Where the hell is it? What's someone doing with my credit cards and my ID right now?* She ran her fingers through what she could, trying to repair her appearance, doing anything to avoid thinking about the pain. Tossing the dirty towels, she got another handful and cleaned her face around the injured skin. When she'd finished, she sat on the bed, much too impatiently waiting.

Do I really need to be here? I've got cold water, drugs and gauze at home. She stared at her bare right foot. A six-inch long wound lay along the top of her instep, deep red. It looked like the center had peeled out, leaving a slimy, sickly yellow mess. Another similar area graced her outer calf. Her right forearm was the worst. Beet red and spotted with oozing blisters.

So I must have moved my leg out of the fire more quickly than my hand. Or my hand was closer, maybe draped over the center console… next to that corpse…

She shuddered and tried to steer her thoughts away from the pain, which seemed to have increased as she took in the damage.

"I can't waste any more time here." She got off the bed, crying out in pain as she inadvertently pulled at her injuries. She reached for the curtain, which was yanked

11

from her hand by a dark-haired man in a white coat. His nametag read "Dr. Giamo Rimon."

He smiled, his imperfect teeth giving him a homely look. "Leaving already?" He continued in, making her retreat toward the bed.

"I-I figured you were too busy and I could deal with this myself." The panic bubbled up again and she fought to keep it at bay.

"Nonsense. It's why we're here." He waited for her to be reseated, then reached for blue gloves from a box on the wall. "Let's take a look, shall we?"

Oh, Lordy, the imperial "we." Trust me, dude, I've already looked. Nothing exciting.

She studied the man, finding him compelling. He wasn't great-looking but he projected warmth. *And I do like his eyes...*

He gestured that she should lay back, then he examined her foot. He followed the damage trail upward, finally touching her cheek with a gentle hand. "This doesn't seem like it happened in a kitchen fire." He eyed her curiously.

Yeah, no kidding. I never said that's what happened, either. "You haven't seen me cook."

He chuckled. "True. Best practices for treatment will come from an honest reveal of how the injury happened."

She frowned. "It's a burn. It came from a fire. Can you fix it or not?"

He went to a drawer and pulled out a tray, which he laid on the rolling hospital table. "I want to help you. What you say to me stays here. You don't have to worry about—"

"Yeah, but it doesn't. People can subpoena records.

Medical reports can be hacked. Can't we just leave it where it is?"

"It sounds like you're in some kind of trouble. I just want to help."

She held up a hand. "I understand what you're saying. I do. But I don't need to be saved."

"Have it your way. I'm not here to force anything on you. You're the one who came here, remember? You can make it as difficult as you want, but we have our duty of care. If I don't carry through, there are plenty of lawyers who will come after my license."

Bet tried not to flinch. "Yeah, lawyers suck."

He studied her. "Indeed." He opened the sealed covering on the tray, revealing the instruments and dressing necessary for burn treatment. "Now, may I treat you?"

His tone was just north of speaking to a child. Bet wanted to be annoyed, but she knew she'd caused his hesitancy. *All I want is for the pain to stop. And for people to stop trying to kill me.* "Yes, please."

"Good." He examined the burns on her foot more thoroughly, every touch making her moan. "You're lucky. Most of this is still blistered. We won't have to scrub it."

She shuddered. "It already hurts. A lot." Her throat caught. Tears scalded her eyes. The pain extended past the wounded areas into the rest of her body, her muscles and tendons. *Well, of course. I haven't had my regular meds for twenty-four hours. Within another twelve, I expect I'll be flat in bed.* She tried to relax, taking deep breaths as he poked her skin and applied some sort of cold medicine that actually seemed to soothe the pain.

"I'm sure." He kept working.

She stared at the white matte ceiling and the bright, bright lights overhead. "Doesn't a nurse usually do this?"

Dr. Rimon chuckled. "As a matter of fact." He finished wrapping her foot in gauze, and then got out another tray, moving up to her arm and hand.

"And you're here…why?"

"The nursing staff was a little concerned when you weren't forthcoming with an explanation." He winked at her. "Maybe they thought I looked more like someone who'd get a confession."

Startled at his humorous candor, she looked at him, then actually laughed. "I see."

He held her hand up to the light, studying the damage to her forearm. "These got scraped a bit. Hang tight." He sprayed her arm with an anesthetic, then carefully debrided the area. Even with the spray, the work was agonizing.

She whimpered, inwardly kicking herself for revealing her vulnerability. *I deal with pain every day. This shouldn't be something I can't handle.*

"You can scream if you want," he said. "But I'd take it as a personal kindness if you didn't punch me."

His smile showed he was teasing. She considered both alternatives, then just bit her lip and breathed deeply.

The curtain pulled open and a tall Black man entered, his white lab coat immaculate. "Someone called for a plastics consult?"

Dr. Rimon stepped away and spoke to the new doctor *sotto voce*, which irritated Bet. Surely, they were sharing secrets about her, and her reticence. *And my likely involvement in something nefarious.*

The new doctor strode across the room, took her

chin in his hand and tipped her head to the side. Bet closed her eyes as the top light glared right into them. Then he let go and studied her arm. He wasn't as gentle as Rimon, and the tug on her burned skin made her cry out.

"Agreed," he said to Dr. Rimon. He nodded to Bet. "Looks like you got off easy. If you follow instructions, most of this should heal just fine." He reached in his pocket and handed her a card. "If you want to have some work done to make sure there's no trace, give me a call." He stepped back, nodded to Dr. Rimon and walked out.

"Nice bedside manner," Bet said.

"Everyone can't be as charming as me." Dr. Rimon continued his debride, then laid a thick layer of ointment on her hand and arm. A third tray came from the drawer, and he carefully patched over her facial wounds. "What kind of work do you do?"

"Not relevant." She felt like an asshole, but self-protection was supreme at the moment.

He gave her an exasperated look. "I was going to write you an excuse, limiting duties, and so on."

"Oh." *Now who's the one being irrationally obstructive?* "I…ah. I won't need that. It's not an issue."

"No problem. How's the pain now?"

"Pretty bad." She hesitated. The beep of the monitor stopped in the next room. The doctor didn't seem to notice, but Bet wondered if the person had left or had died.

"All right. You can take some ibuprofen for that, 800 milligrams every eight hours."

Bet laughed out loud, and then covered her mouth quickly with her other hand.

"That's amusing?" He studied her, brow furrowed.

"It is, actually. I haven't used ibuprofen for a couple of years now. Doesn't touch my situation." As he opened his mouth, presumably to offer her acetaminophen or naproxen, she cut him off. "I have chronic pain and a whole regimen for it. Including Vicodin. I actually take so many anti-inflammatories, I can't take any additional over-the-counter stuff."

He stepped back. "I see. So what you're saying is, you've got this covered?"

"Yes." Her stomach sank as reality hit. "No, wait. Not really. My purse, it had all my meds and it's lost now." Coming up against her missing purse and its contents and all the trouble she'd have replacing it, a wave of anxiety came over her, and the tears began.

He handed her a box of tissues. His eyes were kind. "Sure you don't want to report that to the police?"

"I…can't. I can't explain right now."

"What I can do is give you something strong for pain while you're here. Then you contact your pain management team to get refills or whatever else you need. Is that fair?"

Relieved, she almost hugged him. "Thank you. Thank you so much…for understanding. My life is…let's just say it's a little hard to believe at the moment."

"Miss March, I hope you come to terms with whatever it is. Something tells me you will." He nodded. "I'd like to give you antibiotics as well, to stave off any infections while your injuries heal. I'd prefer to give it as an injection." Though he'd made a statement, there was certainly the hint of a question in that.

Guess I can't be surprised. "Sure. I'm not a complete idiot, you know." She found herself smiling, just a little.

"I never suspected you were, Miss March." He chuckled. "I'll have a nurse come with the meds and instructions."

"Is there…is there a phone I could use? Mine's…well. I have to call someone to pick me up."

"Let me have someone bring one for you. Take care of yourself." He paused on his way out. "Listen, if you get to a point you need to talk about…things, my name and extension will be on your instructions. I don't do this for patients as a rule—well, never—but if you don't have anyone to speak with, you can call me."

That was a first. Bet smiled through her tears. "That's really kind of you, Doctor."

He winked and left the room.

The rest of the hour she spent was routine paperwork and waiting, waiting and more waiting. She called her best friend, Mela Silvani, a former client who had also become her part-time assistant. Mela would take her home.

Mela met her under the brick emergency room portico. Dodging ambulances and other patient drop-offs, she parked her small SUV long enough to come around, long floral skirt flying in the wind, to open the passenger door. The slightly built Cuban expatriate shuddered when she saw Bet in all her bandaged glory.

"What in all the hells happened to you? Where are your shoes? Where is your car? Bettina…" Looking her up and down, Mela burst into sympathetic tears. "Come here." She opened her arms and pulled Bet into them.

"Ow! Ow… Not so tight." Bet struggled to contain her own tears. *Good God, it's been a morning performing like some daytime drama queen with all the weeping. Knock it off.* "I'll be fine. I think. Can we please just get out of here?"

"I'm so sorry…of course, *mi amor.*" Mela stepped back.

Bet got into the car, sniffling. She wiped her face before Mela sat in the drivers' seat. "You still have your keys to my place, right?"

"Yes." Mela pursed her lips. "But I'm not using them until you tell me what's going on here." She pulled away into the parking lot and then made a left on busy Kendall Drive.

Damn. Mela was just stubborn enough to make that stick, too. I'll have to tell her.

"All right. You asked for it. But you can't tell anyone. Any one. Period."

Mela shot her a sidewise glance. "What did you do?"

"Oh, *chica*, I have no idea. Honestly."

Bet told her everything she remembered from the moment she woke in the swamp. Mela listened in shocked silence, nearly hitting the car in front of her a couple times, so distracted was she by the story. She finished just as Mela pulled into the driveway of Bet's pale pink brick Coral Gables home. Bet's green Jaguar XJ6 sat there, in front of the closed garage door, perfectly innocent.

"So until I get a handle on who did this, I've got to lay low. I'll just go inside, shut the door, keep the lights off and tread water. Whoever it was will show their hand at some point."

"But the police—"

"Mela, for all I know the cops are in on it. Or a client. Or…" *A State's attorney, or my ex-husband or…Damn. Let's open a phone book, close our eyes and point out someone.* "Please?"

Mela's face was pale. She chewed her lip. "Did you call Rich?"

"Hell, no."

"Maybe you should hide at my place?"

"I don't want you in the line of fire, kid. I'm responsible for enough trauma around the county already." She patted Mela's arm. "Just let me in. We can have a glass of wine. I've got to get my meds, and report the credit cards missing and all the things."

"I can help with that." Mela reached in her glove compartment for a small candy tin, which she held out to Bet. "Your key's in here. I'm going to park around the corner." She eyed Bet. "But I'm coming back. And you'd better open the door for me. Or I'll let everyone in the neighborhood know right where you are."

Bet smiled. "You know, this is the only normal conversation I've had all day. Come on up and we'll start sorting this out." She leaned over and hugged Mela, wincing as the stretch pulled at her bandaged injuries. "You're the best."

"But I wouldn't be, if you hadn't saved me. I still owe you. Now, go."

Bet pushed herself out of the car, stepping on a sharp rock with her bare foot. "Damn it. Can't I get a break here? Just one?" She limped up to the door, and let herself in, hoping she and Mela could get her life back together.

Chapter Two

May 13, 1995
One year earlier

Bettina stumbled out the side door of the Barracuda Taphouse, straining to focus fuzzy eyes. Leaning against the side of the building, she muttered to herself.

I only took my attention off that pina colada for a minute. Someone dosed it. I've got to get straight. Now.

But she couldn't. Her knees threatened to mutiny and drop her on the pavement. Music pulsed through the wall behind her. She started to spin out of control.

Five things. "Street lights. Blue Lexus. Palm trees. Lady with a purse. Man with a purse."

Should it bother me that his is nicer?

She straightened her back against the bricks, her fingers scrabbling in the grooves for a handhold. Her eyes closed and the spinning got worse. She forced them open again.

Four things. "Bricks. Space between bricks." She tapped her expensive shoe on the ground. "Sidewalk." She didn't dare let go to touch anything else. Her arm rubbed against hard plastic discs down her side. "Midnight blue sequins." Her new blouse that screamed *take me home to bed, stranger.*

Three things. "Um…traffic. Drums. Horns beeping."

Was her breathing easier? She thought so.

Two things. "Cigarette smoke." She cast an envious glance at the couple standing half a block up with cancer sticks in hand. "Diesel fuel."

One thing. She couldn't taste anything at first. Whatever was in her system had taken over. Then bile swirled in her stomach and rose to the back of her throat. Burning, it made its way out as she vomited into a potted plant.

Now isn't that a lovely picture. Up-and-coming criminal defense attorney ralphing al fresco *like a common street drunk.*

She wiped her mouth and faced the wall, drooping against it, one hand propping her up.

The door she'd come out of flew open. "Bet? Oh my God, what are you doing?" Mela grabbed her arm. "Are you all right?"

"Nope," Bet replied. "I surely am not. Someone dosed me. I think it was that suave Nicaraguan." Her stomach roiled and she threw up again.

"The one with the haircut? You think so?" Mela rubbed Bet's back. "Come on, let's get out of here before a *Herald* reporter shows up. That's all you need is for Rich to have proof you're unfit."

Bet reared upward with a scowl. "I'm not unfit. I don't have the children in my custody, do I? He won that round, damn it."

Her head felt clearer.

"Fine, let's go anyway, okay? Senor Pendejo will figure out where you went soon enough. Do you want to go to the ER?" Mela tugged on her arm.

"Who wants to go to the ER ever? Yeah, no." Another wave of dizziness rocked her. *Fuck you, jerk.*

Probably should go to ER. Don't have the patience right now. "I'll just go home to bed. Maybe it'll cover up the pain and I'll actually get some sleep tonight."

"If you say so. Good thing I drove. Come on."

Bet let herself be dragged along to the parking lot, stumbling on her platforms. *I only let you drive because I figured someone would sweep me off my feet. I wanted to dance, so sue me. I miss dancing. I miss someone thinking I'm special. Looking for Mr. Goodbar, dontcha know. I can do the walk of shame as well as anyone.*

I'm damned tired of being lonely.

But drugs are not fair. Screw you, Senor Pendejo.

Mela drove her home, took her keys and let them in, then undressed her and sent her to the bathroom to clean up.

Moving felt like slow motion. She studied her failed makeup in the extra-large mirror, the melted mascara making her look like Alice Cooper on a hot Saturday night. Three wipes later, she'd scrubbed most of it away. *I worked so hard on those damned cat eyes...and it was a total waste.*

Weaving on her feet, she slid open the glass shower door, then paused. All she could picture was her passing out and going right through that glass. "Shower can wait until morning," she muttered.

Her new burgundy-colored nightgown hung on the back of the door. It was low-cut and fit her curves beautifully. It awaited her conquest of Mr. Goodbar.

"Fuck it. I'm wearing it anyway."

She slipped on the silk-and-lace confection, with a little sigh as the slick fabric soothed its way across her hips. Imagining herself emerging from the bathroom in triumph, rather than with an aching head from her evening dose of stupidity, she sashayed over to her king-sized bed. Of course she misjudged the distance and slammed her shin into the metal frame.

"Goddamn it!"

Mela came into the bedroom with a cup of chamomile, and flipped on the small glass light next to the bed. "Are you going to be all right?"

Bet tumbled into bed and climbed under the thick, peach-colored comforter, grateful for the heavy dose of AC coming across her forehead. She stared at the ceiling, still feeling the remnants of the roofie.

"Mela, why does God hate me?"

Mela smoothed the comforter and smiled. "I don't think it's 'hate,' exactly. But you do have a way of getting on people's nerves. Karma, you know."

Only Mela could get away with saying that right now.

"Okay, then. Why do my kids hate me?"

"They don't hate you." Mela straightened up the bedroom, hanging up clothes that lay on the chairs and the floor. "They only live with Rich because he has all the toys. And their home they've grown up in."

"They do hate me. Hell, *I* hate me. My body's consuming itself and I hate that, too." Tears welled up in her eyes.

Mela finished her fidgety straightening and came over to the bedside. She leaned down and kissed Bet's forehead. "Well, *I* love you."

Bet caught Mela's hand and squeezed it. "You're prejudiced."

"Nonsense. You'll be fine. Now get some sleep."

Mela switched off the light and went out, leaving the door halfway open. The sound of glass and silverware clinking came from the kitchen. *She's washing my damned dishes. I'm a total waste of oxygen.* Disgusted, Bet turned to her other side and pulled the covers over her head.

Chapter Three

May 17, 1996
Present Day

Bet woke at noon in an empty house.

Mela had left a note on the bedside table. *Going to open the office so it seems like business as usual. Sleep as late as you want and don't worry!!!*

Good for Mela. That made sense.

Bet eased her way out of bed and limped to the bathroom. Pain settled into her muscles as gravity hit. The bandages reflected in the mirror depressed her. For just a second, she wondered if she'd be happier if her attacker had succeeded.

Now wouldn't Hyacinth find that interesting...

She did what she needed to and washed half her face, grumbling at the discomfort of the burned skin as she moved her arm. *Shut up! You're not dead. That's the part that counts.* Wincing as her hip stretched, stabbing her sacroiliac like an ice pick, she took her hairbrush and climbed back into bed. She flicked on the local news with the remote, muting the sound and adding closed captions. *Never know who's listening.*

The newscaster was talking about the multiple candidates in the Miami-Dade Mayor's race, with Suarez and Ferre still trying to prove they should get back in the seat. Penelas and Teele were coming in close in polls.

All the excitement would come to a head in September in the election.

Bet brushed her long hair thoroughly. Two washings in the shower the night before, bandages protected by layers of plastic wrap, had finally removed the smoke smell. She'd taken the shower in the dark. They'd turned on no lights, doing everything by candlelight behind a few drawn curtains. If all the curtains were closed, it might have raised suspicion if anyone was watching.

Listen to you. If they're listening. If they're watching. If, if, if...

But she didn't know. And whoever it was had been deadly serious. Terrifying.

Distracted for a moment, she glanced up to see a caption: Body in Everglades car fire identified. She froze.

Breathe. Just breathe.

"Monroe County police have identified the burned body found in a car in the Everglades as Jackson Gutierrez, a Kendall architect. No motive in the killing has been determined as yet, but the police have a suspect based on evidence found at the scene. We'll bring you more as information comes in."

Evidence found at the scene? What the hell did that mean? What did I miss?

She mulled over the name of the victim, thinking it sounded familiar. Finally, the architect connection kicked in. Gutierrez had been a client of hers four or five years before, prior to her divorce. DUI. A few minutes' thought yielded more details—she'd pled him out into a first offenders' diversion program and the arrest had been wiped off his record.

So why him? And why me?

A cell phone's unfamiliar ring sounded from her nightstand. Puzzled, she leaned over to check it out. *Not my phone. Must be Mela's.* She hesitated, but then answered it. "Hello?"

"Bet, it's Mela. The police have called here a dozen times this morning looking for you. I told them you hadn't come in yet. What do you want me to do?"

"Looking for me? What the…" Her brain wouldn't process. She couldn't decide what to do. Did the evidence in the car implicate her somehow? Surely, if she was intended to perish in the fire, there'd be no point in planting anything that made her guilty.

A heavy knock sounded on her front door. "Someone's here!" she gasped. Her muscles tightened, all the way down, causing a wave of discomfort.

"It's probably them. They've been very insistent. Call me back after they're gone."

"No, Mela—" But she hung up before Bet could stop her. *Damn it.*

The knock came again.

Bet hobbled over to the window, hiding behind the curtain to peek out. Sure enough. Metro-Dade's finest. *Crap.*

The well-built Hispanic officer happened to look up and spotted her. He spoke to his overweight, balding partner and gestured at the window.

Knowing she was caught, Bet opened the window a few inches. "I'm not dressed. Give me a minute and I'll be there. Please?"

The officer nodded, and Bet closed the window again. She threw on a pair of jeans and a tank top from Goombay, then limped down the hall to face her fate.

She opened the door and stepped aside, inviting the

pair in. The foyer was small, with black and white terrazzo tiles, and seashell décor. There wasn't much room for the three of them.

"Bettina Lenard?" the first one asked. His voice held a hint of a Latino accent. He looked like a television cop, handsome and competent.

Bet nodded. "Can I help you?"

"I'm Metro-Dade detective Luis Ortiz, and this is my partner Robert Brown. We'd like to ask you a few questions."

"Of course. Let me get some coffee. Can I offer you some?" Hoping like hell she sounded nonchalant, she led the way to the kitchen, which had sage green walls and off-white cabinetry, with a wood-tiled floor. The towels and curtains were perfectly matched, thanks to Mela, who'd shopped all over the city to find them. The ever-thoughtful friend had also left the coffee on a timer, apparently—a fresh pot was waiting.

"That's not necessary, ma'am."

She gestured to the oval breakfast table, inviting them to sit, but they awkwardly remained standing. *That's probably a bad sign.* She took her own cup of black brew and sat at the end of the table facing them, and waited.

Ortiz cleared his throat. "Ma'am, I need to ask you some questions about a car found in the Everglades."

"Oh, yes. I saw that on the news. Tragic." She sipped her coffee, holding the cup with both hands to keep from shaking.

"Can I ask, where were you last night?"

She hadn't prepared an answer for this. *Who'd have guessed the police would be on it so quickly? Chet or his buddy must have called them as soon as we left the scene.*

She took another sip of coffee to buy some thinking time. "Am I suspected of something?"

The partner gave her the hairy eyeball, but Ortiz remained calm.

"We're just checking out our leads. So, your whereabouts last night?"

Her underarms filled with sweat. "I'd rather not say."

"I see. Do you know Jack Gutierrez? The body found in the car?"

That one she could answer with honesty, within ethical bounds. "He was a client of mine a few years ago. An architect, right?"

"Yes, ma'am. Can you think of a reason why anyone would want to hurt Mr. Gutierrez?"

She shook her head, wincing as the movement pulled at the taped gauze. "He seemed like a nice enough fellow to me. We didn't know each other well."

"You appear to be injured." He leaned forward, looking at her bare—and bandaged—foot. "How did that happen?"

"I had an accident. Burned myself."

"Burned. I see." The partner, standing behind Ortiz, scribbled on his pad. "Did that happen here, in the house?" He glanced around, perhaps looking for traces of a fire.

Her heart pounded. *Surely he can hear that. Damn it. Why is it they can't always catch the guilty ones, but the innocent ones are just pinned down, looking guilty as hell?* "No."

Ortiz cut off his partner, who'd opened his mouth to speak. "Ms. Lenard, we know who you are. I'm sure you can run circles around us with the avoidance techniques you lawyers like to use. The next thing, I'd offer to take you down to the station, and then you'd call your husband—"

"*Ex*-husband," she interrupted.

"Ex-husband Richard Lenard, and then it would make the news, and everyone would be unhappy." He smiled in a way that seemed legitimate. *Could he be trying to help me?*

Stop it, Bet. He's a cop. A Metro cop. He knows what happened with his buddy who got fired. He's not going to help you.

"Cut to the chase." She put the cup on the table and slid her trembling hands into her lap.

"All right. Your purse was found in the car, under the drivers' seat. Most of it was burned, but enough remained to clearly identify."

Fuck. I didn't look hard enough. That would have saved us a couple hours of phone calls last night. Ugh. "Oh."

"How do you suppose it got there?"

"I have no idea."

"No idea." He stopped just short of rolling his eyes, if his tone was any indication. "All right. When was the last time you saw it?"

She shook her head. She and Mela had tried to reconstruct the day before, but hadn't gone much past quitting time at 5 p.m. An appointment in her book indicated a 6:30 meeting with "K" at Old Lisbon, a restaurant and bar on Sunset Drive. Mela didn't know who it was, since Bet had written it in. Bet couldn't remember.

The trembling got worse. Her anxiety ramped up. *Five things. Cabinets. Coffee. Dirty floor. Badge.*

30

Another badge.

"I don't understand why it's hard to answer. When was the last time you saw it?"

Four things. The chair. My shirt. Bandages. Table leg.

Three things. My heart beating—

"Ms. Lenard?"

"What?" she snapped. Her breath had been stolen away. She took a deep inhale, a gasp for air. Hyperventilation set in next.

The officer glanced around the kitchen and retrieved a plastic bag hanging on the closet door. "Here. Breath into this."

Feeling like a stupid fool, Bet did what he suggested, knowing somewhere in the back of her mind that it would help. It took several minutes to regain control. The two men continued to wait. When she finally breathed normally again, Ortiz took a seat across from her. The partner did, too.

"Now. No one's accusing you of anything. We just want to know how your purse got there."

"I told you. I don't know." She maintained a death grip on the plastic bag.

"Ms. Lenard, were you in the car that burned? In the Everglades?" He looked her right in the eye.

She closed her eyes and nodded, defeated.

Chapter Four

April 19, 1982

The bass line of Joan Jett's "I Love Rock and Roll" pounded off the walls. Colored lights circled over the crowd, flashing in approximate time to the music. A haze of pungent cigarette and weed smoke hung over the South Beach crowd as they moved to the beat. Loud, excited conversations in both English and Spanish punctuated the air.

Bet perched on a bar stool, compact in hand, expertly reapplying her frosted fuchsia lipstick.

Hibiscus wasn't her favorite bar, but it was good for business. Or so Richard said.

She swiveled a little on the padded stool, tilting the mirror so she could catch a glimpse of her errant husband. Though they'd arrived just after 10 p.m., and had two rounds of drinks and a dance, Richard had slipped away to "have a talk." That had been twenty minutes ago. He'd schmoozed it up with several different clumps of Latin men, laughing and handing out business cards. Had they all been drug dealers?

Bet didn't know, and didn't want to know. She wanted to dance.

She'd put Jane to bed, leaving a neighborhood girl sitting in to watch her sleep. It had been weeks since Bet and Richard had gone out on the town like adults, and she didn't want to waste it.

Her toe tapped on the wooden front of the bar, and she gently swayed as the musical notes wrapped around and through her. Before Jane, she and Richard had lived in a small Coconut Grove apartment, close to half a dozen clubs and many "in" restaurants. They'd gone out any night they wanted to, stayed out as late as they felt like. Richard dazzled on the dance floor—he'd taken lessons in all the Latin dance modes, and could switch from salsa to mambo to tango in the blink of an eye. Bet had been a dance virgin before they'd met. He'd paid for her lessons so they could dominate the scene at any club. Knowing they were the center of attention gave Bet a thrill every time.

So why aren't we dancing now?

She sipped her whiskey sour, knowing it was a guilty pleasure she should really feel guilty about. *It's a secret. I haven't even told Richard yet.* She sighed and shut the compact with a snap.

"Hey, pretty lady," came a soft baritone voice near her right shoulder. "I feel like I should call the police."

Bet smirked, sensing the next line would be corny as hell. *Did you hurt yourself when you fell from heaven? Are you a parking ticket? Because you've got* fine *written all over you. Any chance you have an extra heart? Mine's been stolen!*

"Oh? Why is that?" Bet swung around to face the man, adjusting her red wavy mane so it hung halfway down her back, where she knew it would be most attractive. When she gave him her full attention, he took a step back, his eyes widening. His gaze swept her from top to bottom. His mouth twisted, as if it was having difficulty getting words out.

Well, hell's bells, I still got it.

She assessed him quickly, maybe five years her junior, taking in the bleached blond undercut, the carefully-permed cascade of curls over his left brow. The white linen jacket and pale turquoise T-shirt vibed Sonny Crockett. His skin tone indicated Hispanic heritage, and large dark eyes seemed to reach into a troubled soul.

Yeah, he's worth toying with. Besides, if Richard really cared, he'd be sitting with me, right?

Terribly satisfied with herself, she reached in her purse for a dime and handed it to him.

He stared at it in his palm.

"For your phone call," she prompted.

"I-it's a crime," he stammered, dragging his regard to her eyes.

Gotta give him credit for salvaging that landing. "What is?" she said, leaning forward in her hot pink sequined camisole.

He coughed and straightened his shoulders. "That you're here. All alone." He took advantage and checked out everything she was showing him.

There you go.

"Isn't it?" she agreed. The deejay switched to something Latin, all smooth jazzy tones like melted caramel.

He stared at her and pocketed the dime, then held out his hand again. She put hers in his, and let him lead her to the middle of the dance floor. He put his arms around her waist and pulled her close. Her head was at the exact height to rest on his shoulder. The music steered them both, though he was more "prom date" and less "Arthur Murray." It was fine. She felt appreciated—especially when his obvious erection pressed against the black leather skirt she wore.

"You're so beautiful," he whispered. His hand smoothed her hair, his fingers tangling in it for a gentle pull.

She didn't respond, feeling the music, feeling his body next to hers.

He said nothing else until the dance ended. She stepped away from him, a little sad it was over. The lights flashed against his face, pink, then yellow, then blue. He studied her, still holding her hand in his, not moving.

"Another?" he asked in a near-whisper.

Her first impulse was to return to his arms, but she felt obligated to see if Richard had come back. She glanced over her shoulder and spied him at the other end of the bar, sitting alone, blue eyes glittering. He raised his glass of what had to be top-shelf bourbon in a silent toast and grinned.

You know what? Fuck yourself, Richard. I came out to have fun. I'm going to have fun.

"I'd love to," she said to the young man. "What's your name? I'm Bet."

"Carlos. But you can call me Caro." He winked.

She knew what that meant, and thought this was definitely too soon to call him her dear one. "We'll see."

They danced the next several, lighthearted and laughing when Bet tripped over his feet. Breathless, they returned to her place at the bar, where the brunette bartender was just removing Bet's empty glass.

"What can I get you?" Carlos asked.

Bet bit her lip. "Sparkling water." He gave her a sidewise look, and she faltered over an explanation about it being a better thirst quencher.

He smiled. "Whatever the lady says. And I'll have…what's on tap?"

The bartender rattled off a list of beers, and he chose Heineken. When the woman returned with the drinks, Carlos offered her a twenty, but she shook her head. "It's covered, sir."

"Covered?" His brow furrowed and he looked up and down the bar curiously.

Bet, of course, realized immediately what had happened, but she sipped her drink without acknowledging Richard. *The man's arrogant enough. I'm not giving him that satisfaction.*

Carlos gulped about half his glassful, as though he'd been deprived of liquids for hours.

Is he that thirsty, or looking for courage?

Bet felt the beginning tugs of regret, a culpability for leading this man on. She'd wanted so much to feel needed, to feel pretty, and he'd given her that. Now she'd rightfully be expected to consider what Carlos needed.

And while I might feel justified in having a little enjoyment while away from home and child, I'm in no position to give Carlos any more than I already have.

She took her turn at studying him, thinking that before she went to law school, he might have been exactly what she would have considered a possible mate. He seemed nice enough.

So was Ted Bundy.

She shushed her inner voice. The important thing was, she had to do something to make it clear there was no future to this chance meeting. Better, too, to do it before Richard made a jealous scene.

She cleared her throat and turned to Carlos. He turned to her at the same time, his eyes lit with excitement that slowly faded as he read her. Her gaze slipped downward; it was hard to look him in the eye and disappoint him.

"It's been wonderful spending time with you," she said. "Unfortunately, my babysitter has to be home by midnight and…"

"You have a kid?" He stared, glass held in midair.

"I do." *Didn't he notice the silver band I'm wearing? Come on, though. Not like I was acting married.*

After a long pause, he recovered, with a small smile. "I like kids," he said. "That doesn't matter to me. Look, give me your number and maybe we can go out to Metrozoo together, or—"

"No," she said firmly. "I'm sorry." She set the water down, grateful she didn't have to feel guilty for not drinking it since Carlos hadn't paid. She picked up her wrap and clutch and, pushing her way through the dance floor, hurried out of the bar.

A gush of Miami air hit her as she came through the door. It smelled wet and heavy. *Like I will in another five months.* Her heels clicked loudly on the sidewalk as she continued across the road to the parking lot. Music echoed across the buildings from the open doors of several clubs on the block. She dreaded hearing running footsteps behind her, but there were none. Carlos must have been too shocked to move.

Or there was another gorgeous redhead at the bar to move on to…

When she came around the brightly lit corner of the building next to the lot, she spied Richard leaning against the fender of his latest purchase, a shiny black Jaguar. Composing multiple lines she could say to justify her behavior, debating turning the thing around on him, she approached the car ready for a fight.

He stood and walked around the car to the passenger side, then opened her door. "Madam," he said. Like always.

What is he up to? He doesn't want to cause a scene. He's waiting until we get inside. Do I need to have my mace in hand?

But he closed the door once she was comfortably seated and went around to get in the driver's side. Once he fastened his seat belt, he started the car and eased it out of the lot, heading toward the Palmetto Expressway.

She laid her head back, suddenly tired, though she didn't close her eyes. He wouldn't get physical, that was a given. It wasn't his way. He'd rather slice and tear with words.

That was never my way. But I'm certainly learning how from a diamond-sharp teacher.

He didn't speak until they were on the freeway. "Did you see who took our card, Bettina? Miguel Corrado. You know who that is?"

"Uh…no."

Richard's voice warmed with enthusiasm. "In Palm Beach they call him *El Rey Escorpión.* The Scorpion King. He's rumored to have ties in every port from here to Havana. Smuggles products from marijuana to cocaine to genuine Castro cigars." He pulled a well-wrapped cigar from his pocket. "You know what this is worth on the black market?"

Really? That's what you're going to talk about? Cocaine? Cigars? She sighed, confused and a little hurt. "I really don't, Richard."

"Twenty-five dollars." He beamed. His eyes

sparkled and his teeth shone white, illuminated by the passing freeway lights. "He's got our card. If he brings us his business, we'll increase revenue by $200,000 a year."

"That's great." It was great, actually. With a second child to put through college, they were going to need all the money they could make. "Good job, Richard."

"Yeah." He continued driving, his focus on the road. When he rounded the bend and headed south on 826, he said, "I know I neglected you, after I asked you to come out with me. It was wrong, and I'm sorry."

She glanced over at him, not expecting the real sincerity in his voice.

"I'm always worried about providing for this family. I saw an opportunity and grabbed it." He patted her leg. "I'm glad you got to dance."

"You're not…mad?" *Maybe it's the contact high from the weed in the club. Or I'm going crazy?*

"Of course not. After all, you came home with me, right?" He laughed. "Nothing wrong with having a little fun out in the world, is there? You have your fun, then you come home. Where you belong."

He reached for the radio controls and hit the button for the local pop station. Some bubble-gum song came on and ended the need for further talk.

You have your fun, then you come home. Were those words an exhortation to send her looking elsewhere for entertainment? Or did they mean more than that?

Chapter Five

November 15, 1993
Three years before the incident

"Bar meetings" always sounded like more fun than they were. What they actually entailed was sitting around a bunch of white-clothed tables in some cookie-cutter hotel venue. Tonight, it was the Marriott. The tall, good-looking president of the association blabbed on, laying out one boring proposition after another. Bet knew better than to protest—that was a sure way to get volunteered for some committee.

Just when she was ready to declare the meeting an enormous waste of time, the president introduced speaker Hyacinth Martell on the subject of self-care for attorneys.

The psychiatrist wasn't anything like what Bet expected. Her hair was graying blonde, and she was slightly overweight, but seemed comfortable in her shoes. She looked to be of Scandinavian descent, very pale skin and sharp blue eyes. But her voice captured Bet's admiration immediately. It was warm, and smooth like melted chocolate.

"Self-care is not self-ish," Hyacinth began. "It's cliché, but it's true: if you don't care for yourself, you can't care for others. You all have many responsibilities. Family. Clients. Community. If you let them, the sum total of all these things can devour you."

When Hyacinth said those last two words, she looked straight at Bet. The reverberation of that look traced a path through Bet, down to the center of her soul. *What does she mean? Is this personal? Is she…? No. She can't be. My husband's sitting right here.*

With a little smile, Hyacinth continued talking about exercise, better diet, getting plenty of sleep. "But your most important first step is learning how to set boundaries. In order to protect yourself, and your sanity, you have to draw lines."

She picked up a pen, studying it for a moment, then went on. "For those of you taking notes, here's the most important thing you'll hear tonight. Learn. To. Say. No."

A general polite laugh went round the room, and she shook her head. "Really, it's that simple. I would wager that every one of you could look back over this day and count on more than one hand opportunities you had to say no. And should have."

"That's what you need," Rich said, straightening his silk Zegna tie. His tone conveyed parental direction.

"You think?" Bet leaned back in her chair, resentment swelling.

Rich glanced at her, then at Hyacinth, who'd continued talking about boundaries in relationships. "Yeah. All that… pain… you've been having lately, the muscle tension and all. If it's physical, you should work it out of your system. If it's not physical, well…"

Bet chewed her lip. Her frustration at his lack of understanding burned her. She had ongoing pain days at a time. She could find no reasonable cause. Her doctor just sent her for more tests every time she complained, and they'd come back with nothing. Not lupus. Not osteoarthritis. Not Lyme Disease.

But the pain is real, damn it.

It had been so bad that she'd once had to cancel a promised shopping trip with Jane. She'd been curled up in bed, crying, the day the family was supposed to go to the water park. Rich had taken them anyway. Bet didn't know what he'd told the kids, but when they'd come home, they were surly and snappish to her, implying she just didn't care about them enough to get out of bed.

Her attention came back to Hyacinth when the doctor said, "What will you tolerate in your relationships? Make it clear when you feel your partner has crossed that line, if they're expecting too much, if they've even forgotten the true meaning of 'partner.' "

The other lawyers at their table had varying reactions, but at least Lillian Martin, who sat across from them, gave Bet a sympathetic nod.

Rich leaned close. "You should get her card. Maybe meet with her."

Drenched in irony, Bet turned to her silver-haired husband, realizing the doctor's whole point had completely bypassed him. "You think it's all in my head?"

He raised his hands. "Hey, just saying maybe it's an option. What would it hurt?"

Bet had known Richard long enough to know that resistance would be futile, as they said in that space show. Once he "knew" what others should do, he'd harp on it until the cows came home. And then maybe after the cows went to bed, and maybe the next day, too.

She let it drop, knowing they'd ride home in turmoil yet another night.

After the talk was over, and the meeting began to

break up, Bet approached Hyacinth.

"I enjoyed your presentation."

"Thank you." The woman's keen gaze studied Bet as though she were profiling a serial killer. Bet felt seen as she had never been.

"Is that your husband or just a date? I guessed husband."

Bet glanced over at Rich, who was busy schmoozing. *As always.* "We don't bring dates to Bar meetings."

"I figured." Hyacinth stepped close enough to touch Bet. But she didn't. "So much older than you."

No judgment in the words. "Twelve years." She shrugged. "We were in law school together. He was a teacher before he went to law school. Quit because no one would pay teachers enough."

"Hmm." Those blue eyes twinkled bright with curiosity.

Why did I even say that? So personal. "I—uh…I'd like a card if you have one with you." She couldn't bring herself to say it was Richard's idea.

"Of course. I'm sure we'd have much to talk about." Hyacinth reached into her purse and took out a gold-plated card case. Flipping it open deftly, she extracted an ivory card and handed it to Bet. "I am taking new clients."

"Good to know. Thank you." She hesitated, feeling she had more to say, but she couldn't put her finger on it.

Hyacinth put her hand on Bet's arm and leaned close. "Call me," she said. Then she turned to another lawyer waiting to speak to her. Bet was dismissed.

Bet tucked the card into her pocket and returned to

the table. *Now what?* Her husband glanced at her without a smile. *It'll be a long night.* Her muscles slowly tensed, starting at the base of her spine and whittling away her control all the way up into the cervical bones, nerve pain accompanying it like a father walking a bride down the aisle. She slipped a Vicodin in her mouth and chugged her remaining half-glass of whiskey sour.

Telling Lillian goodbye, Bet walked out of the room, down the nondescript hallway, and left the air-conditioned building. The tropical humidity hit her like a wave as she stepped outside. She paused to breathe in the moisture. *The car will be blazing hot.* Rich had insisted on driving the black Ferrari tonight. That meant closing the windows tight so no one stole anything.

No doubt he wanted his buddies to see how his law business prospered. Family law wasn't always a lucrative practice, but criminal defense was. Between the two of them, Rich and Bet had put together a stellar client list over five years, and they had billables well into the six figures. He'd insist, of course, that he personally had accumulated most of their wealth. Maybe it was true, if you measured by percentages. Fifty-five to forty-five. Maybe sixty-forty. It seemed lately that he took credit for so much and discounted her contribution, writing it off to "your hypochondria" or "drug-taking."

So, yes, by all means the Ferrari.

The sound of gunfire echoed off the downtown buildings, not too far away. She hardly twitched. It was part of the grand symphony that was Miami.

Art Lubel walked past toward his car, trailing the aroma of cigarette smoke.

"Hey, Art, can I bum one from you?" She leaned against the Ferrari's fender like an advertising model.

The balding public defender stopped and studied her. "Sure, Bet. Looking good!" He dropped his own butt on the ground and stepped on it.

She smiled in a "come-hither" way. *For the tobacco, not for him.*

Others walked by, murmuring a "good night" or "see ya." She knew that they weren't really looking at the Ferrari. They were checking out her legs, which were, as one said in a colloquial way, "up to there." As usual when not in court, she'd worn a short skirt, so that they would be admired. As a woman of 38, quickly rolling toward 40, she figured she'd better get mileage out of them while she still could.

Clearly Lubel was mesmerized. He hardly looked away as he let her take a cigarette from his pack, and then lit it for her.

"Thanks." She inhaled deeply, then blew the smoke out in a whisper.

"I-I didn't know you were a smoker." He glanced around, nodding to passing colleagues as if he were up to something.

Did he think he'd get somewhere personally with me, just for a cigarette? Or just building his personal appeal? She laughed softly. "I'm not. Just a passing case of nerves."

He frowned. "Everything okay with you and Rich?"

She took another drag and eyed him. "Just fine, Art. Just fine."

Why would he say that? Did he know something? Did he suspect Rich might have something on the side?

That's what I've wondered.

A silence stretched out between them like a single thread of a spider's web, Eventually, he cleared his throat and, hand shaking, put the pack back in his pocket. "Have a good night."

"You, too, Art. You're a lifesaver."

He caught the bone she'd thrown and smiled. "Yeah. That's…ah, that's me." He backed away, nearly tripping over a loose piece of asphalt.

"Careful," she called, trying real hard not to laugh.

Hyacinth walked past, too distant for conversation, but her gaze fastened on the cigarette. She held her hand up to her ear in a "call me" motion. Bet nodded and waved.

Do I really need therapy? Will Hyacinth Martell magically open my mind to some psychosomatic cause for the ongoing pain? Doubt it.

Rich came out of the building, laughing and talking with a couple of the other lawyers. Sure, he was The Guy, always the first with a joke or a compliment, sought out by one and all as friend. *What a man…*

She took another long drag on the cigarette, then put it out. Her self-medication had settled in. The pain had smoothed into a dull roar. She took several deep breaths to clear her lungs. Her statement to Art hadn't been a lie; she wasn't a smoker. A regular smoker. She might have taken it up, but Rich didn't tolerate pollution of his personal air.

Would he make me walk home?

The thought made her chuckle. He wouldn't dare. Leaving her in the downtown lot with the junkies and the homeless crowd would cause people to talk. *And he just can't stand that. Not Mr. Perfect Richard Lenard.*

The resentment bordering on rage wasn't healthy. She knew it. *Maybe therapy wasn't such a bad idea. Unloading all that on someone who's not my assistant, working in the same office, might be a real good plan.*

Having decided to call Hyacinth in the morning, she waited for Rich to open her door, and then she slumped in the padded, low-slung passenger seat.

Rich got in and closed his door. He sniffed deeply. Glared. "Drugs and alcohol not enough for you? Now you've taken up nicotine?"

"Half a cigarette. And I didn't do it in the car." *But maybe I should have.*

"Hmmph." He started the car and roared out of the lot, navigating the nighttime highways in deadly silence. A swath of colors reflected off the solid glass fronts of the buildings, a style that seemed ubiquitous these days. The usual evening traffic as they passed the airport was a blaze of lights and swerving cars, but Rich passed among them like a sharp knife in butter.

Bet snuggled back into the seat, relishing the moments with little discomfort. Stress exacerbated the pain, as a rule. She'd even put two and two together to realize that it escalated weekdays just about six p.m., making it uncomfortable to focus on dinner, homework and all the things that needed to be done as soon as she got home from the office. *And also when Rich and I have to spend every minute in the same house.*

When had she and Rich drifted apart? In law school they'd been inseparable. They'd come back to Florida, not far from her father's house, and opened their law practice together in Miami. Even then, the days had been filled with work, and the nights spent out on the town, dancing in the hottest clubs, or home under imported Egyptian sheets making love.

Not when the children arrived. Although the chaos they added to the mix certainly helped.

Rich left the freeway at Sunset Drive, as the lights became fewer and far between, heading west nearly to the Redlands until he reached their gate. Bet straightened up as he maneuvered down the extended gravel drive through the coconut palms. Fewer trees remained now than when they bought the place in 1988, but then the north edge of Hurricane Andrew had ripped up a number of them in '92. Gradually, the place had started to recover.

Finally, he pulled the car into the second garage. "So, are you going in early tomorrow? The Roberts appellate briefs have to go out by 4."

She sighed. Mornings were hard because the pain was fresh. "I will."

"If you're having trouble getting it done—"

"I said I will." She closed her eyes, irritated.

"Fine." He got out of the car and stalked toward the door. "Don't forget to lock the garage door."

She muttered something uncomplimentary about his parentage. *Don't worry, my love, your precious car won't be taken from you. I only wish you'd be as concerned about your wife, who's going crazy trying to figure out what's wrong with her.*

What will you do when she's taken from you?

Chapter Six

Once she'd admitted being in the car, Bet's sense of vulnerability continued to grow. She completed her two-hour interview with the detectives, and they seemed to believe what she'd told them. She still couldn't answer most of the pertinent questions, like why this had happened, or who might be responsible.

The detective asked for the clothing she wore that night, as she hadn't gone through proper procedures at the hospital. Then he asked whether she had been raped before the fire, if she'd been bruised as though she'd been in a fight. Both of these she answered in the negative, realizing belatedly the scene could have been a lot worse

Yeah, I only got slightly burned. That's bad enough, I suppose.

The most logical conclusion was that she had met the mysterious K. at the bar, and during the course of that meeting, she'd been drugged. Her previous roofie experience had been vaguely similar, with a lack of recall, and so on. But this wasn't a simple date rape situation. She'd been out cold long enough to be hauled to the Everglades, put in a car, and remain so while someone set a fire. What woke her out of her stupor?

49

Whatever it was had saved her life.

Worried, she implored Ortiz not to file the report with the department, not as long as the perpetrator was still unknown. "That's why I didn't call the police from the hospital in the first place, or file any report with the medical staff. I didn't want the perps to know. Just you being here will tip off whoever might be watching. They'll know I'm still alive."

"Ms. Lenard, we can't run an investigation without filing the report. Wouldn't you like to see this person brought to justice?" Ortiz said. "We can try to limit access."

Bet knew exactly how much that meant. *Squat.*

"Besides," the partner said. "It's been on the news. Only one body was found. I think whoever it is has the picture now."

That hadn't occurred to her yet.

Damn it. Why isn't my brain processing like it should? That should have hit me as soon as I saw the report. She sighed. *Whatever plagues my body is definitely affecting my mind, too.*

So she had to accede to the investigation moving forward. There were benefits, of course. Certain things could be done that Bet couldn't do on her own. The police could subpoena the security camera records from Old Lisbon for a picture of the person who'd met her there. They could check National Park security to discover license plate ID on the car, or anyone who might have accompanied it. Extra patrols in her neighborhood could keep an eye on her place.

All this also meant she would have to break down and tell Rich.

A sick feeling settled into her gut. She imagined his

reaction would be that this was another attention-getting ploy on her part. Perhaps he'd even suggest she deserved it if she was drunk. Since the split, he'd been so unsympathetic as to be hostile, and that pained Bet more than she could stand.

She couldn't face it that day. Maybe by the weekend.

Mela closed the office at four p.m. and came back to Bet's house. She brought everything she could find on Bet's desk that might give them some clue as to the identity of the mysterious K, along with takeout Chinese from the place on the corner of South Dixie Highway.

They sat at the kitchen table, all the documents and notes spread out between them. Bet poured them ice water from the refrigerator, served with a generous slice of lemon.

"So, no one suspicious came by the office at all?" she asked Mela.

"Not even your clients." Mela smirked at her own joke.

Bet couldn't even smile. "Could it be one of them?"

Mela waved the spring roll she held. "Why would they kill you? You're helping them. Getting on your bad side wouldn't seem to be in their self-interest."

"You wouldn't think."

She glanced at the kitchen window, the curtains pulled closed. She'd done that early in the day, feeling like the whole world was staring in at her. *You brave enough to come for me again, you bastards? Well, here I am.*

"You should buy a gun."

"What? Why?"

"For self-defense." Mela nodded firmly.

"Well, duh, yeah. I mean how would a gun really change the odds? I'd need to get a permit and carry it all the time." *Would it even fit in my clutch? I'd have to buy one of those big beach totes.*

"Well? Exactly. Let someone try to set you on fire with a hole in their midsection." Mela got up and cleared the food packs and paper plates off the table.

"Maybe." Bet eyed her companion. "I guess it worked for you. After Santos."

"Yeah. It did. But you knew he wouldn't stay away. And he didn't."

"Sometimes it sucks to be right."

Bet drank her water and got more. Her memory pinged. "Where's that dress I had on?"

"What dress? The one from the swamp? I put it in the laundry."

"Did you wash it? I needed something in the pocket!"

"Don't get yourself all *emocionada.* I set them on the shelf." Mela headed for the laundry room and returned with some papers in hand. She gave them to Bet. "The surgeon's card?"

"No." She chuckled. "I have to send Chet gas money." Taking an envelope from the stacks on the table, she addressed it to Chet and stuffed fifty dollars inside with a note that read, "Thank you for doing the right thing."

Mela took it from her and put it in her purse. "I'll send it out tomorrow."

"Thanks." Bet glanced over the piles they'd gone through twice and sighed. "We're not getting much done here. We should watch the local news. Just to be prepared."

The two women went into the living room, where Bet switched on the television that sat against the front wall. It was large and heavy, inherited from her parents. The build-it-yourself TV stand it rested on bowed in the middle. Floor-to-ceiling curtains were sage green with a bamboo pattern. An under-stuffed brown couch and two matching chairs took up the rest of the space. They'd come from some warehouse sale. She'd bought them at the same time as the house, but probably hadn't used them more than a dozen times. *I spend way too much time in my bedroom.*

She'd brought her water in with her and drank most of it before the car dealing commercial was over. *A little nervous, are we?*

Using 'we' to reference herself reminded her of the doctor she'd met in the ER. Dr. Rimon. He'd seemed really nice. He'd cared. *I'm definitely running short on people in that category this week. I'll have to take him up on that phone call one of these days.*

"In this follow-up from our earlier report of a body found in a burnt-out car in the Everglades, Metro-Dade police have confirmed there was a second victim, Coral Gables attorney Bettina Lenard. She escaped serious injury."

Bet rose to her feet, simultaneously furious and terrified. "No way! What the hell are they thinking? What if They are listening to this? What if Rich and the kids are listening? What—" Furious, she paced to the window. "I knew that was a bunch of crap about trying to keep this out of the mainstream. Damn it."

Mela shushed her. "See what else they have to say."

She missed the rest but a photo of her at some court function paired with a photo of the dead architect, and a request for anyone who might have information to call the Monroe County sheriff's office or Metro-Dade.

"That's just great."

"You know, Bet, I think it might be. The more coverage there is, the perpetrators might be afraid to try anything else, figuring you're being watched by the police."

"Or they might want to hurry up and finish the job before I remember anything and tell the cops."

Mela shook her head. "You are always a cup half-empty kind of person."

Bet deadpanned, "Keeps me from being disappointed as often." She came back to the sofa and finished off the glass of water. *Water isn't what I need.* She sensed her muscles tightening from the stress. It was too late to head it off. "As soon as Rich gets wind of this…"

Then the phone rang.

Chapter Seven

July 14, 1994
Two years earlier

Bet finished her case before Judge Ferrer, winning a year-long restraining order for her client against an abusive husband. She waited with her client in the back of the large courtroom lined with wooden benches, while security escorted the husband from the building. Sunlight shone in through the long narrow windows, lighting the dust motes that swirled gently through the air. The other cases proceeded.

The slight woman in a blue dress trembling at the plaintiff's table drew Bet's attention, reading from a paper in her hand. Bet couldn't believe she could even see it, the paper shook so violently. The woman's voice was hardly above a whisper. The judge kept asking her to speak up, which just rattled her more. A fat Cuban sat at the defendant's table next to a high-priced attorney with whom Bet was quite familiar.

He'll destroy that poor woman on the stand.

Bet chewed her lip. *I've got to do something. This woman needs help. She needs…me.*

She turned to her client. "Can you wait here until security comes back? I need to talk to the woman presenting her case. Call me at the office if you have any problems, all right?"

Her client nodded and placed her back to the wall.

Bet strode forward to the gated bar. "Your Honor, if I may?"

Judge Ferrer eyed her curiously. "Yes, Counsel? Come forward."

"Would you be able to move this case to the end of today's session? I'd like to speak to my client." She gestured to the Latina at the table, whose dark eyes had filled with tears.

"Ah." The judge smiled slightly. Most of the judiciary disliked dealing with self-represented litigants. He'd be pleased to have an attorney on both sides. "I think we could—"

The other lawyer jumped to his feet. "I object, your Honor! Ms. Lenard hasn't entered an appearance—"

"You're not afraid of dealing with me, are you, Tim?" Bet asked, with a wicked smile.

Tim Sampson glared at her. "Not the issue." He turned back to the judge, awaiting a ruling.

"I already said we could, Mr. Sampson. Please step back, with your client."

Tim growled and tried to soothe his client, who projected a heated aura. *No wonder this poor little thing's so scared. The man just vibrates with danger.*

Bet beckoned to the woman, who just stared, lost. "Come on, sweetheart. Let me help you."

The woman followed her out of the courtroom, still clutching her stack of papers. Bet guessed they were from the new family court self-help plan which had recently been established. *But just because people could handle a case themselves, didn't mean they should. Especially someone as obviously terrified as this woman.*

They ended up in a small room off the lawyer's

lounge, which had a wall lined with law books, several couches and a small conference table with chairs, where Bet invited the woman to sit. Now that they were close, Bet noticed a scar across the woman's eyebrow, and another on the inside of her left wrist. "I want you to take a deep breath with me, okay? In slowly, and out. Let's do that again."

The woman hesitated, then breathed along with her.

Bet said, "Here's something that helps me. First, think of five things you can see…" She went through the whole practice with her client, pleased to see how she calmed and quit trembling. "There. That's better."

"I-I can't afford a lawyer. Santos has all the money…" Tears rolled down the woman's cheeks.

"Did I ask you for any?" Bet smiled. "I'm Bettina Lenard. I handle these matters all the time. I promise, you're in good hands."

The woman wiped her tears away with the back of her hand. Bet scouted out a box of tissues and set them on the table.

"May I see your paperwork?"

The woman handed it over, and then blew her nose, trying to compose herself, while Bet looked through the pages.

Holy mother of God. The man isn't an abuser; he's a terrorist.

The petition revealed, in carefully hand-printed sentences, that this couple had been married for ten years, in living hell. The history of abuse included physical altercations, substantiated by four sets of hospital records; mental abuse, including segregating her from friends and family and constant bullying. He'd insisted that she submit to him sexually, since he was her husband. She had filled out in painful detail some of his more deviant perversions.

Bet glanced in surprise at the petite woman, who sat, tearing pieces off the corner of her tissue. *I can't imagine spelling this out on paper, much less enduring it in person. Makes me want to go out there and punch the guy.*

The final straw apparently came the day before this court appearance, when a friend had given her a small puppy. When she'd brought it home, Santos had been angry that someone else made her happy, and had twisted the puppy's neck, killing it.

Bet gasped and looked up. "He's a monster."

The woman nodded.

"How old were you when you got married?"

"Fifteen. My father…he insisted I marry Santos. He said Santos would treat me well and bring me to America."

"From Cuba?"

"*Si.* I mean, yes."

"Well, he was half right." Bet sighed. She could win this case, if she put the woman on the stand and dragged her through the testimony, word by word. It would be agony for them both. The judge would likely grant a permanent restraining order on these facts, depending on the testimony of the husband.

"What will Santos say about this? Would he admit it?"

The woman looked down at her lap. "He always says it's my fault. That I make him do these things. That he can't fulfill his promises to my father if I won't be a good girl." She wiped her cheeks. "I try so hard to be what he wants. But I just can't any more…"

"Of course you can't. You shouldn't have to." Bet got an idea and looked over the documents again. "What does Santos do for work? Is he in business?"

"He is kitchen manager at a restaurant in Little Havana. He works many hours."

Hmm. Too bad he doesn't have a more public position. We could negotiate him into an agreement. She shrugged. *Maybe we still can.*

"All right. I'm taking everything you put in your petition as true. Right?"

The woman nodded, relaxing a little. When she wasn't a nervous wreck, she was actually pretty.

"I'm ready to take this case into the courtroom. Then you'd have to answer my questions on the stand. Then his attorney will have the chance to ask you questions. He'll try to confuse you, get you to say things that help his case and so on. Did you bring any other witnesses?"

"No. No one is brave enough to stand up to him."

"But you are." Bet reached across the table and squeezed her hand. "I can't imagine how much courage it took to file this, but you are one strong woman. You hear me? We can do this."

She squeezed back and nodded.

"What I'm going to do now is speak to your husband's attorney and see if we can get an agreement that will save you from having to testify. Can you wait here and just keep breathing deeply?"

"Yes, I can." She sounded much more confident.

"Good. I'll be right back. Keep the door closed."

Bet picked up her briefcase, the Satchel and Paige leather one Rich had bought her when she graduated, and marched out to the hallway to find Tim. She and Tim had battled several cases before; Bet was four to one in the winning column. *And that loss was a dud anyway.* Surely his client had told him it was all lies, as they usually did. *But I can sell this woman's testimony. And he knows it.*

She walked in the direction of the courtroom, pausing when she spotted Tim at the end of the corridor, leaning on the marble windowsill. His client wasn't in evidence. She nodded at him, and he came to join her.

"Nice guy," she said. "Surprised he's not up for husband of the year."

Tim shrugged. "What can I say? Some of my clients are dirtballs."

"I hope you got paid well. Maybe that'll help you sleep at night."

"I sleep just fine. What do you want?"

"A three-year order with no contact. None. Zero." She eyed him quite seriously. "And he owes her a new puppy."

Tim snickered. "Judge isn't going to order that."

"He'd honor an agreement." *This boy had best start taking me seriously.*

Bet didn't expect to get the puppy. But she had to start somewhere. "And he pays her $200 a week for support pending the filing of a divorce complaint."

"He won't agree to that. If she leaves him, she's on her own."

Well, that isn't the law. But there are other avenues to get her alimony. "There are no kids, very little property, they don't own a house. Easy for them to go separate ways."

"But he loves her and wants her back." Tim spoke very sincerely. Maybe he even believed what he was saying.

"He wants a housemaid and sex object, you mean.

He blew that one. You go run the three years past him. I'll ask the judge for five. And when Ferrer hears the testimony, hc'll probably recommend filing criminal charges. So yeah. Tell Santos he's getting off easy."

Bet turned and walked away before she said what she really felt. *The man should be broadsided by a Mack truck. I even know people who would do it.* Still seething, she took the elevator down to the third floor and used the antique-fixtured restroom with the stone stall dividers and softly worn wooden stall doors. The geometric floor tiles always cheered her up. *As much as a bathroom visit could.*

Returning to the corridor outside their courtroom, she found Tim waiting for her.

"He won't buy a three-year order. He's sure she'll be back home in a matter of days." He paused.

"But?"

"But I explained the value of not hashing this all out on the record, particularly if there ever *is* a divorce. So he'll give her six months."

Bet considered that. Getting the order was the important thing. Once you had one, it was easier to extend it if there were violations. *And this guy is bound to violate it. I just have that feeling.* "One year and we've got a deal."

"Let me talk to him." Tim sighed and went off to find his man.

A year would do. That would provide her a chance to begin again and realize she didn't need to take the abuse in order to have food and shelter. *My good deed for the day.*

Sure enough, Tim managed to convince his client to take the deal. Twenty minutes later, Judge Ferrer dictated the order and got Santos's sworn statement that he understood all the no-contact terms. As she had earlier, Bet waited with her client until the abuser and counsel had cleared the building.

"What do I do now?" the woman asked, when they were sitting on a bench in the hall.

"What was your plan when you filed the papers?"

"I just wanted to get away."

"Okay, we've got that down. You've got to have a place to live, somewhere he can't bother you. What did you have in mind?"

"I thought maybe I could stay with a friend." Her voice had fallen to a whisper again.

"There's a shelter downtown where they lock the doors and keep the place secure. He couldn't get you there."

"What about my clothes? My things at the house?"

Bet straightened her shoulders, feeling a twinge of pain drift down her back muscles. Now that the adrenaline of the fight had passed, reality always snapped back. "You'll have to find a time when he won't be there to go. Or send your friend to pick things up for you." *Or realize that he was likely to destroy all your personal possessions by way of punishment.* Bet just couldn't tell her that, not while she was so fragile.

"What about you?" she asked. "Aren't you afraid? He could kill you for helping me. He's a dangerous man."

Bet considered the tragic fate of the puppy and guessed it might be true. "That's not part of my math. I helped you because you needed it. That's all I need to know."

The woman shuddered and chewed her lip.

New subject. Quick. "When's your next check coming from the drycleaners?"

"Not until ncxt Friday."

Bet considered some options. "Can you type?"

"Yes. I learned at school."

"All right. You can temp in my office this week. Do you drive?"

"Santos didn't let me."

"The office is near the University stop off the Metrorail. Here." Bet gave her a card. "I can drop you at the shelter on my way home." As she protested, Bet raised a hand. "You don't have to stay there. But they have a social worker who can get you hooked up with food stamps and Section 8 secure housing, and other services to help you. Counseling, medical and so on. It won't be big money, but you'll be safe at night. All right, Mela?"

A long pause. "All right."

"Come on, let's go. Maybe we'll get ice cream on the way there. I feel like ice cream, don't you?"

****

November 25, 1995
Four months later

Mela continued to work at Bet's office two days a week. Since Rich managed the finances of their two offices, he'd objected to taking on a new staffer, but Bet agreed Mela could start at part-time with no benefits or unemployment, and he finally backed down. They put another desk in a corner, and life went on. Over time, the woman became quite valuable, having a strong memory and the ability to retrieve almost anything that had been filed, even if it had been sorted incorrectly.

Even more important, she had become Bet's friend

and confidant. Now, it wasn't always advisable to befriend clients. Or employees. For most, even if she liked them very much, Bet preferred to maintain a businesslike relationship, keeping them at arms' length. It certainly rendered the subject of fee payment into a much more professional level.

But Mela pays me no fees. So that's one issue not on the table.

The two often went to dinner together after work, as neither had much to return to in the evening. Mela had obtained her own small apartment after a few weeks, but had never become involved with anyone, since Santos wouldn't sign divorce papers. Bet, on the other hand, had concluded her divorce, with Rich keeping the family law practice, box seats for the Miami Heat, their home, the children and the majority of the debts. A cash settlement allowed her to buy her little house in Coral Gables, and at Rich's insistence, she'd changed her specialty to criminal law, something the firm had more than dabbled in previously. He had decreed he'd rather have the family law clients—less muss and fuss.

Bet found the social evenings with Mela fulfilled her need to see people, for the most part. Other than Bar meetings or continuing education, Bet didn't go out often. *Except for evenings when she just got too lonely and wanted male companionship. Like the night at the Barracuda Taphouse.*

One night about 11 p.m., about four months into Mela's restraining order, Bet got a phone call when she was in bed, nearly asleep. "Ms. Lenard, this is officer Reyes with the South Miami Police. I'm here with Mela Silvani. She asked me to contact you."

Her stomach sank, and she sat up, pulling her covers

back. *I've got to go.* "Is she…all right?"

"Oh, yes. Here, let me put her on."

Bet expected Mela had been hurt, and thought she'd hear hospital sounds in the background. But it sounded more like a television.

Mela's tentative voice. "Bet?"

"What the hell's happening? You're all right? Shall I come over? Where are you?"

"Hey, hey, don't worry. The police are here. Santos is under arrest. It's handled." She paused and answered a question asked by someone wherever she was. "Just get him out of here."

"Santos is there?"

Bet was powerless to help, but her conscience urged her to get up and get dressed. *I knew it. I knew he'd violate that order, as sure as I was born.*

"He's just leaving. Listen, I'll have to extend the order, I think. Can we do that Monday?"

"Sure, we can. He broke in? What happened?"

"He came to my apartment telling me he thought he'd like to get back together. I've convinced him it's not a good idea. Ever."

Mela's voice didn't waver. *She's calling her own shots. Good for her. I'm so proud. Some of them, you can save.*

"I told you that you were the brave one. Are you sure you don't need me to come over?"

Mela took a deep breath. "No. I just wanted to check in. I feel better now. Thanks."

"Sure thing. You call me any time."

"As long as you promise to do the same." Mela spoke to someone with her. "I'd better give the phone back. I'll see you Monday morning."

"All right. Thanks for letting me know."

Bet got up anyway, feeling at loose ends. She stopped in the bathroom, then went downstairs to get a glass and bottle of wine that she took up to bed. The ibuprofen the doctor had prescribed was doing nothing for her pain. If she were to get some sleep, she'd have to add something stronger. She tucked herself under the covers and watched old reruns until the bottle was empty and she finally could let go.

Chapter Eight

Mela stared at the ringing phone. "Aren't you going to pick it up?"

"You know who it is." Bet crossed her arms, suddenly chilled. The fury dissipated, and her body turned on itself. The bandages pulled at her skin. Her painkillers were wearing off.

Have I pointed out I hate my life?

The ringing stopped.

"See, I was—"

It rang again.

He wouldn't give up. Not when he was on to something, like a bird dog on a hot scent.

Bet rolled her eyes and picked up the receiver. "Hello?"

"Bettina?" Rich's voice was soft with relief. "Bet. My God. Are you really all right?"

Has Rich finally gone on drugs? What the hell…

"Not *all* right. But I'll live."

"I'm so sorry. Bet…I…"

Mela's eyes lit with curiosity. She relaxed into the chair and sipped her water, a smirk on her lips.

For her part, Bet was flabbergasted. This was totally not the response she'd expected. Rich had hardly said a kind word to her in six months. "Sorry about what?"

"The Everglades…the car. I had no idea."

She stretched the phone cord so she could sit on the couch, and then she muted the television with the remote. "Well, how could you have an idea, Rich? It's not like it's your fault."

No response.

Why didn't he come back with some sarcastic response? What was he really saying? Her heart squeezed tight in her chest. Her nerves tingled all the way to her fingertips. "Rich? You didn't have anything to do with it, right?"

"I hope not."

Good thing I'm sitting down. Just…good thing. "What the hell does that mean?"

"We should probably talk. In person."

What in heaven's name had Rich done? Still processing this odd turn of events, she realized he'd nearly admitted doing something that could have caused her death. *And NOW he wants to talk about it?*

He added, "Look, Bettina, don't tell the police about this until you and I can sit and discuss it. All right?"

Stranger and stranger. She tried to draw him out. "I don't know, Rich. The police are all over me for information. I spent two hours trying to prove that I wasn't the one who'd set the car on fire."

"I'm sure it wasn't you. I'll tell them that."

"Well, that's just great." She glanced across at Mela, whose eyes had grown wide.

"Rich?" Mela whispered.

"Apparently he's done something bad," Bet said aloud, not caring if her ex heard. She leaned back on the sofa and crossed her legs at the ankle, propped on the narrow coffee table.

A hesitation. "Who's there?" Rich asked.

"Not that it's any of your business, but it's only Mela."

"Don't tell her, either!" Rich's voice was tight and a notch higher than usual. "Don't tell anyone."

"How can I tell people what I don't know, hmm? Call me tomorrow." She hung up.

"Rich?" Mela asked again.

Bet took a deep breath and let the last five minutes settle, ignoring the pangs in her muscles the best she could. Then she recapped the conversation for Mela. "So it's bad enough he knows the cops will come after him. What. The. Hell."

"So horrible. If he thought you might be in danger, what concerns should you have for the children? Surely they could be targets, too."

Bet's blood went cold. For her, anger wasn't a flame but an icicle. She drew all the frozen pieces of her wrath together and held them close inside. "He dares to make me feel sorry for how my pain has impacted Jane and Jeremy, and he pulls whatever this is?"

"But he wouldn't tell you what?"

Bet shook her head. "He wants to talk in person." *Did that mean he thought her phone was tapped? Or his? What the—* "I should go over there. Right now."

"*Mi amor,* the children are there. They don't need to hear all this."

"I forgot to ask him if they saw the report with him." She tried to force calm through her body. "I'd just hope they'd call on their own if they were worried."

"I don't know any kid their age who cares about watching the news. They were probably off on their computer or playing video games. Don't worry, Bet. You know what that will do."

Bet sighed. "Yeah. I know."

The phone rang again. She answered it to find a colleague practically in tears with shock over the report. Bet calmed her down and got her off the phone. Then it rang again. She picked up the receiver and pressed down the button, hanging up, then left the phone off the hook. It beeped loudly for a minute, then changed to a dial tone. She put a pillow on top to muffle the sound.

"This is going to be impossible." Bet slumped on the couch, pulling her legs in, knees bent. Everything in her world had just changed. *And someone still wants me dead.*

"Should I go? What do you need?" Mela asked.

"No. Yes... I don't know."

"Even when you survive a deadly situation, it takes a long time to feel safe again. I know this." Mela got up and came over to hug Bet. "Lock your doors. Get some sleep. Tomorrow you can get your gun."

Bet pulled herself together and stood up. "We'll see. Thanks for bringing the paperwork over. I'll give it another run-through tonight."

"All right. Call me if you need anything at all. Anything."

"I will."

Mela let herself out, and Bet shut off the television and the lights, retreating to the sofa as night set in. Shadows slipped in, caused by the street lights out front. The windows were open a few inches, and the breeze caused sudden, random movements that fed into the fear she'd held off all day. Was someone out there, watching? Now that the news had broadcast her well-being, would they come for her, here?

And what was this with Rich? Was he part of the conspiracy that had left a burnt man in that car? What was so bad he couldn't tell her? Mela's reminder that the children could be in danger horrified her. Rich had convinced her to walk away from Jane and Jeremy, but that didn't mean she didn't love them. What if something happened to them—and it was Rich's fault?

She realized with a start that tears were streaking down her cheeks. *I'm not in control. I have to be in control. I have to be in control…*

But she couldn't find a way to get on top of all this. Her heartbeat picked up, broadcasting the syncopation of her terror. Lastly, she picked up a rough-edged throw pillow and held it over her face. She screamed again and again, until she was wrung out like an old beach towel.

Taking a breath, and running through her five things, she regained some composure. She put the phone receiver back quickly and picked it up again. She dialed a now-familiar number and waited.

A sleepy voice answered. "Hyacinth Martell. Is this you, Bet?"

Bet smiled with relief. "Of course it is. Can we talk?

Chapter Nine

December 10, 1993
Three years earlier

Bet arrived at the lobby of the terra-cotta-toned Coral Way building that held Hyacinth Martell's office, but couldn't make herself enter the elevator.

I made it this far, what's another dozen steps?

She crossed the lobby and eyed the *faux* marble stairs, the tastefully placed real potted plants, the abstract paintings. She paced back, wondering what the pricey address and neighborhood said about the psychiatrist. Did she need the hot location to establish her confidence? Was it a justification for her rates? Did she come from money, so it really didn't matter?

Do I truly need to analyze the analyzer?

Back across the lobby, studying the little lighted numbers atop the elevator door. *Right there. Number 3. Let's go.*

But she found herself marching in time with the troop of butterflies careening around her stomach.

What am I worried about? That she'll find something wrong with me? There is something wrong with me. That's why I'm here.

She just has to find the right *thing wrong with me. Otherwise, I'll just write her off like all the other doctors who can't figure it out. Can she do that?*

Or is it all just mumbo jumbo, and I'm really just doing it to shut Rich up long enough to stay married?

It was true that difficulties with Rich had come to a head over Christmas presents for the children, of all things. She didn't know how long they'd last as a married couple.

That's worth therapy, right?

The elevator door opened, and a dark-suited man in good shoes exited, startled to find her standing there. She stepped back and he hurried out the door, not looking back.

"Oh hellfire," she muttered. "Let's get it over with."
. She went in. The MUZAK played James Taylor, and Bet felt impossibly old.

The plush gray carpet on the third floor swallowed any sound of her heels as she walked along, looking for Suite G. The door bearing Hyacinth's name on a gold plaque was closed. Bet reached for the handle and found it locked.

Did I have the wrong day? Or is this a sign?

She paused, ready for flight. Then the door opened, and Hyacinth herself stood there, wearing a conservative navy suit with a scarlet scarf accessory.

"Right on time!" she said. "Please, come in."

"Great." Bet forced a smile and followed the psychiatrist inside.

No outer office? No secretary? That seemed odd, considering the implication of upper strata the building carried. The only time Bet had worked without a secretary was in the first six months of the practice, when they'd been saving everything to move more upscale.

I could swear John said Hyacinth had been in practice for a number of years. Or maybe I just wasn't listening.

The office was cozy, but felt old, from another time. Hyacinth had no "psychiatrist's couch," but instead had two large, overstuffed leather chairs that sat across from each other. A thick Persian rug in reds and blues lay between them—and it looked and felt like real wool. The far wall was lined with windows. A heavy cherry desk sat at the far end of the room, its top neatly stacked with baskets full of work. Bet walked along the floor-to-ceiling bookshelves, glancing at the titles and the small, odd dried skeletons of sea animals scattered here and there.

"I like to use aromatherapy in my sessions," Hyacinth said. "Do you have a preference of scent?"

"I'm not sure I know much about aromatherapy," Bet said with an uncomfortable smile. *Actually, that's kind of "out there," right? With crystals and chakras and all that jazz....*

Hyacinth studied her. "You seem a little nervous. Why don't I start with vanilla? That usually calms people." She turned to a small round object on an end table and put some drops inside. When she turned it on, a mist came out of the top. Before long, the office smelled like cookies baking. Bet approved.

"Would you like some tea? I have herbal and black—and I might have some instant hot chocolate."

"No, thanks. I had coffee on the way here."

"Fine. Let's sit down, shall we?" Hyacinth gestured to the two large chairs.

Bet took the one by the window, sinking into it. "This is nice. You sure we aren't just going to have a nap?"

"This is your session, Bet. You may use it as you see

fit." She smiled. "But I think we can get more accomplished if we plan to work."

"Probably," Bct mumbled. She adjusted herself into the seat, running her fingers over the soft leather. *Maybe I'll just concentrate on this tactile experience. Delightful.*

"I received your intake papers last week. Thanks for sending them ahead of time. It saves us having to go over the basics during this hour. Let me just verify a few things." She spent several minutes asking some questions and writing down answers. "After reviewing this, I feel like I can help you deal with your anxiety."

Bet raised an eyebrow. *What was she talking about? Anxiety was for the weak.* "Anxiety? Who says I have... I'm just stressed. High powered job, family and all."

"You're a litigator, aren't you? Big-stakes divorce cases?"

Bet nodded.

"I'm assuming you make some enemies doing that. No one really 'wins' in those cases, even if they get a judgment in their favor. Isn't that true?"

Frowning, Bet shifted uncomfortably in the chair. "We pursue our clients' requests, yes. It's an unhappy time for the families anyway."

She eyed Hyacinth, still burning from the armchair diagnosis of anxiety. To her, that was a cop-out, just a catchall term that was applied more often to soccer moms and table servers who couldn't handle their jobs. *It isn't what I have. I can handle things.* "That's why we send them to your colleagues. We're not here to solve every problem in their lives. Just the ones prescribed by law."

"The firm also has a lucrative criminal law practice,

isn't that so? I imagine with some of the criminal types in this area, you could rack up some dangerous opponents as well. Even among your so-called 'friends.'"

Wouldn't be the first time I'd thought that, especially with some of the clients Richard has brought in. But that isn't my problem.

"I don't understand. What does this all have to do with the pain I'm fighting?"

"'I'll tell you. Issues we have no control over, like enemies, like stress, like conflict, lead naturally to anxiety. And anxiety can manifest in many ways." Hyacinth leaned forward, elbows on her knees. "I'm guessing that's what your body is trying to tell you."

Natural defensiveness crushed her like a tidal wave. She stiffened and sat up straight. "It's not all in my head, damn it."

"Is that what you heard?" Hyacinth paused, then made some notes. "I said, 'your body.' "

Bet bit her lip. She had heard exactly what Hyacinth said. She was just so used to *that* being the next implication, she provided it for herself. *Now isn't that pathological?*

"Right."

Hyacinth studied her coolly. "Why is this pain such a hot-button issue for you?"

Bet shrugged, forcing herself to relax, and dug her shoulders farther into the leather. "I wrote it all there. Over the past year, the pain has inundated me. Most days I can manage. Some I spend in bed, crying."

Did I just admit that? Man, she's good. I need to take notes so I can make my clients confess.

Rewinding the conversation, Bet went back to her

point. *"*No one can figure it out. I don't believe in something that doesn't have an answer. Someone must be able to identify a cause."

"And you're sure it's not in your head. Apparently."

"No. It isn't." *Could I make that any clearer? I hope she heard that determination.* "We have a problem with that. Rich and I."

"He doesn't appreciate that you understand your own body? He'd rather come up with a solution so the two of you can just move on. Even if it's not the real thing."

Bet blinked, surprised. "Exactly."

Hyacinth's face broke into a smile. "Don't be shocked. It's a common characteristic of lawyers. They're problem solvers. You know that. Do you think it makes Rich uncomfortable not to have an answer, just as it is for you?"

Why is she lumping all lawyers together? Do I lump all shrinks… well, maybe I do…

"He's just tired of it. Which is fine for him. He can go through his day and pretend it's not happening. I can't."

"And you're tired of it too."

"Well, of course I am," Bet snapped.

"Mmhmm." Hyacinth made some notes.

What does that mean? What did I say that she thought was relevant? Am I exposing something I can't see?

Hyacinth took a sheet of paper from her folder. "I've got a release here that I'd like you to sign, so I could get information from your medical doctor." She handed it to Bet. "Before you tense up and hurt yourself, I'm not spying on you or 'double-checking,' just opening the door so we can all work together."

Too late. She'd already felt the spirals of pain shoot through her muscles at the hint of conspiracy.

"I'm sure Dr. Moore will be thrilled to hear I'm seeing a shrink." Bet rolled her eyes.

"Has he suggested that before?"

"Yes. But I couldn't see how it would help."

"What does help, Bet?"

Bet squirmed, knowing this part would come sooner or later. "You know. Painkillers."

"Prescription?" Hyacinth's eyes glinted like blue steel when she looked up.

"Now. OTC stuff stopped helping. So now I get some minimal pain meds from my primary doctor. He's not happy about it. It sure doesn't deal with the extent of the pain."

"And before that?"

Why is she persisting in this? I came about the marriage. didn't I? Bet sighed. "Self-medicated with alcohol. Still do, sometimes. Happy now?"

Hyacinth shook her head. "Whether I'm happy or not isn't the issue. Let's guess, what, three years' consumption of alcohol for pain-numbing?" She waited for a response, but Bet just looked away. "It's probably a full-bore addiction by now. You'll need to deal with it."

"You mean rehab?" It was all Bet could do to stay in the chair. This was not what she had signed up for.

"Let's hope not," Hyacinth said quickly, with a warm smile. "One thing at a time. We don't have to solve that today."

Hyacinth gestured to the paper. Bet dug in her purse for a pen, signed it and handed it back.

"Let me ask you something else. You didn't fill in the line for 'family' on your intake sheet."

"I didn't?"

No, I didn't. Maybe that should tell you I don't want to talk about them.

Bet sighed. *As if I can get off the hook that easy.*

"Perhaps you'd like to fill me in. Rich, obviously. How long have you been married?"

"Fourteen years." She rushed on, wishing to get through it. "Two children, aged twelve and nine. They live with Rich and don't see me. I'm not talking about that now."

Hyacinth made notes and didn't push it.

"I'm not asking to cause you pain. I'm assessing your support system. I'm guessing you feel like you have to handle everything on your own. Maybe you do. I need to know, however. What about parents? Siblings?"

"No siblings. My parents split when I was about sixteen. My mother went off—we never did find out where. My father pretty much gave up on family and threw himself into work. It got him a grave at forty." Bet was surprised to find herself choked up. Usually she kept her past at a comfy distance. *Not today.*

A few final notes, then Hyacinth set all her papers aside and sat up straight.

"I want to share with you a method I found that may help when you feel yourself becoming anxious—or stressed. Let's use your word. Can you try this with me?"

Oh, yay. Fun and games now. Bet sighed. *I'm the one who chose to come. Might as well play along.* "Sure." She sat up, facing the doctor.

"When you first feel things starting to move out of your control, I want you to take a deep breath. Go ahead."

They breathed in and out together.

"Then first, I want you to take note of five things around you that you can see."

"Seriously? Just anything. Like…desk, chair, doctor, expensive shoes…um, folder."

"Good. Those are all things that are here, that are real. They can anchor you to this reality, calmly. Next, note four things you can touch. Let them ground you."

This is ridiculous. Her fingers twitched on the arm of the leather chair. She smoothed them along. "Soft leather. Hard floor. My purse. The chair."

Hyacinth made a face. "Cheating to pick the same thing twice. But yes, those chairs are good and solid, very real. Very safe." She cleared her throat. "Three things you can hear."

"Ah, you talking. Cars outside." Bet glanced at the aroma thing, where the mist was coming out in little puffs. "That thing."

"Inside and outside. Good. The world continues on. Now, two things you can smell."

"Vanilla. Pretty much vanilla." The leather, of course, had a rich aroma, but she wasn't about to say the chair again after being scolded.

"Fair enough. One thing you can taste."

"Taste? Uh. Coffee, from when I drove over."

"All right. Those last two are right down to you. Drawing in from what you can see, which may be far away, closer through touch, through sound, and now you're back in your body. Everything is solid. Everything is under control. You are grounded. From here, you can calmly make decisions and move forward." Hyacinth studied her a long moment. "You think this is bunk."

"Yeah. I'm afraid so." *I'm used to controlling things with my brain. I don't need any new-agey gobbledegook to make decisions. I know what I need. This isn't it.*

"That's all right. It's just a tool. Some people find it works for them." She glanced up. "I see our time is up for today. I'll challenge you to use this tool a few times this week, when you feel that tension begin to rise. And I'd like to see you next week. Is Thursday a good day?"

Bet wanted to say she wasn't coming, but something compelled her to pull out her calendar instead. "Thursday, same time? I could make that."

"Great. I'll see you then." Hyacinth stood in dismissal.

Bet gathered her things and left the office, not even hearing the MUZAK in the lobby as she passed through. *I expected to spend an hour talking about how I hated my mother and how my childhood ruined everything. This woman wasn't anything like that. I think…I think she really heard me.*

Tears welled up in her eyes as she slid into the driver's seat. *She heard me.* A small fountain of joy rose in her midsection. Some sappy song came on the radio, and she turned it all the way up and sang along. For the first time in a long time, she felt like maybe things would turn out all right. Hyacinth Martell was going to save her life.

Chapter Ten

May 19, 1996
Present Day

Had it only been three days since she'd woken up and found that she should have been dead? It seemed a lifetime.

Bet's kitchen table took the place of her desk this morning, and every inch of it was covered. She'd finished one pot of coffee already, something delicious with hints of pecans and coconut. The brew had fueled another pass through the paperwork Mela had brought, but she'd found nothing with the initial "K" or a hint of what else had happened at the bar in South Miami.

Her other "lead" at the moment, Rich's mysterious non-confession, was on hold until that evening. He'd called first thing and arranged to meet her for dinner. *At the 94th Aero Squadron, yet. That used to be only for anniversaries and special occasions. A place where no one dared cause a scene.*

Oh, boy.

She boxed up the paperwork and set it by the front door. She could have gone to the office, now that the police had exposed her as alive anyway. But she didn't feel up to it. Her normal pain had ramped up, thanks to the stress, too much to sleep through it. On top of that, even after changing the bandages, the burns alternately hurt and itched. Damned inconvenient.

Not as much as it was for poor Mr. Gutierrez…

The thought hung in the air, dripping guilt like warm honey until the phone rang. The sudden noise split the silence like a klaxon, and she jumped. Feeling a little stupid, she answered it. "Bettina Lenard."

"Ms. Lenard, this is Detective Ortiz. Would you have time to come to the station today? We've pulled the security video from the Old Lisbon restaurant and wanted you to take a look."

That meant the police had already reviewed the content. What had they seen? "Was it helpful at all?"

A pause on the other end of the line. "We'd like to get your take on it, ma'am."

Hellfire. What did that mean? And what if the person who was after her worked at the station? The hostile looks she'd received over the last year from officers who knew her client had ratted out one of their dirty comrades felt like they could have killed. Would she be walking into a trap?

But if she refused to go, who was she hurting but herself?

"All right. I'll be down in half an hour or so."

"Thank you."

She hung up, bemused. Part of her couldn't wait to get there, unravel the clues and put this thing behind her. The other part feared what she'd find. Putting a face on the evil that had been done was frightening.

Her closet contained probably $10,000 worth of clothes, but for the life of her, she couldn't choose what to wear to the station. *Should I dress in a designer suit, so they take me seriously? Do I want to look like a victim, so they'll feel sympathy? Something girly?*

Androgenous? What serves me best?

Most of all, she just wanted to feel pretty and free again.

When was the last time I felt that way? Certainly before the incident. Before the divorce? Before we had children? Before I knew Rich at all?

She picked a sleeveless seersucker shirtdress in blue and white, with a scalloped hem. The white bow at the front waist was probably too young, but today she didn't care. She popped the collar, put on some gold hoop earrings, and let her hair hang loose. Her makeup—carefully edged around her bandage—took nearly fifteen minutes, but she wanted it to look "suburban soccer mom" and not "lounge club lizard."

With all this armor in place, she felt ready to go.

Downstairs, she opened the door and peered around the corner, half expecting an assassin to be waiting in the modest, unmowed front yard. The scarlet buds on the royal poinciana tree teased a full blossoming in the next week or two. It would be spectacular, as it was every year. The sun blazed through her clothes, creating a small sizzle on her skin, as she walked from her house to the car. It wasn't even officially summer—hurricane season was still two weeks away—but blistering heat announced its domination over the southern peninsula once more. Drips of sweat crept under her bandages and made her itch.

She slid on her CK sunglasses, and cranked up the air conditioning in the car. According to his card, Detective Ortiz worked at the main station in North Miami, so she took the most direct route to SR836, then joined the traffic lines and swung around the big curve to head east. It was the same drive she took to the courthouse, and she'd made it hundreds of times. Something about her mission today made it seem surreal.

Would any day ever be the same after what had happened?

The police station lobby was quietly institutional, light green walls, metal desks, and a row of chairs for those who inevitably waited. After checking in at the front counter, she paced, listening to the officer answer calls. When he wasn't yakking on the phone, he alternated with interoffice banter in Spanish. Bet wouldn't call herself bilingual, but she knew enough Spanish to know the men were talking about her, *la gringa,* at first in a sexual manner, then as they put two and two together, speculation that she might be a superhero. Or a murderer.

Trying to ignore them, she wished she'd worn a hat with a broad brim, so she could hide her face. *Might as well get used to it. The next…however many weeks…will likely be a replay of the same. My colleagues, friends, and enemies will all have the opportunity to bathe in the glorious scandal of it all. My God, will judges have to battle over sympathy decisions or step too lightly, not wanting to make it worse?*

"How exactly could it be worse?" she muttered aloud. The office conversation cut off abruptly. Fortunately, Detective Ortiz came to the counter and invited her to the conference room.

She followed him, wondering how she'd missed how good-looking in that Andy Garcia-Robert DeNiro style he was at their first interview. *Must have been preoccupied with my world vanishing into the toilet…*

"I'm glad you could come so soon," he said. The two had to step aside several times as driven colleagues rushed by with files in hand. "I've got a team out at the site this afternoon, taking track marks, and so on." He watched her face. "How are you feeling?"

"Like I've been picked up out of my life and dropped in someone else's."

"That's understandable." He opened the conference room's glass door for her, then showed her to the long rectangular cheap-office-store table, with half a dozen chairs around it and a television set on the far end. There were no windows. The carpet was the same generic gray that lay in most of the county buildings. *Must have been some sale on bulk carpet that year.* She took a seat near the TV.

Ortiz smiled and looked like he didn't know what to do with his hands. "Detective Brown will join us in a moment. Can I get you something? Coffee? Water? Cola?"

Do I make him nervous? That's almost laughable. She didn't really want anything. But she asked anyway. "You have *un Cubano*?"

He grinned. "Actually, I do. Be right back."

He stepped out, leaving her staring at the TV, which displayed only gray and white static. Her future depended on that small screen. A part of her history existed there, one that had been hidden, perhaps erased, from her mind. Who would she find revealed?

And what did it have to do with what Rich wants to tell me?

Was it too late to go mad? Seemed as reasonable as any of her other alternatives.

An officer walked by the glass windows with Tim Sampson. The attorney stopped right there, and his eyes widened. He made a "call me" gesture with his thumb and forefinger. She half-smiled and nodded.

Yeah, I'll get right on that.

He moved on. The other detective came in and had a seat, soda in hand. Ortiz came back with a tiny white cup and saucer, which he sat in front of her.

"Thanks." She picked it up and took a long whiff of the bittersweet brew. *So good.* Cuban coffee blended a strong espresso with *espumita*, or sugar foam. Normally served in one-ounce cups, it carried a blast of caffeine. *Un colada* was a four-ounce Styrofoam cup people bought to share among several friends. Bet and Mela often drank a whole *colada* each to get through a long afternoon. She sipped the coffee. "Perfect."

Ortiz almost wagged his tail, and took a seat, pleased with himself. "Has anything else come back to you, Ms. Lenard?"

Yeah, apparently my ex-husband is involved in shady dealings... "No, I'm afraid not."

"Nothing at all?" Ortiz seemed disappointed.

"The last couple of days have been their own special sort of hell, as you might imagine, Detective. Believe me, I'm as interested in recovering the truth as you are."

He made a few notes and nodded. "So, are you ready to see the video?"

"Might as well." She took another sip and began to wish it was bourbon instead.

"Very well." He hit the button on the VCR.

The customer area, particularly the bar where the cash register was located, came into view. The black-and-white video was hard to follow at first, but gradually she could make out people moving, a waiter, and finally, herself, in sunglasses, her hair up in a bun, making her way to a table next to the bar. Two people sat at that table, a burly bald man with his back to the camera, and a woman in a long-sleeved jacket, with dark hair that hung down into her face. In-the-film Bet paused by the table, speaking to the two for several minutes, before she joined them.

Ortiz paused the video. "Can you identify either of these people?"

Bet shook her head. "Hard to tell, not seeing his face. But, no."

"All right." He started the video again. A conversation ensued between Bet and the man. The woman said nothing, but sat sipping from her tall glass. Bet couldn't get a full look at her face, either. She didn't seem to be a familiar client. A waiter brought Bet what looked like a Manhattan with an orange-and-cherry spear. The man drank a beer, and gestured broadly as he talked.

Who were these people and what did they have to do with what happened? Her heartbeat quickened. Her head felt light and floaty. She finished the small cup, knowing it wouldn't help.

In the video, Bet suddenly reached into her purse and took out her phone, then said something to the two, and stepped away from the table, talking to the caller. The man and woman looked at each other. The man reached into his pocket and dropped something into Bet's drink, stirring it with the spear.

The horror of seeing just how easily it was done made her gasp. *That's the last time I'm answering a call in a restaurant. Ever.*

The men both looked at her with interest. "Should we take a moment?" Ortiz asked.

"No," she whispered, her stomach churning. "What

happened next?"

The video went on to show Bet returning to the table, speaking to them both, then taking the spear and eating the cherry off it before draining the drink. Another several minutes of conversation, and Bet-in-the-film dropped her hand on the table, nearly knocking her glass over. The waiter came by, leaning over to hand her a napkin. He spoke to her intently. She shook her head. The woman stood up and gestured to the back of the restaurant.

The restroom? Bet thought a minute about Old Lisbon. She had to have been to the restroom at some visit or other. She, Rich and the kids had eaten there many times. Yeah, that was the direction.

The woman came around to Bet and took her arm, helping her up. Bet was talking, talking, talking, and didn't seem to want to go, but eventually walked away, unsteadily, with the woman. A few seconds later, the man threw two twenties on the table, picked up Bet's purse, and walked out of camera view toward the front door.

Ortiz turned off the machine. "That's it."

"That's it?" Bet burst out. "That's nothing!"

Brown interjected, "It's clear that you were drugged, that you weren't complicit with whatever happened."

"Complicit?" Cold flooded over Bet. "You had me come because you thought I was complicit? Knowing I'd be without counsel? I thought we were all working on the same side." She placed her hands on the table and shoved straight up to her feet.

Ortiz shot Brown a dirty look. "No. NO. Please, Ms. Lenard. My partner misspoke."

"I'll say." She glared at Brown.

Ortiz refocused the discussion, moving a seat closer to her. He reached out as if he would pat her arm, but apparently thought better of it.

"I know it's hard to identify the two individuals, but I hoped perhaps seeing the scene would jog your memory, even if we don't know who they might be." He locked gazes with her until her breathing slowed and she returned to the seat.

She shook her head. "I'm sorry." She chewed her lip. "You'd think a guy like that would be memorable."

He agreed. "Exactly."

"Nothing else? Nothing in the parking lot?" she asked.

"They didn't have a camera that caught either of these individuals or you."

She sighed. *I'd hoped—and feared—this would solve the case. And we don't know much more now than we did.* "Can we run it again?"

"Certainly." Ortiz gestured to Brown, who reset the video to the beginning.

Bet watched as intently as the detectives did, but she saw nothing new. "No, I'm sorry. I'll think about it." She stood, stretching muscles that had spiraled in tight. "If there's nothing else? You'll let me know what the techs find?"

"Of course." Ortiz stood.

"All right. Sorry I couldn't be more help."

Brown grunted and drank his soda. Ortiz came around the table and opened the door for Bet, walking her back to the front. "Again, I'm sorry about Brown. He was a friend of Jellico's."

Ah. Figures. Jellico was an overweight, corrupt loser, too. "Blame your crooked co-worker, not me. I didn't make him take the bribes."

"I-I…right. Of course." He coughed uncomfortably and stopped at the door to the lobby. "Anyway…"

She cocked her head and studied him. He seemed like a good guy. And he looked good, too. *But as a criminal defense attorney, Lord knows I've learned not to trust the cops farther than you can throw them.* "Partners can be problematic. That's why I have an ex-husband."

He laughed, then looked embarrassed. "I'm sorry, that's—"

"No, it's okay. I meant it that way." She shook his hand. "You know where to find me." With a glance toward the curious office staff, she turned and walked into the brilliant Miami sun.

****

She stopped by the office, waiting several minutes in her car to get a good look around for possible danger before she went inside. Mela was on the phone when Bet walked in, but her expression was one of surprise, and she quickly took a message and got off.

"What are you doing here? You should be resting!" she said.

Bet waved a hand and continued into her office, plopping into her wheeled chair with a wince and a groan. She sorted through the mail on her desk, opening the letters she knew she wanted to see. Wishing she felt safe or comfortable, she looked around the room she'd been forced to rent when Rich booted her out of the plushy office at Lenard and Lenard. Bet hadn't done much to personalize it; she hadn't even bothered to hang her diplomas. *Did clients really think you were smarter because you have a frame and embossed piece of paper hanging on the wall? If someone really wants to know, they could go look it up.*

"I drafted some continuances," Mela said, following her in like a mother duck. "I guessed you'd be home at least a week—"

"Screw it," Bet said. "What's the point? I'm a target wherever. Might as well get paid."

Mela studied her. "What's happened?"

Bet sighed. "Apparently the police still thought I was a suspect. Until we watched the video from the bar." She explained the futile effort of Ortiz's tape.

Mela sank into the chair opposite the desk. "And you have no idea who the couple was?"

"Couldn't see either face, so no. The man's form was distinctive. You'd think I might have some idea who this square block of a guy was." She leaned forward. "Sound familiar to you? Someone who's come by here?"

"No. Not at all." Mela crossed her legs and brushed off her skirt. "Maybe Rich should go watch. I mean, if he thinks something he did was the cause. When are you meeting with him?"

"In about five hours. At the 94th." She glanced up with an ironic smile.

"Whoa." Mela sat back. "This is serious."

"Yep."

"Did you tell the detectives what Rich said?"

"No. I'll give him the benefit of the doubt. Until he confesses. In full."

She stayed only an hour, distracted by the creeping pain. *Maybe Mela was right. I should recuperate at home. I've got more control over my work environment there.* She gave Mela the satisfaction of knowing she'd been right, then took her laptop and a briefcase of mail and case files home with her.

At home, she marched swiftly to the door and let herself in, locking up bchind her. A quick trip to change into a loose caftan necessitated washing her face and changing the bandages yet again. She stared at the angry red blisters with a mixture of disgust and rage. Who were those people and how dare they? *How dare they?*

Too uncomfortable and anxious to work, she debated calling Hyacinth, but settled for a thorough meditation with the Five Things. A Vicodin dialed back her pain, and a shot of Jameson's topped it off. Instead of working, she curled up in her living room chair and watched a TV rerun of *Heathers.*

She'd always identified with Veronica. Part of the wrestling cheerleader squad, Bet had played the game just long enough to establish it on her high school resume, then she'd left the group. *These days, I'd just rip the rug out from under those mean girls.* She'd purposely chosen a small school, Muskingum College, and joined a sorority dedicated to serving others rather than being popular.

Bad enough still having to play games as an adult. At least now, I have weapons of my own.

Her first weapon for the evening was a spritz of Joy, by Jean Patou, a perfume Rich had bought her years before. The combination of jasmine and rose was once a favorite of Jackie Kennedy; it certainly was Rich's favorite, too.

Her second weapon was a short maize-and-navy dress with wide diagonal stripes, a real eyecatcher. If Rich thought he'd shove Bet under the rug—or perhaps the bus?—he had another think coming.

Her most valuable weapon would be the small

recorder she slipped into her clutch before she left. If she had the chance to get information that could finally give her the upper hand over Rich, she intended to grab it.

Maybe I'm a Heather after all…

****

Dusk set in as Bet pulled into the 94th Aero Squadron parking lot next to the Miami airport taxiways, a layered pink sunset in her rearview mirror. Airplanes roared in the sky around her, which was one of the attractions of the restaurant, watching the air traffic. But tonight, the view didn't matter.

Wearing flat gold Valentino sandals instead of the high heels that made her legs look muscular was disappointing. But the blisters hadn't healed, so she couldn't wear any of her favorites. *If Rich did this, he'll owe me for that, too.*

She walked in, admiring the wide-beamed ceiling. The quiet clink of glasses and silverware, the buzz of conversation, the spotless white tablecloths, all were comforting and familiar. She spotted Rich, sitting at a table for two back by the kitchen. *Probably didn't want to be overheard. As long as I can get him on the recorder, that's all I need.*

She nodded to the maître d' and walked across the room to join Rich. He stood up as she came to the table, but didn't pull out her chair. A caprese salad plate and a whiskey sour sat at her place. Rich had a glass of what looked like bourbon—probably Pappy van Winkle, if he was true to form—next to the basket of rolls. She took her seat and eyed the salad.

"That's Bushmills Black in your drink." He smiled. "And you know you're always starving by the time they bring food. I thought I'd get ahead of the game."

"Thoughtful." She set her clutch on the table to the left of her place setting. Three minutes was all she could hold out before she dug in to the salad. *Damn him for being right.*

Rich set his phone on the table, watching the people around them, nodding to some, raising his glass to others.

Bet studied him between savory bites, thinking he had a few more lines on his face since the split two years before. He still looked good in that aging-tennis-pro way. Was his hair grayer, or did that new comb-over expose more roots? Ten years' difference between them—she'd definitely be coloring her hair before it got to that shade, though.

He fussed with his glass, swirling the amber liquid and taking angry little sips. Giving her the side-eye, he said, "That's what you meant by 'not *all* right'? Are those burns?" He leaned over to look down her arm and leg.

"Yes, they're burns," she said, eyeing him with a bit of salt. "And I can't wait to hear why you think it could be your fault."

He cleared his throat and fingered his fork. "Well, you'll have to wait because I'm hungry. Every condemned man gets a last meal. Let's order." He flagged a server, who stopped at the table immediately.

"Bettina?" Rich gestured impatiently.

"I'll have the branzino," she said. "No rice. Extra lemon."

The server nodded. "And for you, sir?"

"The Churrasco steak. Extra chimichurri. Baked potato, sour cream, butter and shredded parmesan. And another of these." He shook his glass, now empty.

The server left the table and Bet chuckled. "You're

working hard on that coronary, aren't you, dear?"

He shot her an ugly look. "Well, I don't carry a jug of Vicodin with me."

She forced herself not to flinch. *That hurt.* She said nothing, just picked up her glass, focusing on the cool droplets of condensation wetting her fingers.

A moment later, he reached for her other hand, startling her. "I didn't mean that. I'm sorry, Bettina. This meeting is in truce territory." He squeezed her fingers and let go.

"We'll see about that. After the big reveal."

I should have known nothing had changed. He's just feeling guilty. And maybe he should.

"What are the kids up to?" she asked, wanting to avoid the maudlin tendencies he was showing.

"Jeremy's decided to play soccer this summer." He glanced up at her. "Practice and games will be on Saturdays."

"Of course they will." Saturday was her scheduled visitation day, although Jeremy usually declined the opportunity.

"You can pick him up and take him."

"I'm not much of a sports fan, Rich. I'll let you have the honor. And Jane? I expect she's done the same?"

"Actually, she's trying out for JV cheerleader." Rich leaned back in his chair. "Taking after you."

"Do you think she'll be a Heather?" Bet asked idly.

"A what? What are you talking about?"

The server dropped off Rich's new cocktail and spirited the empty away.

Bet just laughed softly. "Never mind."

He picked up the glass and drank half at once, then grabbed a roll and bit into it viciously.

The two sat in silence until their food came, then ate in silence as well. Anyone watching would certainly have guessed they were a long-married couple who no longer had a need to communicate. *Well, the long-married is right. Fifteen years is hard time, in our business.* Bet enjoyed the branzino, which was simply baked with olive oil, lemon and white wine. Rich attacked his meal as though it really was his last.

What the hell is it he wants to tell me? If he chickens out, I'll embarrass him in front of this whole place. I swear I will.

When the server had cleared the plates, along with Rich's third and fourth drink glasses, and Bet's half-finished sour, when they'd passed on dessert and settled for a civilized cup of coffee to finish the meal, Bet excused herself to use the ladies' room. As she'd expected, the mid-thigh length dress, or perhaps Bet herself, was a magnet for people's attention all through the restaurant. She glanced over her shoulder to see that Rich noticed, too.

Well, isn't that special…I'm pleased.

She touched up her makeup—which was definitely *not* suburban soccer mom—and checked her purse for the recorder. Angling it so she could activate it with a tap, she made final adjustments and returned to the table. Coffee steamed in white cups on white saucers. She sat and hit the button as she set her purse down. "Well?"

He paused, staring into his coffee. Then he turned and looked her hard in the eye before he blurted out what he had to say, practically all in one breath.

"Two years ago, John Lee came to me with a request—no, a demand. He had some dirty money and he wanted me to make it right."

"John Lee." The name was familiar. The man had been in the offshore drug business for years, lived an extravagant life on Star Island. His yacht was worth more than her house. He'd been a client of Rich's when Rich ran the criminal law part of the partnership. *Wait, this has been going on for two years, and he never said a thing?* She growled internally, her emotional temperature dropping.

"Yeah. All I had to do was quote him retainer fees of $9500 for a number of different cases. He'd pay them to me; I'd put them in escrow. Several months later, I'd mark the cases settled, keep 10%, and refund him the rest."

"Ninety-five hundred, because the federal reporting level is 10K."

He nodded and picked up his coffee. She was gratified to see his hand shook a little.

"I didn't do it all the time, Bettina. Just on occasion. I didn't see any need to tell you because…well, because you never had a head for all the math anyway. You still got paid all your percentage from the partnership and it didn't matter."

"Oh? Laundering money didn't matter?"

"Shh! Keep your voice down." He set the cup back in the saucer with a clatter. Several people turned to stare.

She smiled and leaned closer as if he'd just told the most fabulous joke. "So why are you telling me now?"

He hesitated. "Damned if I know."

"You can't stop there. What happened?" she hissed.

A sigh as deep as Biscayne Bay. "About four months ago, I told him I didn't want to do it any longer. I felt like I'd honored any debt of…friendship…or at least loyalty, I owed him." He shifted in his seat. "And you know, the state Bar proposed new rules on escrow accounts, and…"

She clicked her tongue. "Tsk-tsk. And you thought you'd get caught."

He just stared, a hangdog expression on his face. *If he thinks I'll feel sorry for him…*

She waited for him to go on. When he didn't, she kicked him under the table, regretting it immediately because he was on her right side. *Those burns HURT, dammit.*

"He said if I pulled out, he'd make me sorry. You and I both know he's got the connections to pull off almost any criminal endeavor. So, when I heard about the…thing…on the news, that was my first thought. Maybe he found you a lesser target, since you were my ex."

"Ex as in expendable? For Christ's sake, Richard. Where the fuck is your brain?"

"Do you think I don't realize this? He could have gone after the kids, or…"

Her blood turned to ice. She pulled her chair closer to his and leaned in, close enough she could bite his ear. She whispered, "You may have just killed us all because you have exalted yourself above the law. I hope you're happy."

Flicking her tongue around the inside of his ear, she breathed warmly, slowly, knowing exactly what it would do…what it had always done. She looked into his lap and smiled.

"Now I'm going to walk out of here without getting *you* killed—see how easy that is? And you'll have to sit here until you get control of your dick."

She shoved her chair back from the table with a screech that made everyone look, then grabbed her purse and stalked her long legs all the way to the door. Once outside, she broke into a run, glad she had left the heels at home after all. She jumped into her car, slammed and locked the door. One finger turned the recorder off. Then she peeled out of the lot.

Intending to nurse that burgeoning fury all the way home, she was surprised when she only had one thought: *Wait.... even after all we've been through, if I can give him an erection with just a whisper, does that mean he still loves me?*

Chapter Eleven

September 23, 1990
Six years earlier

Bet stretched out on the blue-flowered chaise lounge in the huge screened-in porch, half watching the kids play in the pool. Rich sat with her feet in his lap, gently rubbing them, while they read different sections of the Sunday *Herald.* Sun filtered in through the tree branches overhanging the enclosure, and the light breeze just carried the scent of gardenias from the pots on the west side. They each had a fresh cup of coffee, and the soothing sounds of Love94's weekly jazz program came from the Bose speaker at the far end of the porch.

Heaven.

"Mom! Mom! Watch!" Jane prepared to jump off the deep end of the pool.

"I saw you last time," Bet mumbled. *That flat-bellied slap hurt my cranky muscles, just listening to it.*

"I'll be better this time!"

"All right." Bet laid the entertainment section across her lap and turned her head to watch. "Go ahead."

Dark-haired Jane, with her long pigtails, wearing her new pink two-piece suit, posed with her arms straight in front of her, like the swimmers they'd watched in the last Olympics. The pool wasn't deep enough to permit dives; but Jane wasn't likely to succeed anyway.

She didn't. Another painful belly flop, just as Bet had predicted.

"Keep practicing," Rich called. "You'll get it one of these times, Janie."

"Love you, Daddy!" Their daughter pushed herself out of the water, onto the side of the pool, and beamed.

"Love you, Daddy," Bet said, just loud enough for Rich to hear. Her mocking tone was intentional.

"What? Being supportive of the kids' efforts actually contributes to their improvement, Bettina." He glanced over the newspaper at her. "It wouldn't hurt you to try."

She rolled her eyes. Why was it he never missed an opportunity to criticize her relationship with the children? *Not like your wife can be a full-time stay-at-home mother and hold up her contracted end of a 24-7, 365 days a year law practice in Miami, dear...* "I'm sure."

Drawing her legs up, she scooted to the other end of the lounge and sat straight, wincing at the pain that zigzagged through her tendons. She took a long sip of coffee, letting the flavors layer across her tongue. *Nothing like good coffee. No matter what it costs. Isn't that why we made the sacrifices to go to law school?*

Though some days I wonder exactly why we did that. Why I did that.

"Mom! Come swim with me."

Sometimes, when the water was this warm, swimming helped relax the tension in her muscles, but Bet had a feeling it wouldn't help much this day. The pain had continued at a slow build since she got out of bed. "Jane, I'm really not feeling well."

Jane's expression tightened. "Again?"

It's not like I want to ache this way, kid. Cut me some slack.

"It's just water, Bettina. Give the kid five minutes, for Christ's sake." Rich practically growled. "Honestly, sometimes you're the most unnatural mother—"

"Fine!" Bet got up, her lower back screaming. She threw the paper down and stalked inside to put on her bathing suit. The muscle contortions caused by pulling up the slim one-piece brought a tear to her eye. She grabbed a thick turquoise beach towel from the bathroom and returned, stopping in the kitchen for a generous shot of straight whiskey to help ease the discomfort. Then she added another for luck.

Jeremy ran out into the yard to kick his soccer ball around as she came through the door. She tossed her towel on a deck chair and walked into the pool via the three steps at the shallow end. The water was warm, not bath temperature, but it was summer's end, and the sun had beaten down on the pool every day. When she reached waist depth, she let herself drop forward, and in a few long strokes, she was side by side with Jane at mid-pool.

"Look what I can do, Mom." Jane folded in half and dove for the bottom of the pool, her skinny little legs sticking up as her hands reached the painted concrete.

Bet treaded water, wishing peace into her body. When Jane came up, Bet gave her a high five. "Wow. That's really something."

"You try, Mom." Jane looked at her expectantly. When Bet didn't move, Jane added, "You can do it in shallower water, if you want."

"Honey, I'm really not up to handstands today." She paddled into water where she could reach the bottom.

"We could…race? Laps?"

"Sure! Let's start at the shallow end."

Jane swam several strokes until she, too, could stand, and then ran to the steps. "Daddy! Call 'on your mark, get set, go.' "

Rich grinned. "All right, ladies. On your mark, get set, go!"

The two hit the water, Bet taking a leisurely pace, allowing Jane to reach the end a few seconds before she did.

"Janie wins!" Rich said.

Bet reached out to scoop her daughter into an embrace and kissed her cheek. Jane hugged her back briefly, but pushed her away.

"Mom, you're drinking already? It's not even afternoon!"

Guilt pulsed through Bet. *How did she know? Could I smell like liquor after only two?* She caught Rich's disappointed eye and sighed.

Jane swam to the ladder and climbed out, grabbing her towel before marching inside.

Furious at maybe herself, maybe life in general, Bet launched into a series of laps. She swam the forty feet back and forth, back and forth, muscles burning. Punishing herself was stupid. She knew that. But she couldn't face Rich, or Jane, and she needed to do *something*.

After a while, she didn't know how long, when she reached out to the steps at the shallow end of the pool, Rich was there. He pulled her up, into his arms, and held her.

"I know you tried," he said close to her ear. "Jane's not old enough to understand."

The moment of unexpected kindness was too much for Bet, and she broke down in tears. Rich gently helped her out of the pool and wrapped her in the towel, then sat beside her on the lounge chair. "You're hurting today? That bad?"

Bet nodded.

"Let's try another doctor at Jackson Memorial, all right? Some specialist there must be able to figure this out."

"Okay." Bet calmed herself and sniffed.

"Why don't you go in and lie down a bit? You've probably dinged every muscle in your body after that performance," he said, with no derogatory tone. "I'll make the kids lunch and maybe we'll ride out to the farmer's market. Get ice cream. A movie. Something."

She nodded and let him help her up. She went inside, shivering in the AC, and stripped off the wet suit, hanging it on the lowest nozzle in their double-size shower. Wrapping herself in a thick bathrobe, she climbed into bed, wishing herself to sleep to escape the nibbling stabs of pain.

Chapter Twelve

May 20, 1996
Present Day

Bet woke as a shaft of sunlight hit her face through a crack of the beige-tinted bedroom blinds. For a few moments, she lay still, checking in with her body. Nothing hurt. She was cocooned in a sense of well-being that she wished would continue forever.

Then she moved. And it began.

Muscles pulled with long aches that made her wince. Knee and elbow joints stabbed with ice picks. The bandaged burns tickled and simmered under the gauze she'd replaced the night before. By the time her feet hit the floor, she was already reaching for the pill bottle on her bedside table.

A shaky twenty minutes until the Vicodin would kick in. She had no choice but to wait.

She threw on a bathrobe and went down to the kitchen to put on the coffee she'd forgotten to set up the night before, when she'd returned, triumphant from The Grand Confession.

Much too much to think about after my talk with Rich. He's unbelievably stupid to try to launder Lee's money through the bank. The escrow account! The inviolable trust account that contains only client money. The one that we can be disbarred for screwing with.

Disbarred.

She'd signed the yearly joint statement to the Florida Bar, verifying that the trust account had been purely managed, never contaminated with firm money. *Or ye gods, criminal money.* Rich had handed the form to her, and she'd blindly put her name on the verification. *So now I'm just as guilty as he, in in the eyes of the Bar.*

"Damn him."

Bet tried to find a comfortable way to stand while she waited for enough coffee to brew that she could pour off a cup. It seemed like wherever she put her weight, a steady painful ache would settle in her limbs. Calling the doctor seemed like the rational thing to do, but she'd already bugged them three times this week, arranging to get her lost supply of pain meds replaced. What she'd had in her purse was locked up in some evidence room downtown.

I probably should have them check the burns anyway. Maybe I'll start there and see if they've got anything else that will help the stress pain that's accumulated, dealing with this mess. And that mess. And...

When she finally poured her coffee, she took it through the sliding glass door to the small cement porch out back and sat gingerly on a turquoise-cushioned Adirondack chair. Settling in, she eyed the thickly clouded skies that echoed her own morose outlook. The humidity was up; that could well explain the increase in pain. Any time a front came in, a painful twang in her muscles and joints came, too.

Unlike the beautiful fruit grove behind the former marital home, here there was no view, only the neighbors' back yards with their above-ground pools and swing sets. Her yard was mostly grass, with a few raggedy trees. Several scrawny potted schefflera and other poorly-tended plants grew in colorful ceramic jars on the cement, but Bet mostly forgot to water them or take care of them at all, really.

Why is it I can only nurture clients? Plants, pets, kids... it just doesn't come naturally.

Hyacinth said some people were not cut out to be parents. The psychiatrist herself had no children. When Bet asked her why not, she'd demurred with a simple "That's not relevant." Bet thought it was. *How can she direct or counsel me on my feelings about having children if she's never had any? You sure as hell can't learn that kind of thing by reading black and white off the page.*

Or maybe that's just me.

Bet liked to use her mother's disappearance as an excuse for not connecting with Jane and Jeremy as deeply as she'd like. In fact, she and her mother had enjoyed a relatively warm relationship in childhood, and even in her early teens—the years Bet was experiencing with her own kids. She recalled happy memories with her mom, with her mom and dad. And then her mother left.

It had been a painful, broken time for Bet, and no one to share it with but her father, who was equally shattered by the separation.

The one thing I was determined to never do to any children I would birth. And it happened anyway.

Not that she didn't try. But as the years passed, the alcohol had interfered, and in the last few, she couldn't cope with the pain any other way. Sometimes, it even felt like Rich was always riding herd, cutting her out when she got too close. But that could just be paranoia. Rich ended up cutting her out of a lot. But she'd deserved it.

With a long-suffering sigh, she stretched out her legs, frowning as the big bandage around her right foot came into view. The burns had healed to the point that her regular dose of pain medication covered them, unless she did something stupid, like kick Rich. Despite the plastic surgeon's confidence, she was sure she'd have scars. *I'm vain enough to know I'll probably do something about them, too. When you're used to being known as a pretty girl, it's hard when that stops.*

Her coffee smelled wonderful, and she paused a moment just to take in the aroma before she drank some. A bit of movement caught her eye, off to the right, in Rainy Ketelman's yard, kitty-corner across the yards on the next block. A silver-haired man in a black T-shirt and jeans stood next to the end of Rainy's little porch enclosure, watching Bet. He wasn't someone who belonged in the neighborhood; Bet was sure she'd never seen him before.

Trying to be nonchalant, even as a *frisson* of fear slithered through her, she looked away, off to the left, stealthily checking to see if any of her other neighbors were out. But, no, it was noon on a weekday, and all the good people of the world were off at work. *Figures. It's not like anyone borrows a cup of sugar from the house next door these days. The least they could do is spectate if I'm about to be assassinated.*

Her standard sarcastic response did little to reassure her. Damn it, she was still scared. Glancing up at the sky as a pair of seagulls winged their way toward the Bay, she slid her gaze to the right again. *Still there. Okay. That's enough,*

She sat straight and finished her coffee, then got up

and walked inside, in no hurry so as not to spook the voyeur. The screen slid closed with its usual ease. Bet leaned against the door jamb, looking out. The man remained where he was, still watching. With the lights off, it would be hard to see inside the screen, so she wasn't worried he'd catch her at anything.

Not like he had a weapon in his hands, either. Not a threatening sound or movement. No sense calling the cops. Maybe it's just Joe-Bob, Rainy's cousin. Hell, who even knows anymore?

That reminds me, I forgot about buying that gun. Better put that back on the shopping list.

She pulled the glass door closed, too, and locked it. *Just in case.*

On her way past the table to get more coffee, she spied the hospital paperwork. She could give Dr. Rimon the call he seemed to want so desperately that he'd broken the unspoken rules about personal contact with patients.

Surely he'd seen the television reports by now. He'd know what I didn't say, if not why. But he appeared smart enough to guess.

Somehow, she felt comforted that he might, in fact, not think she was as crazy as she must have seemed that morning in the ER. At least he'd been concerned for her. She'd been lacking something of that nature for a while now. It felt good.

Feeling a little giddy, she dialed his office number. His service answered.

"Dr. Rimon's answering. Is this an emergency?" A calm, alto voice. Very soothing.

"No, not at all."

"All right. What message is there for the doctor?"

"Ah…" She'd known, in her depths somewhere, that he certainly wouldn't answer himself. But she hadn't really thought far enough ahead about a message. "This is a patient of his…um, Jo March. Here's my phone number. If he could just call me when he's free?"

The woman repeated the name and number. "I'll leave this for him. Thank you." Click.

Feeling a bit sheepish, Bet hung up. A moment later, she picked up the receiver again and called Mela at the office to see if anything interesting was happening. Since there wasn't, she decided to work on the files she'd brought home the day before. She hauled them upstairs and made a comfy little nest of soft blankets and pillows in her bed, setting the laptop on a bed tray. It wouldn't knock her pain out, but it would certainly be more comfortable than a hard kitchen chair at the table or trying to find something that put her arms at the right height to work from the couch. She flipped on the TV news at minimum volume as white noise, and plowed into her brief.

The phone rang just after 2:30. She rubbed her eyes, burning from her intense screen scrutiny, and hit 'save.' "Hello?"

"Miss March." A smile infiltrated his words, and she detected some amusement at catching her out, as well.

She straightened up. "Dr. Rimon."

"Giamo, please."

Better to get the lie out of the way right from the start. "And you can call me Bet. Bettina Lenard."

"Yes, I surmised as much. How are you doing?"

"All right, considering. The police are…well, you've probably seen." She leaned back into the stacked blue pillows.

"I may have taken a personal interest, yes." He still sounded entertained. "I hope you're pleased with my work. Since you are one of those lawyers we discussed."

She blushed, belatedly remembering that part of the conversation. "Well, takes one to know one, right?" She laughed softly.

"I've just got a few minutes on my break now, but I'd love to get together outside of work and just give you an outlet to vent, if that would be helpful. Do you know the Fuentes coffee shop off Coral Way?"

Was he asking her for a date? Was she crazy enough to go?

Yes.

"I've driven by. When?"

"My day off's Friday. About 9 a.m.?"

Her smile was so wide, it pulled her bandage loose. A line of pain rippled along her cheek. With a hiss, she winced and patted it back on. "Sure. I can't promise you'll be safe. Someone's trying to kill me, you know."

He gasped. "I can't believe you can joke about it like that."

"Yeah, well. What else can I do?"

"Maybe that's what we'll talk about. We can find you some help." He cleared his throat. "Have you seen your regular doctor about your injuries? Let me guess. No."

Am I that predictable? And he only knew me for an hour. "I'm going to. When I have time."

"Uh-huh. Let me give you a piece of advice. Maintaining those coverings on the wounds is extremely important. Infection can set in on very short notice. You need to get to your doctor for follow-up ASAP."

"Yes, Doctor," she said meekly. "I'll see you on

Friday."

He hung up and she did too, delighted. Expecting nothing, because she didn't know what kind of future she had coming, she was still pleased that something enjoyable had happened today. It had to happen every so often, just on odds, right?

Her rhythm broken, she decided to stop in the bathroom, and she removed her bandages, studying each wound for any hint of the anticipated redness or pus. Nothing yet. Promising herself and the absent doctor that she would make an appointment as soon as she could, she taped fresh gauze over the injuries, as he'd recommended.

Now what? Her work rhythm had been interrupted, so a walk around the house would help loosen her up. *Maybe a cold drink?* Stretching painfully, she groaned her way to the kitchen. On her way back, she checked the living room for her favorite pen.

The front door knob rattled. The sound froze Bet where she stood. *Was it that man…?* It rattled again, then someone knocked, hard.

She backed away from the door, unable to swallow, her throat tight as a clogged drain.

"Mom! Open the door! I know you're here."

Bet blinked. "Jane?" She put herself in forward gear, hurrying to peep out the tiny hole. *What in the…*Jane and Jeremy appeared in the fish-eye view. She unlocked and opened the door.

"What…what are you doing here?" she asked softly. "Come in, quick." She stepped aside and beckoned them in, then re-locked the door behind them.

Jeremy stared a moment, then threw his arms around her. "Mom." He held on for dear life. Jane smirked and headed for the kitchen.

When did my boy get tall enough his hair tickles my cheek? She'd seen them what, two, maybe three months before? She hugged him tightly, grateful for his affection. Then he let go, so she did, too, studying his dark eyes, so like his father's, his curly mop of red-gold hair, like hers. His face seemed thinner; his shoulders broader. *He's growing up, damn it.*

"The kids at school were talking about the accident," he said. He stared at her bandaged injuries. "Is it true you almost died?"

"That's what the police say." She slipped her left arm around his waist. They followed Jane, to see what she was up to. "How did you get here?"

"Marty dropped us off."

"Did you let your father know? He'll be worried." *Probably much more worried about you than me. You're not EX-pendable.*

In the kitchen, Jane was standing before an open cupboard door, frowning at the liquor bottles inside. "Still at it?" she asked, disappointment dripping from her tone.

Bet sighed to her depths. "Not today, Janie. Please? Could I have a hug?"

After a pause long enough to demonstrate she was not capitulating, Jane closed the cabinet and crossed the room for a perfunctory hug that gradually relaxed into the real thing.

Teenagers. Ugh.

"So, what happened, Mom?" Jeremy pulled them both toward the living room, where they sat on the couch together, one kid on each side of Bet. Jane laid her brunette head on her mom's right shoulder, her dark eyes closed. *She was her daddy's girl in appearance, too.*

"I wish I could tell you," Bet said. "And before Jane says something rude, no, I wasn't drunk. The police have determined it wasn't my fault." She hesitated. "I'm not sure I can give you any details, though. The investigation is active. Usually, they like to keep the information to themselves until they make an arrest."

Jane snorted. "You always say the cops are full of shit."

Bet chuckled. "Well. Yes. But then, I've never been the focus of an investigation."

Jeremy sat up straight and clutched a throw pillow. "Was the guy your boyfriend?"

"No. He was an old client of mine. I hadn't seen him for years."

"What was he doing in a car with you, then?" Jane asked.

"No idea. Not my car. Certainly not my plan."

Was that what Rich thought? That Gutierrez was her boyfriend? Is that what he told the children? Something about that troubled her.

Jane lifted Bet's arm and studied the healing burns that remained in the open. "Do they hurt?"

"Not as much as they did." She removed her arm from Jane's grasp. "I'll be fine, you guys. Thanks for worrying. Thanks for letting me know you are." She slipped an arm around the shoulder of each and hugged them. "Do you have homework?"

"Really, Mom." Jane rolled her eyes.

The first time they'd been here in ages, and she had to pull Mom rank? She sighed. *I'm not sure how to even be with my own children any more.* "Okay, you can do it later. I'm just glad you're here. What do you want to do?"

"You have any games?"

Bet had to stop and think. "I don't know. If you brought any over, maybe. Check the hall closet, on the top shelf."

It turned out at some point they had left a VCR game about TV shows at her house, and they all three hung on the couch and played the game amid a rush of small talk, catching up on each other's lives. Bet was pretty stunned at the relaxed atmosphere, and the fact that Jane in particular was really trying to be a "good daughter."

Doesn't mean I'll try to get myself blown up again any time soon, just to get the same result.

I'm still grateful.

It got to be dinner time, and Bet debated takeout, but decided she felt safer keeping them all safely inside the house. She threw together some macaroni and cheese, and salad, and they ate at the kitchen table, telling stories they remembered from years past and laughing. Jeremy washed the dishes and stacked them on the counter. Jane raided the freezer and discovered an ice-crusted container of Chunky Monkey in the back that contained enough for each of them to have a tablespoonful. They licked the ice cream like it was a cone and then had a contest to toss the spoons across the room into the sink.

Bet lost. It didn't matter. She was just happy the kids had come to see her. They still cared.

Rich knocked on the door about eight o'clock. Bet went to answer it, and he quickly stepped inside.

"Feeling like there's a target on your back?" she asked sweetly.

His eyes narrowed and he scowled. "Next time you decide to take the kids on a school night—"

Jane popped her head around the corner. "She didn't do it, Dad. We came over on our own. Since you didn't bother to tell us about the accident."

Rich coughed and looked guilty. "I didn't want to worry you kids. Especially since your mother seems to have retained all her—faculties." He eyed Bet, and Bet smiled, with an edge.

"It was a nice visit. I'm glad you came," Bet said. "It's probably time to go home and get your homework—"

"Mom! You're supposed to be the fun one." Jane grimaced, but she grabbed her backpack from its place by the door.

Bet hugged Jeremy, then Jane. "Really. Thanks for coming." To Rich, she said, "Any news on the matter we talked about last night?"

Rich shook his head. "Not like that will just jump out onto the table, Bettina."

"That's a shame."

He growled and opened the door. "Let's go."

Bet was gratified to hear Jane ask, "What's she talking about? Did something happen? Did you do something?" She continued all the way to Rich's car, and looked determined to go on after they got inside. *That's my girl. She doesn't miss a thing. She'll hang on like a bulldog.*

And this time, she's biting Rich's leg.

Bet locked the door, then went to turn off the kitchen light, and smiled, thinking of the evening they'd had. Was it the impromptu nature of the visit, or the relaxed atmosphere without Rich hovering that had made it so magical? *I haven't taken a pain pill since this morning. And I feel great right now. Better call it a day before I go and screw it up.*

She poured a glass of mango juice instead of wine, and retreated to bed, taking refuge in some soapy medical drama on the television. *Now those people have REAL problems....*

Chapter Thirteen

November 23, 1995
Six months earlier

Hyacinth welcomed her into the office, taking Bet's heavy sweater with a faint smile.

"I know," Bet said, feeling a little silly having outerwear in Miami. "It's insane to be cold on a sixty-five-degree day. When I went to school in Ohio, this was practically bikini weather. But after a few years here, sixty-five is freezing."

The doctor's expression remained blandly amused. "As you say. I've got tea. Chai or chamomile?"

"Chai, please."

Bet took her usual seat. A few minutes later, Hyacinth brought her a steaming thick-walled ceramic mug of spicy liquid. "That will warm you nicely, I believe."

"Thank you." Bet sank back into the wonderful leather chair, sniffing the cinnamon and cardamom.

"Of course." Hyacinth flipped open her ubiquitous notebook, scanning a couple of pages. "Now, when we were last together, we discussed your feelings of lack of control in the work environment. Are we finished with that topic? Would you like to revisit it, or move on?"

"I thought about the points you made. I guess I do yield to Rich on most management decisions."

"You agree that he doesn't 'take' those choices from you?"

"Yes. I actually never handled most of the business decisions even before the split." *Absolutely not. So much of that was tedious and mind-killing. Give me the drama and excitement of client contact and courtroom battle anytime.*

Hyacinth nodded and made notes.

"So, if he wants to carry all that burden, more power to him."

"Good. What else is on your mind? How have you been doing with stress reduction through meditation?"

Bet choked on her sip of chai. "Um, it's been going…slowly."

Hyacinth looked at her over the top of her narrow tortoiseshell glasses.

Bet sighed. "All right. I tried. I can't just sit and do nothing. It makes me crazy."

"To the contrary. Millions of people have found that meditation specifically makes them *not* crazy. In particular, medical professionals find that meditation is better than medication." She gave her usual small, tight smile that Bet took to mean she knew she was being ironic.

"Ha-ha. I'll try again. Promise."

Why do I promise something I know I won't do? My word is more than that, isn't it? Well, isn't it?

Hyacinth watched her intently, almost as if she were trying to pierce Bet's skull to read her thoughts.

Bet set her mug on the small table next to the chair. "All right. Maybe I will."

Hyacinth nodded and wrote some notes. Then she smiled.

Damn it.

"Look, maybe we could talk about Jane? I mean, I know teenage girls are supposed to go through that 'I hate everything and everyone' phase, but what can I do to get her aligned again with me, like she was for about five minutes when she was twelve?"

Hyacinth sat forward, eyes wide. "Interesting. Before the split. Before she caught on to your use of alcohol as pain management. What could you do differently now?"

Before Bet could answer, Hyacinth's phone rang. The doctor stiffened and glanced over to her desk.

"I'm so sorry, I'm expecting a call from the Board. Do you mind?"

"Go ahead, please. This chai is plenty entertaining." Bet grinned.

The psychiatrist walked to her desk and sat down before she picked up the receiver. "Yes, this is she. Who?" A long pause. "What?" Alarmed. "Where?" She stood up. "I'll be right there. Yes. Thank you."

She hung up and stared for a moment.

"I've got to go. My mother's been in an automobile accident."

Bet stood, setting down her empty cup. "Of course. Is there anything I can do?"

"No. Nothing. Just…I'll call you to reschedule." Hyacinth practically tossed the sweater at Bet as she hurried to open the door. She closed the door behind them and scampered to the stairs. Bet followed more sedately, forming a small wish in her heart that everything would turn out fine. Hyacinth was one of the few positive notes in her life now, after the divorce. Bet only wished her well.

****

Bet didn't receive a call the next week, or the week after. Finally, a little worried, she called and left a message saying that she hoped everything was all right, and she'd like to know how Hyacinth was doing.

She received a call from an answering service a few days later that simply said the psychiatrist was making arrangements for her mother's memorial service and she wasn't taking appointments.

How awful. Some of their discussions had led to Hyacinth revealing that she and her mother had been very close. The mother lived north of Miami—Boca, maybe? Bet couldn't remember. *I'll send flowers to the funeral home…or maybe the office.*

She checked the *Herald* obituaries, but found no one with the last name Martell, or that had a daughter listed named Hyacinth.

Odd. She called the number again, leaving a message with the service requesting that information. The service called back, saying they were unable to provide it.

No one is required to have an obituary printed. Maybe the mother was a private person and didn't want it listed.

She asked Mela to call around to the funeral homes and check. Not knowing more than the mother's name was Judith made identification difficult, and Mela came up dry.

Very odd.

More than a month passed before Bet heard anything from Hyacinth. Finally, just after New Year's, Bet got a message on her answering machine at home, inviting her to make an appointment. She called right away.

Hyacinth answered, as usual. "Dr. Martell."

"It's Bet Lenard. How are you? I was so sorry to hear what happened. I tried to send flowers, but—"

"Are you calling for an appointment?"

Bet frowned. The cold question seemed to reject any sympathy she might share. "Ah…yes."

"I've got next Wednesday at 4. Will that work for you?"

Bet consulted her calendar. "Yes. But—"

"Great, I'll see you then." She paused. "Listen, Bet, I assume you're trying to follow the whole condolences rigamarole. But you and I know we can't change what's in the past. What's done is done."

"Of course. I didn't mean to make you uncomfortable."

"No worries. See you Wednesday."

Hyacinth hung up, leaving Bet wondering what on earth had happened to change the doctor's outlook on life. Losing a parent was painful—Bet's loss of her father had torn a piece of her heart loose. But this seemed extreme.

Maybe it'll just take a while. What is it Hyacinth always says? "Stop acting as if life is a rehearsal. The past is over and gone. The future is not guaranteed."

Bet decided to bring Hyacinth a nice gloxinia or something for the office, anyway. *If it doesn't make her feel better, at least it will make me feel that way.*

Chapter Fourteen

May 23, 1996
Present Day

It had been a week since she woke up in the Everglades, not dead. Knowing that most investigation is done in the first forty-eight hours, Bet wanted to review the analytical reports. Unfortunately, there was no official way to obtain them—she hadn't been charged with anything, so she had no rights to discovery through legal process.

But I'm not completely without means of persuasion.

Betting on a long shot, she got dressed for the office, then made a call to Luis Ortiz. His voice when he answered was warm, encouraging. She remembered the warmth in his eyes, even when his questions had her pinned down in her kitchen. *He could be a nice guy. Maybe.*

"Good morning, Detective. I've been up most of the night worrying about this horrible thing that's happened. I know the tape didn't show us anything we wanted to see. It's really got me down."

"I'm sorry to hear that. I imagine it's impossibly stressful."

"It is. I just need information to work with." She stretched the truth into taffy. "I—I think my memory might be filling in. If I just had something…"

"I'm not sure what I can do, Ms. Lenard."

"You've got reports from the arson people by now, don't you? I can come right down and take a look over them and see if that helps."

He hesitated. "That's not SOP, you know that."

Tread carefully. "This is hardly a standard operating case, Luis." She waited to see what use of his first name would do.

"Ah…I'm not sure."

I think I've got him.

"I could meet you right in that conference room. You could stay there the whole time and watch me. I don't even need to take anything away when I'm done. I just want to see what they've found so I can fill in these holes in my memory. That will likely help your investigation more than anything else, wouldn't it?" She actually had tears come to her eyes. She milked them until her voice cracked. "I just don't know if I'll ever be able to sleep again…"

Sympathy infused his tone. "All right. A brief look. And not the originals. I'll have select copies for you. You understand this is very preliminary. We've asked for a rush because a homicide is involved, but we may not have everything figured out for weeks or even months."

"You're an angel, Luis. My police angel." She grinned like a fool, pleased with her success. "I'll be there in twenty minutes."

"See you then."

She could hear the regret in his voice as he hung up. Maybe he was rethinking his decision. *I need to get there right away.*

Even though it was morning rush hour, she made it in twenty-one minutes. Ortiz met her in the lobby, and escorted her quickly back to the conference room, where he closed the blinds on all but the glass door.

"I'm not sure how these will help," he said. "But for what they're worth…"

"I just have a feeling this will pull things together." She sat on the same chair she'd been in last time, sitting back, crossing her legs. The slit in the side of her skirt showed everything it was supposed to.

He set down a stack of papers. Two regular Styrofoam cups awaited them on the table. He shoved one in her direction, and took the other, sitting next to her.

"You're so kind," she said. The coffee was black, and sweet—not how she usually drank it—but it was meant kindly so she didn't complain.

"Go on and read," he said, shifting uncomfortably. "You need to be out of here before the shift commander gets back from his meeting downtown."

She nodded and dove in to the reports.

First, she reviewed the photos and list of personal items found in the car. The tattered remains of Gutierrez' clothing brought back the vivid memory of the smell when she'd opened that door. She shuddered. A gold cross on a neck chain had sunk into his skin. The dead man's wallet was found, singed, packed between his body and the seat, likely in a back pocket. The cards and IDs in there remained mostly intact, once they'd been peeled apart where they'd melted. *That's how he was identified, then. But still no explanation of why him.*

Her purse had been similarly wedged under the driver's seat, and some of her credit cards weren't completely destroyed. The investigator noted that an accelerant had been poured into the right back seat, which is where the fire began. Traces of the accelerant were also located on the backs of the front seats, allowing it to spread forward.

When…how…did I figure this out? I got out of the car. Did I do it on my own? Surely if someone had helped me, they would have rescued Jackson as well. Could I have done something to save him?

"Anything?" Ortiz asked softly.

"It feels close," she replied, gripping the papers until they crinkled.

"Have you seen one of these guys work?" he asked. "They examine the vehicle in reverse order, from the areas of least fire damage to the worst. They study the parts most likely to generate evidence first. Fire patterns indicating the direction a fire burned are of evidentiary value. People expect everything to be black after a fire. The things that aren't black tell the story."

"No autopsy results?" she asked. *Not that I want to see the gory details. Just wondering if the fire killed him, or if the people who set the fire did.*

"Not yet. My guy said something about that, though." Ortiz tapped his forefinger on the table, staring at the ceiling as if trying to remember. "He said the fire might have gone out but for the fact the driver's door was opened. That provided enough oxygen to allow the rest to burn."

Realizing these implications brought a wave of nausea. "You're saying that because I escaped, I condemned that man to die?"

Ortiz's jaw set. "Not necessarily. The autopsy will show if he was dead when the fire was set. We'll have to wait and see." He gestured to the papers. "On one of the subsequent pages, it says that because the door was standing open, the techs were able to recover the VIN number. So they'll soon know the car's owner. That should help move things forward."

Bet couldn't get the image out of her mind. This was beyond survivor's guilt; she could have contributed to someone's death.

"Ms. Lenard, please. We don't have much time. Would you review the physical details on the last page and see if anything there is familiar?"

She forced herself to turn to the page he indicated. Pictures of her purse and contents. Pictures of broken windshield glass, of the scorched engine compartment, trunk and undercarriage, of the tires. More photos of the molds taken from the ground outside the car, revealing what appeared to be two different cars and several different shoes. Rust already forming on the parts that were directly in the fire.

"Those are my shoe prints," she said at last, pointing to impressions clearly made by someone wearing high heels. She studied the ground around the driver's door, following her erratic steps away from the car, and to the place she eventually woke up.

But, wait. Where's the ones leading to the car? How did I get in there if I didn't walk?

A fuzzy sequence came to her, being carried, hitting her head on the car frame as she was being shoved in. Thick, strong arms around her. A conversation in Spanish, a man with a deep, scratchy voice and a woman's measured speech. She shuddered and looked up. "I remember something."

She told Ortiz what she'd seen and heard in her mind's eye. That little bit wasn't particularly incriminating, if true. *And being all doped up, who knows if it's even accurate?*

"A conversation in Spanish." Ortiz nodded and made notes. "Did it sound like native speakers?"

She nodded.

He glanced at the clock. "All right. You've got to go. The boss will be back any time."

She nodded again, still trying to grasp the wispy trails of memory. "Thank you." She gathered her keys and purse and followed him to a side entrance, where he let her out.

"If you recall any more details—the more the better," he said. "Write them down. Review them before you go to sleep at night. Let your subconscious work on them." He put a hand on her arm. "I know we both want to put this in the 'solved' case file ASAP."

She appreciated his sympathy more than she'd expected. "Understood. Thank you."

Concentrating on putting one foot in front of the other, she made it to her car and locked herself inside before her frustration burst loose in a nerve-chilling scream. *It's so goddamned hard not to be able to remember. Chemicals burn those neural pathways and then…zilch. Makes that roofie attempt by that would-be date all those months ago look like one hell of an amateur.*

She closed her eyes and took in a deep breath. Too agitated for real meditation, she turned instead to her five things, and counted down silently. The practice brought some semblance of peace, and she paused to be thankful that she'd remembered something. The detail was very clear in her mind now, that rough-voiced Hispanic man. The question was, how did he relate to any of the potential suspects? He could be one of Santos's friends, acting on orders from the fat Cuban. He could be someone recruited by John Lee. If he was just a run-of-the-mill hit man, he could have been hired by anyone she knew, friend, colleague, client, opposing counsel. Even the police. She had to do something to jog the rest of her stubborn memory loose. And soon.

****

Bet began seeing clients again at the office, knowing some had court dates coming that shouldn't be postponed under the criminal court rules for speedy trial, or other timing issues.

She hadn't intended to take on new clients while dealing with the investigation, but Mela made an appointment for one particularly insistent man on Thursday afternoon. Mela handed her a note sheet saying that Mark Gordon had been arrested and charged after a physical altercation that appeared to the police to be a drug deal gone wrong.

Mark arrived promptly, wearing a wrinkled suitcoat with jeans and no tie. His face was bruised, and his nose wide and lumpy as if it had been broken a few times over the years. He sat opposite Bet and told her "his side of the story."

Somehow, I knew he'd say the police misunderstood and that nothing was his fault. What a surprise.

Bet made notes and looked at the police report and the list of charges, which ran from public nuisance to assault and battery, with a side order of possession for sale.

Mark leaned back confidently in his chair. "Yeah, I know the cops always throw everything at the wall and see what sticks."

"Are you interested in pleading to any of these

minor charges to get rid of the felonies? Is that something you think the State's Attorney would consider?"

"Do I look guilty?" he asked.

Bet assumed it was a rhetorical question and didn't answer. She shrugged. "Most of the time that's not the issue. It's what we can get in by way of testimony, and what we can block from the State." She eyed him. "Truth doesn't always matter."

He laughed raucously. "John Lee said you were a practical woman."

Bet stiffened, one vertebra at a time locking into painful place. "John Lee?"

"Sure. You know him, right? He said you were a real badass in court, and that you'd have a special rate for me, if you get my meaning." His blue eyes pierced any shield she might have been able to erect.

"A special rate? I see. Let me look up your history first, and see what I can do."

As she tapped into the statewide criminal records, Bet's mind flew in a very different direction. *Why was John Lee promising people I'd do things for him, just if his name was dropped? Is this his way of moving forward with the corruption of our firm now that Rich halted the laundering? Are we going to hear him say that if we don't cut his henchmen a financial break, he'll reveal what we've already done? Or that more bad things will happen? Or…?*

Her heart beat faster, and an adrenaline rush of fury burst through her. *That's a crock.*

I'm not doing it.

Pairing up Mark's name and social security number with the records, she found pretty much what she'd expected. He had a full jacket of offenses, most charged but not convicted. The pattern indicated that with priors, the SA would nail this guy at sentencing. *This case is a loser.*

"Well, if you want me to take the case, I can. It'll be a retainer of $10,000 against $350 an hour. I'll need the names of all your witnesses so I can do a full vet."

You want a special rate? I'll give you a special rate. $100 more an hour, just because you said the name John Lee.

Mark's smile faded. "I was thinking something more like half that."

She nodded. "That was before I saw the priors. You're no freshman at this dance, my friend. You play, you pay." She looked him right in the eye.

He got to his feet. "You don't have to be a bitch about it. I'll let you know."

"Have a nice day."

She sat still as he slammed out the door. Mela peeked her head in after he went. "Is everything all right?"

"Peachy. John Lee sent him."

Mela's eyes widened. "Oh."

"Yeah. I'm going to have to have a talk with Rich. I'm stopping this right now."

Mela nodded. "At least he paid the consultation fee."

"That may be all we see. But I've worked too hard to have my reputation in this town sunk by a slimy drug runner."

"Bet, it's more than your reputation on the line. If Lee's the one…" She held on to the door frame as though it were propping her up and chewed her lip.

Bet sighed. "I know. But whoever it is has to be

more careful now. They've played their hand. Surely, we'll hear something soon, and they'll catch the perp."

"I hope you're right," Mela said. But something in her voice told Bet she really didn't believe it.

****

Bet woke up at the crack of dawn on Friday.

No alarm necessary.

Though her meeting with Dr. Giamo Rimon wasn't until nine, she couldn't force herself back to sleep for even twenty minutes. From the moment her eyes opened, she alternated her usual pain and a sparkly, effervescent feeling that burgeoned right from her midsection.

One decision was not difficult: what to wear. She'd been pondering that since he'd called her back. Considering when she'd been in the ER, she'd been at the end of her rope and totally *dishabille*, she wanted to be well put together and calm.

She pulled out a pair of light gray slacks and slipped into them, the linen cool against her skin. Adding a deep green blouse with oil-painted flowers around the hem, and silver dangle earrings, made her feel attractive. She tried putting makeup on her whole face, since the blisters had subsided and closed over. The healing abrasions remained, though, and her foundation couldn't cover the ravaging of her skin. She did the best she could, shading a beige and lavender eye style. She wore her hair up in a bun, which showed off her earrings.

Too much for a coffee date?

She couldn't decide. *Not like I want to show up in pajamas or bike shorts. This will do.*

When she was ready, she left the house and headed for Fuentes' coffee shop. The place seemed like a little hole in the wall. But there was off-street parking, which in any neighborhood near downtown was a plus, and she found a place easily, glancing around the lot and wondering which was the doctor's car. She checked her hair in the rearview mirror and went inside.

Giamo waited at a table next to the storefront window, a colored coffee mug in front of him. He stood up when she entered, his polo shirt well-worn and paired with khaki shorts from one of the mall stores. "What can I get you?" he asked.

"Let me see what we've got," she replied, the smile stuck to her face. The shop's pale-yellow walls were cheerful, decorated with painted farm animals in assorted colors, ones that matched the mugs. The counter was stacked with dishes and silverware and several trays full of cheesecake, *Pastelitos de Guayaba,* coconut bread, Trinidadian hops bread and so many other Cuban and Caribbean sweets. She found a guava one with white stripes of thick frosting and knew it was meant for her. "Coffee, black. And one of these."

He chuckled and paid for her choices. "I got here early to eat one before you came."

"Hiding your treats? Do you feel like you don't deserve them?"

Now that sounds like something Hyacinth would say.

He carried her items to his seat, weaving through the other dozen small tables. "No. I just didn't want to have a chest strewn with crumbs while we talked." He set them down and pulled out her chair.

"Thanks. I guess that will be me instead."

She sniffed the coffee, a strong Cuban espresso blend, and sighed contentedly. *This will definitely get the day started.*

"So, how are you doing?" He slouched in his wooden chair and studied her face, which wasn't bandaged, and her arm, which was. "You look good." He said it in a non-creepy way.

"All right. Getting readjusted to a new, strange life. As you can imagine, having the police all up in my business is less than pleasant."

"Which, I understand now, you were trying to avoid."

"Exactly." She broke off a piece of pastry and shook loose some flakes, then ate it. The guava and cream cheese blended perfectly. It was a bit of heaven.

They both watched people pass by on the sidewalk, people without all the debt of a doctor's education or a death sentence hanging over them.

"No answers yet?" he asked.

"Nothing solid." She debated telling him the part about the oxygen likely lighting up Jack, but couldn't bring herself to actually say it.

"Your family? I heard something on a news channel about your children?"

"They're fine." Memories of their visit surfaced, and she smiled, though the smile faded. "They stay with their dad most of the time."

His face froze. "Oh. I'm sorry, I didn't know."

She waved a hand. "Water under the bridge." She leaned closer. "He's a lawyer, too. You know what they're like."

Giamo smiled. "I've heard." He sipped his coffee. "Have you seen your doctor?"

Bet mock-scowled. "You're a pest, you know that?" She paused. "But, yes. I did, yesterday. We've got everything on track." *Well, mostly on track. Meds are back in stock, and the doctor is worried about my stress. Ha! Join the club.*

He grinned. "Good." He looked ready to lecture her again, so she jumped in first.

"What about you, Doctor? Children? A wife?" She glanced at his left hand.

"No time," he confessed, shaking his head. "I've moved around some since medical school in Pennsylvania, and just settled in Miami a few months ago. Working the ER doesn't allow much extracurricular activity."

"That's a shame. You'll find Miami has a lot to offer culturally—if you ever get time to go out." She drank coffee and finished her delectable pastry, wishing she could afford another. *You remember what they say. One second on the lips, a lifetime on the hips. Gotta stay pretty.*

"What do you like to do? When you're not getting chased down by some bad guy?"

He spoke lightly, and she appreciated his picking up her tone on the subject. *Sure, we could dwell on the horror of it all. But isn't it better to just do what we can to solve the problem and get past it?*

"I've done less since the divorce," she admitted. "A lot of nights, I'm happy to go home, put up my feet and veg out."

"The chronic pain doesn't help." His eyes were moist, sympathetic.

The reminder tore at her, but she nodded. "Also true."

"Can I ask about that? I know you've got a pain control regimen, but have you got a diagnosis?"

He was a doctor, after all. She'd seen so many, she

doubted he'd have anything new to offer. Everyone had their own "solution" for her—yoga, heavy meat diet, vegan diet, hot showers, Epsom salts, vitamins, supplements, walk more, walk less… *You name it, they've all got just the thing.*

"So far, they're talking fibrositis. But there's no test to prove it. And believe me, we have done many tests." She gave him a quick rundown of what her own doctor had done, and also the specialists in Kendall, South Miami, Atlanta, and Jackson Memorial. "They thought it could be Lyme disease, but I never had the target signature or the rash."

"What about rheumatoid arthritis?"

"Tested negative. And I don't have the big bony knobs and twisted fingers."

He wrapped his hand around the mug, a pensive expression on his face.

"False negatives are pretty common. Not everyone gets the same indications. So they haven't treated you with methotrexate?"

Bet shook her head. "Never heard of it."

"Pity. They're just treating symptoms, then, not getting at the underlying causes. I've been reading in the journals about new studies involving glucocorticoids that seem to be promising, and they're on the edge of developing biologic targeted therapies that will work much better than DMARDs…"

Bet listened in amazement at the medical jargon she didn't understand. Finally, someone who acted like they really knew what was happening with her. *Could I really get back to normal again?* "Where can I find these doctors?"

"My colleague Sahire Bhatti in Palm Beach has

specialized in RA for years. I can get in touch with her and ask her to see you." He eyed her. "Under your correct name and insurance."

She blushed, caught. "Of course."

"Good. I'm happy, actually, to be able to share her name with you. There doesn't seem to be much I can do to help you with the rest of your situation."

"I'd appreciate it. I've been looking for answers for years. If there is something that really helps…" She finished the remainder of her coffee, enjoying the last bitter sip.

He grinned. "I'm glad to do it. I'll call you when I get word back." He drained his cup. "Now, I'm afraid I've got to go home and get some sleep. It was a long night."

So soon? It's been a long time since someone's met with me without some agenda or other. I don't want it to end!

"Of course. You've been delightful. And helpful." She stood up and offered her hand to him. They shook as if making a satisfactory bargain.

The doctor pushed his chair in and gathered their dishes, taking them to a heavy rubber tub sitting nearby. He came back and walked her out to her car. Bet surveyed the lot for anyone who looked threatening, but the cars were parked and empty.

"Call me if you need to talk," he said. "No strings, right?"

"Seems only fair I offer you the same outlet," she said. "You have my number—and you know I'm a sucker for fresh pastry."

"You can't go wrong with that. Have a pleasant day, Bet."

He waited to see her safely in her car, then once her door was closed, he crossed the lot to a Honda motorcycle with blue trim. A black helmet awaited him. He pulled it on and fastened the strap. Bet watched in her rearview as he started it up and roared out of the parking lot.

Oh, baby, now that's a lot of power between your legs...

She chuckled, realizing belatedly she wasn't sure which appealed more, applying that term to the machine, or the man.

Either way, I just may have to try them out.

Chapter Fifteen

May 28, 1996
Present Day

The day after Memorial Day, Mela brought in the morning mail with a rush of sultry air, but withheld one envelope from the stack she tossed on the desk, waving it at Bet.

"This was stuck in the door when I came to the office this morning."

"What is it?" Bet sipped her coffee and reached for the letter.

"It's marked 'personal and confidential.' I didn't open it." She handed it to Bet and slid into the chair across from her, eyes sparkling.

Bet chuckled. "You need to know now, right?"

"Of course." Mela watched the plain white envelope with bated breath. "In case it's full of white powder or something."

Hadn't thought of that... Bet shook it carefully and held it up to the bright light that shone in the east-facing window. It seemed the proper weight for a letter in an envelope. Nothing shifted. "Guess we'll find out. Sure you don't want to watch from over there?"

Mela shrugged. "All for one, one for all, right?"

"You're as crazy as I am."

Bet reached for her letter opener and ripped the end

of the envelope in one bold slice. Nothing inside but sheets of folded paper. She pulled out the stack and unfolded it, eyes opening wide as she realized what it was.

"Well?" Mela demanded.

"It's the autopsy report from the…from the accident. The…you know." She scanned through, guilt wrapped around her throat like a noose. *Where is it? Cause of death? Where?*

Finally, she found it. "Blunt trauma to the head," she read aloud. "No smoke in lungs."

The words brought tears to her eyes. *It wasn't me. He was already dead.*

"So. 'They' killed him," Mela said.

Bet nodded. She went back to the beginning of the document and looked at each page, but neither the papers nor the envelope bore any indication of who had left it for her.

It has to be Ortiz. He'd know I was waiting for this. Maybe someone noticed last time I went there, and he's trying to keep me out of sight.

She double-checked the signature page and found the name of the Medical Examiner, Dr. Bruce Hyma, in its usual scrawl. *At least this is legitimate, but can I trust the rest of the evidence? I hope so. I very much hope so.*

One page contained only the information that the car's VIN number showed the registered owner was Wesley Hicks, of King City, California. The car, a 1989 Ford Taurus, was reported stolen about a year before, and had not been located before this.

Well, that's no help then. Other than to assume if the perps have access to stolen cars, then they obviously have criminal connections.

"I'll let you study the rest." Mela paused at the door. "Don't forget I've got an appointment at noon. I'll lock the door behind me, so you won't be disturbed."

"Great. Thanks." Bet returned to the M.E.'s report. Blood tests performed showed a normal level of carboxyhemoglobin, which confirmed Gutierrez was dead before the fire. Examination of the trachea showed no soot in the throat, another indicator he breathed none of the smoke. The post-mortem X-ray revealed blunt trauma to the skull which ultimately killed the man, despite the damage from the fire.

I am so lucky. If They had tried to kill me first…

And why didn't They?

Not that I'm complaining, but why would They do this to Gutierrez, and not to me, if their goal was to kill us?

I must be missing something.

I'd better figure out what it is. Sooner rather than later.

Bet set aside the papers, wanting to look over them the next day when she was fresh, to see if clues remained to be found. *Plenty of other work to do here.*

She hadn't heard from either Mark Gordon or John Lee. Inside her was that feeling of one shoe left to drop, but she remained adamant that she wouldn't give in. She could have asked Rich about it, but that would mean asking Rich for help, which she refused to do. For all she knew, Lee had gone straight to Rich, over her head, and made a different arrangement.

I knew I should have fought to keep the family law practice. Sure, it's full of hate and bile and dirty tricks, but divorce is less deadly than working with some of these criminal types.

Shuddering, she dove in to the files on her desk that needed attention, drafting pleadings and assorted letters to opposing counsel. Losing herself in these processes for a few hours, she finished the last one just before two o'clock, and decided to take a coffee break.

She walked out to the reception area, which was empty. The door was locked, as promised, with a sign taped on it that said "Knock for entry." No one had.

Swinging her arms and rotating her shoulders, stiff from being hunched over her desk, Bet went to the small kitchen area in the back and made a fresh cup of coffee, then carried it to her office. Instead of her chair behind the desk, she sat on the small paisley-covered loveseat where she interviewed clients. She stretched out and read over the morning paper, which she'd put off all day.

No details on my incident, thank the heavens. Miami generated enough crime that any particular event hardly lasted two days in the press. The one she always remembered happened about ten years before, where a man was caught carrying his girlfriend's head—which he threw at the police—after stabbing her 111 times and decapitating her. Even that was relegated to the back pages of the front section after the initial splash.

But she did find something interesting in the police reports.

Santos Silvani, 59, of Little Havana, was charged on May 18, with violating a protective order, and attempted burglary and assault. Silvani allegedly attempted to enter the home of his estranged wife, who held the order. This is the third such order against Silvani, and the second time he is charged with violating the order against his wife. He remains in Dade County Jail pending a bond hearing.

Bet picked up her phone and called Mela.

"Hey, it's me. Is there something you forgot to tell me?"

"I-I don't think so. Your messages are all on the spindle. Something in particular?"

"Santos?"

A pause. "Is he there?"

"No." Bet puzzled over her answer. "Should he be? The paper says he's in jail."

Relief in a sigh. "Oh, good. Yeah, I didn't tell you. *Dios mio,* you have enough on your plate this month. I handled it."

"Why would you ask if he would come here?" Bet sipped her cooling coffee.

"Oh, I don't know. When the police came, he got irate. He shouted something at me about making sure I didn't bring 'that bitch attorney' to court. So I..." She trailed off.

What date was that again?

Bet rechecked the report. He went to jail May 18. Two days after the incident. *It could have been him.*

Mela gasped. "You don't think that—"

"Who the hell knows what to think?"

"I'm so sorry, Bet. Do you want me to come back?"

Now I feel pitiful. Damn. "No, of course not. You do whatever. I think I'm going home. Let's close the office tomorrow and each take a mental health day." *That's a good idea. I'll call Hyacinth and make an appointment to see her.*

"All right. Take care, Bet."

Mela hung up and Bet left a message with Hyacinth's service.

"Mental health, that's what I need," she muttered to

144

herself, folding up the paper before disposing of it. She took her cup to the kitchen and washed it out, then grabbed her things and headed home.

Chapter Sixteen

May 29, 1996
Present Day

Bet had talked with Hyacinth by phone a few times since she'd first met with the police, but one thing or another had prevented them meeting in person until today, almost two weeks after the incident.

"The incident." Sounds...I don't know. More interesting and less deadly.

Waiting in her car, she prepared herself to go inside. Because she still hadn't remembered what had happened, she could see Hyacinth doubling down on her demands for Bet to get better control of her life.

"You can't just go through the days freewheeling things, especially now," Hyacinth had scolded her on the phone. "You need to be worried. You have to have a plan. You have to be safe."

No kidding.

Bet looked around carefully, as she had every time she exposed herself to the public since it happened, feeling she was doing the best she could to protect herself. She hadn't bought a gun yet; she was waiting for a firearms training class to open. She'd have to complete that before she could apply for a concealed-carry permit. And frankly, she hadn't had time to really think about it.

I'm sure I could shoot someone if they were

146

threatening me. Certainly without all that arguing and posturing about "stop or I'll shoot." If they're already threatening, they've asked for it. POW. One shot, then keep shooting until they don't get up.

But she couldn't do that without a gun.

Maybe Hyacinth would have some practical advice.

She took a long, deep breath, trying to ignore the pain ricocheting along her ribs. This was her most recent symptom. Even breathing hurt. Her doctor suggested it was something called costochondritis. Bet didn't care what the official name was. She just wanted it to stop.

I should call Giamo and see if his friend has an available appointment yet.

"Okay. Time to go."

She got out of the car and walked quickly to the building. The MUZAK selection of the day was Eurhythmics.

Sweet dreams are made of this, my ass.

She'd given up on sweet dreams at this point. The more she pondered her lost memories, the more nightmares she had. With all the medications she was taking, she hated to add something prescribed for sleep. So far, alcohol had made the difference some nights. The others, she tossed and turned. Lack of solid sleep would exacerbate her condition, the doctor said. *Great. So* now *the doctor's prediction has to be correct.*

Hyacinth's door stood open a few inches. Every time Bet had come before, it had been closed and locked.

This is what occurs when a police officer comes to retrieve his protected witness on TV. Then he finds that person dead.

She approached the door slowly, stress tightening her muscles until she winced. She raised her hand to knock, then the door swung wide open. Hyacinth reached for Bet's hands and took them, squeezing them firmly.

"Bet, I'm so glad to see you in person, alive and well."

She drew Bet inside, then closed the door. "How are you? Dealing with everything?"

"Sure. Not like I get a choice." Bet studied the psychiatrist, wondering what was behind the change in routine. A glance around the room showed her nothing that gave her a clue. "How about you? Everything all right?"

"Fine, fine. We're here to talk about you, remember?" Hyacinth smiled tightly and gestured Bet to her usual seat. "Can I get you something? Tea? A cola? Water?"

"No, thanks. I'm good." She took the chair, reveling in its comfortable squish as she sat down. *I need to get a chair like this for the living room. Or maybe not... I'd never get up.*

Hyacinth sat across from her, notebook in hand. "So, how are you handling today? You're back to work, you said?"

Bet nodded. "Not full days yet. But putting out fires right and left."

A raised eyebrow. " 'Putting out fires'? Interesting metaphor. Considering."

Bet closed her eyes against a flashback of that charred car. "You know what I meant."

"I do. You're right. That was uncalled for, wasn't it? So, tell me, are you looking out for yourself? Making sure you have access to medical care, to self-care?" She studied Bet's remaining bandages.

Bet shrugged. "I could go without these, I suppose.

The injuries aren't nearly as painful any more. But they aren't pretty, and I don't want people seeing them." Hyacinth nodded to her to continue. "And I don't want people to stare for *that* reason."

And I'm sensitive and vain and want to be pretty and perfect.

But somehow she couldn't admit that aloud.

"How are people treating you?"

Bet sighed and shifted in the chair. "Colleagues are mostly acting like I should be wrapped in layers of tissue paper. Same with the bench, except for Judge Wilton. He barked at me that I'd better not expect sympathy or undue consideration because of what happened."

Hyacinth sat up straighter. "My. That seems extreme. What did you say?"

" 'Yes, sir.' What else was I going to say?"

And the worst part was, I hadn't even asked for a favor. I just showed up for a status conference.

"Hmm." Hyacinth made some notes. "Have Rich and the children been supportive at all?"

This was a more comfortable conversation. She shared the story of the kids' impromptu visit, which seemed to please the doctor.

"And Rich?" Hyacinth persisted.

"He took me to dinner."

"Interesting. How did that go?"

I know what I say is supposed to be confidential, but I just can't tell her about this. I don't imagine the truth makes any difference to my 'treatment.' I learned I can't count on him to make decisions in my best interest. That's for me to chew on.

"It was all right. We went to the 94th Aero Squadron. It was almost like a date." She smiled, but it was the memory of how she'd put him in his place that pleased her.

Hyacinth's pen paused in midair. "How does it make you feel to be with him again? Are you considering a reconciliation?"

Bet frowned. "Fuck, no!"

"All right. No need to get excited." Hyacinth wrote furiously. "It happens, sometimes, after a trauma. Reverting to a once-comfortable pattern. People re-complicate their lives."

After that came a period of silence. Hyacinth spent it reviewing her notes. Bet considered how she could manipulate the session to help her the most. Why had she wanted to come?

She cleared her throat and crossed her legs. "It's hard to deal with the uncertainty."

The doctor nodded. "How does that feel? What would you like to do about it?"

"I've stayed as close to the investigation as I can. Got some information from the team."

"That must be reassuring."

"Not really."

Hyacinth raised an eyebrow.

Bet pouted. "They're waiting on my memory to come back. I have remembered a few things, but not anything that's particularly helpful."

"That's too bad. You've told them about Mela's stalker husband, right? The dirty cop? Anyone else? In the time we've been meeting, we've discussed many potential enemies you may have. So many…"

Bet didn't like the way Hyacinth trailed off. *There weren't that many, were there?* "A couple of clients who've been hostile over the years. You know how it is.

People expect a certain result when you're working together. When it doesn't happen, they flip out."

"Indeed, I do." The doctor rolled her shoulders and stretched. "I've had several clients like that as well. How can I help you?"

I'm not the expert, damn it. You are. "I was going to ask you that. Do you have any suggestions for me?"

"If you're primarily interested in memory recall, we could try reconstructing the scene—perhaps going there in person, seeing it, smelling it, experiencing it as it was at the time you were there. Fear is a very powerful feeling. It might evoke vivid memories."

"I'd thought of that. I suppose we can't visit the scene in the Everglades until it's been thoroughly vetted for evidence."

"Surely, they're done with that by now. It's been weeks."

Bet shrugged. "That would be something Detective Ortiz could tell me."

"Good. So that's something positive you can do."

Time passed with more questions. Hyacinth continued to make notes. Suddenly she looked up, her blue eyes sparkling. "Have you ever tried hypnosis?"

"Oh, I don't know—"

"I'm not talking the 'barking like a dog' stuff. I mean a professional who regularly regresses people to a different spot in their memory by making them relaxed and receptive to getting around any barriers created by their mind."

"What about the drugs?" Bet asked. "If I was roofied with something that blocks my memory, is that something they'd be able to get past?"

Hyacinth cocked her head, thinking. "You know,

I'm not really sure about that."

"So, you don't mean yourself?"

"Goodness, no. But I do have a colleague who does this on a regular basis for the police, in missing persons cases or childhood abuse, things like that."

For the police? Is that something Ortiz was considering if I can't come up with it on my own? He hadn't said anything like that. What if what I said incriminated me—I certainly wouldn't want the police getting hold of that transcript/video.

"Would they have to tell the police the results? Is there protection of confidentiality?"

"My colleague isn't a psychiatrist—so I'd have to check and see." Hyacinth studied her. "Are you worried what might be revealed?"

Bet's fingers tapped in staccato rhythm on the arm of the chair. "I don't know what the hell they will reveal. So that leaves me hanging out on a ledge."

"But it's better to know, right? You told me on the phone the other night that you wanted to resolve your feelings of guilt about the death of the architect. If you could recall exactly what happened to get you out of that front seat, maybe you could do that."

"I suppose."

Hyacinth glanced at the elegant silver-framed clock that hung over the desk. "Our time's about up. Let me put in a call, and when I have solid information, I'll get back to you."

Bet nodded. "Sounds reasonable."

Hyacinth leaned forward, her hands clasped on top of her notebook. "Bet, you are a beautiful, successful woman. You have been blessed with a pair of wonderful children. You have a nice home, a solid career. There is no reason why something like this should take you down. We'll get to the bottom of things, I promise."

Bet felt the smile on her face, a correct social response. But she experienced no joy inside. Until this was over, she expected happiness wasn't something that would come to her so easily. Getting to the bottom of things seemed to be the right goal. But the harder she looked for answers, the more she found things she didn't like. It might just be that pursuing the truth would be even more dangerous for herself, and her family.

It might just make everything much worse.

Chapter Seventeen

June 1, 1996
Present Day

Pulling into the driveway of what had been her home for eleven years was always a punch in the gut.

The long drive through the palm and fruit trees held so many memories. The first time she and Rich saw it, and marveled at every turn. The way Jeremy had squalled in Mom's arms all the way home from the hospital—until they hit the driveway. Cleaning up after Hurricane Andrew. Bet and Jane learning to ride bikes at the same time.

But that's all they are, memories.

Bet frowned as she noticed Rich had pulled up her ruby bromeliad bed on the east side of the house. She'd planted them when a client had been broke but owned a tropical farm, so he bartered new plants for service. He'd promised that they were easy to grow, native to the landscape, and they'd beautify her property in no time.

Well, in no time, they were dead.

Seems to be a theme in my life lately.

She drove up to the carport and turned off the engine, waiting. Jeremy and Jane had agreed to come to a street art festival in Coconut Grove, as long as she took them for lunch to some new trendy burger place all their friends had been raving about. Some bribes were less arduous than others. Bet always loved a good burger.

With….avocado, thin sliced red onions, sliced dill pickle, and a gourmet cheese, if possible. No mayo. Definitely not ketchup.

Even the thought of ketchup made her shudder.

The kids weren't waiting. Both the screen door and the inner door were closed. She didn't want to go up and knock. Rich would ask her in, because he'd feel he had to, to be "civil." He'd be uncomfortable, and she'd be more so, and then she'd have to smile and ignore the other changes he'd made that screamed, "Bet doesn't live here anymore."

Her tires had crunched all the way up the gravel drive. They must have heard her.

She sighed and beeped the horn twice.

Her dad had always taught her it was rude to honk for passengers. *Maybe so, but it's a shortcut I will take advantage of to spare myself crap. Sorry, Dad.*

A few seconds later, Jane peeked out the window, then she and Jeremy came out. Jane took the front seat and Jeremy slouched into the back, drenched in some frothy teen boy cologne. It reeked. Bet's first impulse was to open all the windows, but it was too damn hot.

"Sorry," Jane said. "We didn't hear you."

"I said eleven o'clock."

"Yeah, but…"

A lot of weight in that "but." Bet immediately stiffened, knowing Jane referred to Bet's history. Before the prescription pain medication, when over-the-counter drugs just weren't cutting it, she used alcohol to control her pain. When she drank, she wasn't very reliable. It was that simple.

And it's why I don't live here anymore.

"Anyway," Bet said with forced brightness, determined to make the visit work, "I called and they don't take reservations at the Burger Bar."

"It's pretty popular," Jeremy said. "Shawn had to wait two hours for a table last week."

"I guess we'll take our chances." She gunned the engine and did a three-point turn to head out the driveway and onto the main road.

"So, Mom, what's new on the investigation?" Jeremy said. "Have they nailed the perp?"

Bet snickered at the police jargon coming from her son's mouth. *Too much TV, that kid.* "Not so far, Jer."

Jane swung around in the seat and eyed her. "What were you talking about to Dad the other night? What does he know about all this? He wouldn't tell me."

Big surprise there.

"I really can't say, Jane. Like I told you the other day, investigations are kept quiet so they don't spook the criminals."

"Is Dad a criminal?" Oddly, Jane didn't sound shocked, only curious.

Bet's breath caught. Rich was this child's father. It was Bet's first line of advice to all her divorce clients with children. She couldn't disparage him to her. Jane needed to be able to respect her dad. *And yet...*

Traffic burgeoned around them, and she stalled off the answer with a raised forefinger. "Let me get out of this mess, Jane."

Jane grunted. "Never mind. That tells me enough." She put her feet up on the dashboard.

"Jane, you know you shouldn't do that. It's dangerous. If we get in a wreck—"

"Then don't get in a wreck, Mom. Geez."

Bet muttered in frustration. "Fine. You were warned."

"We can still collect against the auto insurance. Don't worry, I won't end up a cripple."

Contributory negligence, you little shit.

The snappiness was something the kid came by honestly. Restraining the impulse to reach over and smack the girl, Bet took deep breaths and concentrated on avoiding the mass of cars on South Dixie Highway. Saturdays were always crazy on Miami streets. All that culture she'd raved about to Dr. Rimon. *Giamo.* She smiled, thinking about their conversation, then let the smile fade before Jane's discerning eye suspected something she needed to root out.

Jeremy jumped in with some minor bragging about his soccer team's games. Bet half-listened, adding interested nods and "mmhmm"s every so often as she guided the car through South Miami and on to the Grove.

She parked in a public lot near the festival, backing into the parking space for easy exit. She made sure the Jag was locked up tight, then the three of them strolled along the sidewalk to Peacock Park to see what art had in store for them.

The afternoon sky was Chamber-of-Commerce blue, spotted with a few fluffy white clouds. Small booths lined the pathways of the park, each containing a creative person and their colorful wares—paintings, sculpture, even pinatas swinging in the wind. Latin music came from a stage set up under a huge cypress tree filled with green parrots providing syncopation.

The sun bore down as usual, but Bet found relief in the strong breeze that came off the ocean to the east. She reached up to put a band around her hair, giving herself a youthful ponytail. Jane cruised the paths from one jewelry crafter to the next, keenly interested in anything with turquoise or blue stones. *I guess that gives me ideas for her birthday in August.* Jeremy, on the other hand, followed her dutifully, eyeing the crowd like a Secret Service agent on alert.

When Jane was occupied at one abundantly stocked jewelry stall, Bet pulled her son aside from the chattering crowd. "Jer, what are you doing?"

"I—just watching out. You know, in case…" His wide eyes looked up at her for a moment, then looked away.

He was growing to be such a…man.

The thought made her proud, at the same time she tsk-tsked herself. *I'm the parent. I'm supposed to be taking care of him, not the other way around.*

"Babe, this is a huge crowd, hundreds of people. If anyone was intending to come after me, they'd have to do it with all these witnesses looking on. It makes no sense."

The reminder brought back a sudden whiff of burnt flesh, a glimpse of charred corpse. The flashback startled her. She grabbed Jeremy's arm out of instinct, momentarily terrified.

"Mom! What's the matter? Did you see someone?" He grabbed her right back. "Jane!"

"No, Jer. It's okay." Her breathing was out of control. *Get hold of that. Five things…sky, trees, Jane, yellow tablecloth, green grass…four things…my boy, my gauze skirt, edge of a fingernail, the solid ground…three things, music, birds, the wind…two things…hot churros, Spanish food…not really tasting much, but there…* She took a deep breath and let go.

"It's okay." She forced a smile. "Just a bit of PTSD. I'm fine."

He studied her, the tight angle of his jaw reminding her of his father. "Are you sure?"

Jane joined them, looking from one to the other curiously. "What did I miss?"

"Nothing, Jane. We're all good. Come on. Let's get something to drink."

Bet steered them to the food truck that had fresh-squeezed lemonade, and fifteen dollars later they each walked away with a tall plastic cup full of icy sweet-tart goodness. They sat on a bench under a tree in full red blooms, watching the people.

And hoping the people weren't watching them.

Though it passed quickly enough, the moment of terror caused her some concern. She'd had dreams where she'd revisited the deadly scene, but she hadn't faced it in broad daylight before.

Guess we know what I'm talking to Hyacinth about this week.

She tried to make light of it, throwing herself into admiring the displayed watercolors and oils. Try as she might, she couldn't work up the enthusiasm to actually buy any. They were lucky enough to see some of the exotic birds for which the park was named, one male peacock in particular strutting and fanning out his tail as photographers gathered around. Into the second hour of their excursion, though, her kids were dragging their feet and whining. *Aren't they supposed to grow out of that after they're toddlers?*

"All right," she said. "Enough culture for one day. Let's head over to the burger place. "

Both Jane and Jeremy perked up as they headed

back to the lot.

"I'm getting the biggest veggie burger they have," Jane said. "With provolone. And no tomatoes or onions."

"Rag says the fries come in a huge basket. And you can have all the sauce you want." Jeremy pumped his arm. "Honey mustard, right?"

"Ugh. No. Korean barbecue." Jane shot him a sidewise look.

Bet dug for her keys as they came around the corner to the lot where the Jag was parked.

"Mom, there's people by our car," Jane said. She frowned and stopped.

Bet looked up. Several men were indeed standing along the right front fender. None looked Hispanic— more like suburban soccer dads and trade investors. "Huh. That's odd."

Jeremy marched up to confront the men. "Hey! What are you doing—oh my God."

The distress in his voice made Bet break into a run. As she came up beside him, she saw what he had seen. In the center of the driver's side of the windshield were three bullet holes, evenly spaced. The glass around them had splintered into spiderweb cracks.

Jane caught up and grabbed her mother's arm. "If you'd been sitting in the car…"

Bet nodded slowly. "If I'd been sitting in the car, I'd be dead."

The men murmured sympathetic platitudes.

"Were you here? Did you see what happened?" Bet demanded. "How long ago did this happen?"

One man, in a peach-colored polo shirt, said, "Was just walking along and saw this. I mean this is a fine car, ma'am. What a shame."

"Yeah," another man said. "Your husband is gonna be mad as hell."

Bet shot him a look that could kill. He just smiled, oblivious.

One asked if he should call the police.

"You didn't see anyone else hanging around? No one with a gun?"

Peach shirt chuckled. "Ma'am, this is Miami. Pretty much everyone carries here."

The shame of a public scene clashed with a personal sense of deep loss inside her, and she fought back tears. She'd lusted after just this car, a green Jag with tan interior, since her first day of law school. How dare anyone desecrate it?

"Go on, get out of here," she growled.

She reached for her phone, noticing that the men stared a little long at her before they backed away. *Probably realizing I'm THAT woman, and this is part of a larger, famous tragedy they've now been part of. What a thrilling thing to go home and tell the little woman. Or man. This is Coconut Grove, after all.*

The voice that answered the phone dragged sleepily. "Ortiz."

"Detective, it's Bet Lenard. I'm sorry if I woke you."

He cleared his throat. "Ms. Lenard? What…why are you calling?"

"We have a little problem." She took stock of the children while she waited for the man to wake up. They seemed disturbed, but were handling it stoically, leaning against the next car, arms crossed in stereo.

"I don't understand."

"My children and I are at Peacock Park. Someone's

left bullet holes in my car windshield."

"Damnation. All right, I'll be there as soon as I can. I'll send a local squad out to meet you. Are you somewhere safe?"

The gravity of what happened had begun to set in. "Is there any place safe?"

A hesitation. "Don't touch anything. I'm sending someone." He hung up.

Bet stood with the phone in her hand, wanting nothing more than impetus. Where to go? What to do? How to protect herself and her children? Her impulse was to scan the area around them, but those banyans and purple-flowered jacarandas could hide those who wished her harm. Had they followed her here? Had they followed the little family into the park? Why shoot the car instead of Bet herself?

They just wanted me to know it could happen. We have our eyes on you.

She glanced at the kids. "You should probably call your dad to come pick you up. The police are coming, but I don't know how long they'll take."

Jane cast the look around Bet had chosen not to. "You think they're still here?"

She walked over to join them. "Honestly, I don't know. They'd be idiots. This is a hit-and-run kind of job. But in light of the big picture, I'd rather have you safe at home." *Assuming they are safe at home, and Rich's bad business decisions aren't following him there…*

Jeremy took her hand. "You should come, too, Mom."

His words struck her like a brick. "What? No."

"Yes. If they found you here, they know when you're home alone. You shouldn't be alone."

"Honey, your dad and I…" She just shook her head. "That's not a good idea."

"I'll tell him. He needs to say yes." The boy's voice cracked. Tears filled his eyes. He wiped them away with a frown.

"That's sweet of you." She fumbled for something else to say.

"We're staying," Jane said, her tough tone cutting through any emotional folderol. "If they want to take you on, they're taking us on, too. Right, Jerro?"

Her brother didn't look nearly as convinced. "Uh. Right."

Jane gave him a sharp nod and took Bet's other hand. "All three of us."

Bet squeezed their hands. *They make me proud. But a good mother would not let it come to that.*

So I will never let it come to that.

Chapter Eighteen

September 28, 1982
14 years earlier

The call of the criminal list in Miami courts could be compared to a highly organized cattle stampede.

The courtroom was huge, one of the biggest in the Dade County Courthouse, with row upon row of wooden benches, most of them at least partially occupied. Bet sat in the tenth row with her file on top of her protruding belly. Next to her was the firm's client, Tom Hall, a charming rogue originally from Australia. Tom wasn't *her* client, he was Rich's. But Rich had stayed up until four a.m. preparing his appellate argument for the District Court this morning, and he'd asked Bet to cover for him.

"Look, it won't be hard," he'd promised. "Cop didn't appear the first time, so the State got a continuance. You know the cops don't want to show up because the county cancelled all the overtime, so they don't get paid. You'll go in, present yourself as ready, and the cop won't show. The judge will dismiss. Piece of cake, honey."

Like anything is a piece of cake when you're 39 weeks pregnant and your ankles are the size of tree trunks. HONEY.

She tried to beg off, again, but he eyed her with

164

disdain.

"You're the one always saying, 'I'm not handicapped, I'm just pregnant.' Come on. Prove it." Implied but not said, *Be a man.*

I'm not a man, dammit.

But she was unable to face that lack of compassion with the strength to argue. So, she got dressed and went.

"You don't look crash hot. You feeling all right, love?" Tom asked.

"I'm fine." The man was endearing. She loved listening to him talk. Aussies had an appealing way with words. He'd even brought her an amaretto cake the day before to celebrate the impending birth.

It figured, really, because the man was here for his third DUI. She flipped open the file again and glanced over the police report.

"This officer found the suspect in his car, crashed into a concrete abutment. When this officer approached, he detected a strong smell of alcohol. This officer spoke to the suspect, to assess his condition. The suspect leaned against his door and said, 'I'm drunk as a goddamned monkey.' "

Yeah. This case is a sure winner.

Bet rolled her eyes and shifted in her seat. She'd given up on fashionable clothing. All she could hope for was comfortable. Today she wore a red dress with a white sailor collar that must have been created by Omar the Tent Maker.

Ugh.

Most of the attorneys were corralled into a tight bunch up front, regular defense attorneys and the Public Defender's guys. That way when the 120 or so cases got called in order, they could just pop into their seat at the defense table with their client and tell the judge whether they were ready for trial or not. Some, like Bet, expected their cases would simply be dismissed and they could go on their way.

She rocked forward, her back aching. *Remind me to kick Rich in the ribs tonight so he knows how it feels.*

He'd been insistent on trying for a boy, now that they had Jane. What was it about men and sons? Most of the fathers and sons she'd known tended to be at war for many years of their lives. Who'd want that on purpose? But the idea of another child had appealed to her at the time.

I must have blanked out all this crap about actually being pregnant. The falling asleep at 7 p.m., the utter exhaustion, the sore ribs, the running to the bathroom every twenty minutes. Yeah. Never again.

She'd already made arrangements for having her tubes tied before she left the hospital after little Junior or Juniorette was born. If it wasn't a boy, that was too bad for Rich. He could get a dog.

One hour into the calendar mess, and they had just reached case number 65. Tom Hall's was 111.

She grabbed the bench seat in front of her and pulled herself uncomfortably to her feet, setting the file aside, hoping to relieve the backache. All it did was transfer pains to the front as well.

"Miss Bettina?" Tom stood and took her arm. "I don't think I believe you're fine. You look like a dog's breakfast there, no offense intended. You right?"

"I'm fine," she snapped, jaw clenched. *This is not labor. This is not labor. I'm standing in a courtroom, miles from my hospital. This is not happening.*

She stepped into the aisle of the huge room packed

with people, to see if walking would help. *Just six feet back and forth.* The pains faded slightly and Bet sighed with relief. "Better," she said. They took their seats again, the droning of the judge and lawyers from the front fading into routine.

Nearly ten minutes later, a wave of pain swirled from back to front and held on.

Just kill me now.

Of all the reasons to get a continuance, she hated the fact she might have to use one that men always threw out as a reason why women shouldn't do jobs of importance: getting pregnant. *C'mon, Bet, be a Man.*

The clerk called case 100.

Over the next half hour, as they inched closer to Tom's case, there was no doubt what was going on. She was going to have to admit it.

The clerk called case 111. "State of Florida vs. Tom Hall; Driving Under the Influence, operating a vehicle in an unsafe manner, damage to public properties…" She went on while Bet got to her feet, gathered her things, and gripped Tom's arm as they walked toward the bench. People in the aisle took one look, and the crowd parted like the Red Sea. The buzz of conversation clearly centered on her imminent crisis.

Judge Ferrer looked down from the bench and raised an eyebrow. "Is the State ready to proceed?"

The State's Attorney gestured to the police officer by his side. "We are, Your Honor."

Bet cursed under her breath. So much for cake.

"Is the defense ready to proceed?"

"Bettina Lenard for the defense, Your Honor. I'm afraid we won't be able to proceed today. I'm pretty sure I'm in labor."

The judge paled. "Granted. Get out!" He turned to the bailiff. "Help her out of here. Now!"

Bet gave the SA an apologetic shrug and let the tall, uniformed bailiff assist her down the aisle, clearing a path, Tom carrying her briefcase and file behind them. They cleared the doors, and the bailiff stopped, undecided.

"Can I call someone for you? Do you need help to your car?"

Bet gritted her teeth. "I'm right downstairs. I should be able to make it."

He nodded. "Well, good luck." He disappeared back inside.

Tom stood next to her, his slightly Sad-Sack face wearing a puzzled frown. "So? Time to do a Harry, eh?"

****

The next twenty minutes was a blur. Tom got her to her car. The pains continued, and she had to lay the driver's seat back to take a break and breathe. She called the office, and asked the office administrator, Delia, to reach out to Rich, if he could be contacted, and tell him she was on her way to the hospital.

"Oh, my God, is it time? How exciting!" Delia purred.

How exciting. Right. "Ow!" she said, as a tightness gripped her midsection like a short belt after Thanksgiving dinner.

"Okay, okay, I'll get him. You go!"

"I'll do that," Bet replied drily. A few minutes later, when the contraction had passed, she put the car in gear and headed to the hospital where her doctor had privileges. It was farther away than Baptist or South Miami, but she and Rich had agreed to go with it.

About halfway there, she mused that she could have called an ambulance. Certainly her driving was not enhanced by ongoing labor. But she would have had to wait, and there would have been a huge fuss, and she'd probably have argued with the medics anyway. *So, there you had it.*

At the hospital, she pulled up to the emergency room door, parking just far enough ahead that she wasn't blocking the entrance. She took the keys in with her, figuring some orderly could move the car out into the lot if it was necessary. No way she was going to walk from the back of beyond, as Tom would have said, not at this point.

After several pauses for contractions on the way in, she stopped at the triage desk. The emergency room was filled with waiting patients, but she got moved up on the list because of the imminent issue. Her relief was tempered when the clerk insisted she go through the whole patient entry rigamarole. The doctor had suggested earlier that they pre-register, but she wasn't due for another week. *Yeah, okay, so I procrastinated and put it off. Sorry.* Soon enough she was in a hospital gown, on a semi-hard mattress in the room on the third floor, monitor wrapped around her middle and obstetric nurses poking and prodding at her.

"Water hasn't broken yet, right?" one asked.

"Not that I know of. But it didn't last time." Bet tried to keep her mind occupied in her quiet place, a beach at Matheson Hammock Park, listening to the water burble up onto the beach in tiny waves. She'd selected the place in the Lamaze class that she and Rich had attended, even if they only made some of the sessions. *Couldn't waste those box seats to the Dolphins' opener, hmm, Rich?*

Finally all the "preggo just landed" stuff was behind her, and she could try to relax. Now that she was flat on her back, the contractions slowed down, and she could feel every inch of them as they progressed up and around. The heartbeat of the baby remained strong at an average 130 per minute. *The books say that means it's a boy. Let's hope so.*

Some twenty minutes later, her OB, Doctor Dan, showed up, a smile on his tanned face. The man looked like a country club tennis pro, and had the same bountiful charm. "Someone tells me we're having a baby today!"

Bet eyed him. "You let me know when it's your turn for 'having,' will you? I'm glad to let you take the glory."

He just patted her arm and turned to the machinery, studying the patterns. "Everything looks good, Bet."

"Contractions have slowed down, I think. Is that a bad thing?"

"It's not a terrible thing. What were you doing when labor began?"

She explained her situation at court and he laughed out loud. "I bet the men were jealous of that excuse."

She didn't bother to answer. Dr. Dan was pleased with himself enough for both of them.

"Is Dad going to join us?"

"He's supposed to. He was in appellate court this morning."

"All right. We'll wait as long as we can. The nurse says you're about fifty percent effaced. It'll be a while yet."

An aide slipped in with a cup of ice chips. She ducked back out without saying a word.

"Okay, Momma. Rest up. We have a couple hours

of hard work ahead of us. They'll let me know when you're ready."

He left, and Bet was alone again. She breathed through the contractions, letting herself slide during the valleys, visiting her quiet mental beach, and lulling herself into half sleep.

Sometime later—there wasn't a clock in the room—a voice woke her from her meditation.

"Bettina? Sorry it took me so long. I was next to argue when the message came in. I didn't think you'd mind me being half an hour later."

Coming into full wakefulness along with the arrival of another contraction, she took the hand he offered her and squeezed it so tight he yelped. "I. Don't. Mind," she managed.

"Good." His face got red and he groaned. As she gradually released her grip, he gently pulled his hand loose. Then he took off his jacket, pulled a side chair up to the bed and dropped into it. "Did Tom's case get dismissed?"

"No. This happened first." She took her cleansing breath. "The SA's witness was there, anyway."

"Damn. We tried. I guess we'll see what happens when it's re-calendared."

"Really not the first thing on my mind, Rich."

The rhythm of the contractions changed over the next hour, a steady five minutes separating them. The time blurred between Lamaze breathing, sucking on ice chips and Rich dozing off, depleted from his two hours' sleep.

After she'd been there another hour, Rich finally got enough naps to focus. He got up and walked around the room. "Sorry, Bettina. I'm really trying. It's life, right?

Figures it would be today, of all days." He came back to the bedside. "You're amazing, doing this mostly by yourself. We will have our new child soon. Really soon."

Bet glanced at the monitors. "Another one coming—hold on!"

He grabbed her hand and breathed with her. This one was worst of all so far. When it was over, she said, "Get a nurse. I think it's about time."

His brow furrowed. "All right. Wait here." He ran out the door.

Where the hell do you think I'm going to go?

Another contraction came, and another almost immediately after. A nurse came in and checked her after the second one passed.

"Ten centimeters. Let's go!"

The machinery was detached, and the bed rolled down the hall to the delivery room. Bet lost track of all the people who came in and out. The wires were attached to new machinery. Someone in scrubs pulled a paper gown over Rich's court clothes. He rejoined Bet and took her hand, an encouraging smile on his face.

"Here we go, love."

"It's a good thing I love you," Bet said. She smiled to take the sting out of her words. *Rich knows me after all this time. At least I haven't offered to make him a eunuch for putting me through this.*

She was tugged this way and that as the nurse put her legs in the stirrups. The doctor came in, gowned and gloved, and took his place at the foot of the table. The sounds around her blended into a minor electronic orchestra. Too hard to focus on the beach now. She just had to trust the others with her body and that of her imminent child.

"Whoa, there's the head!" The doctor's eyes widened and bent to his work.

Rich looked across the table at the nearest nurse. "Should she push or not? I don't remember!"

"Don't!" the doctor warned.

"Don't push," Rich said to Bet, as if she wasn't right there, listening.

The next few minutes blended into one long, awful contraction, and then it was over. The few seconds of non-action after the baby came out was followed by the expected wail.

"Bettina," Rich said, breathless. "It's a boy."

The doctor concurred. "He sure is. He's just perfect." He passed the baby to a nurse who took him aside to clean him up. Bet fastened on the sounds of the nurse and the baby, and then he was brought to her, wrapped in a blue towel.

Everything after that didn't matter. She'd gotten through it. Rich had his son. Life as they knew it would change all over again. She didn't care. She held the boy they'd decided would be named Jeremy, and let herself fall in love.

Chapter Nineteen

June 10, 1996
Present Day

Frustrated with the lack of progress in the police investigation, Bet decided to follow one of Hyacinth's recommendations. Half asleep in bed, she woke with an idea about 10 p.m.—which was, of course, when all good ideas surfaced—and called Mela, asking her to wear old clothes and shoes the next day. "Come here, not the office."

Mela's voice wasn't sounding confident. "Because…?"

"Because we're going to take a ride south. To check out the scene. Maybe it'll jog something loose in my head."

"We're going to tromp around in the 'Glades? Really?"

"Do you have a better idea?"

"Where do you want me to begin?" Mela scolded. "Alligators? Mosquitoes? How about let the police do their jobs?"

"Detective Ortiz said they'd recovered all the evidence they could from there. Not like we can hurt anything."

The detective had also said the car had been hauled away and examined at great length after the body was removed. Whoever had done this was thoroughly professional. The lab retrieved not a single fingerprint or stray hair. No stray fibers on the vegetation in the area. No gum wrappers, cigarette butts or any outside traces other than the shoes and the tire tracks. All of those were common enough that discovering them gave the investigation no traction.

Nada.

Enter Bet as Nancy Drew and Mela as her sidekick Bess.

Mela drove, since Bet's car was in the shop.

The Jag was in sad shape, needing the front windshield replaced and also the driver's seat. Ortiz and his team found the three bullets buried deep in the stuffing, which led him to believe the weapon used was some sort of handgun.

"If it had been automatic, they could have gone through into the rear seat." Rumpled and unshaven, he'd still perused the Peacock Park scene in a thorough manner. "I think you're right. This was just a message."

"How do I tell them it's a wrong number?" Bet asked, tongue firmly in cheek.

He smiled. "Guess we'll have to catch them first."

Again, the team found no fingerprints, no shells, no trace of evidence. Ortiz was kind enough to give Bet and her kids a ride to Bet's house, and the car was towed to the repair shop. Where it sat.

"Coffee," Mela said, as they pulled onto South Dixie Highway. "We need coffee."

Bet agreed. They stopped at the drive-through Cuban coffee shack and bought two coladas. Drinking those provided a quick adrenaline rush, one Bet expected she would need to face the place where she nearly died.

Mela drove south on the Turnpike to Florida City. Heading west on Palm Drive, they turned left at Robert is Here, a local produce stand that had become quite the tourist trap, selling *batidos,* and all sorts of tropical fruits that would only grow this far south.

"We can stop on the way back," Mela promised when Bet looked longingly at the sign for sugar cane juice. "I want some black sapote."

"I expect I'll need a reward by then. Something mango?"

She forced a smile, but the momentary memory of sweet fruit on her tongue vanished as quickly as it had come. Bet's body became increasingly resistant to this expedition, tensing proportionately as they came closer. Despite a strong dose of pain medication, muscles burned and her head was pounding. She said nothing to Mela, who would likely have called off the trip.

They sped along the back roads the last five miles to the national park. As Mela paid their car's entrance fee, Bet noticed the security cameras at the gate. "I wonder if Ortiz had them run this feed."

"You should ask him." Mela pulled away smoothly from the gate and headed down the main road. "Now where is this place again?"

"Fifteen miles in, the boys said."

"All right. Here we go."

Bet watched the scenery pass outside the window, wishing she could relax and enjoy the beauty of it. Though much of it appeared to be grasslands, she knew from prior visits--not just *that* one—that much of the ground was marsh. An assortment of birds perched on the trees closest to the road, squawking their love calls to each other, and signs indicated there might be alligators or even wildcats crossing their path.

"What possessed you to come out here today, anyway?" Mela asked.

"Thought it might jog my memory."

"Just out of nowhere that came?" Mela glanced sidewise at her. "After nearly a month?"

Bet scowled. "Fine. Hyacinth suggested it, after I told her about the insight I had at the police station. She thought if I remembered one thing, perhaps I could remember even more."

Mela snorted. "You should have made her haul *her* ass all the way down here."

"I don't know. The last meeting we had, she seemed a little too interested in the whole incident. I mean, more so than just as part of therapy. She wanted to know about suspects and exactly how much I remembered. She even suggested hypnosis."

"Oh, great. Yeah, they use that on *The X-Files* all the time."

A flash of inspiration. "Did it work for them?"

Mela burst out laughing. "That's television, you idiot. Look, I know you. Do you really want someone poking around in your head? There's some scary stuff in there."

Bet sat up straight in the seat and crossed her arms. "Says you! Like what?"

"Like—wait. What did you say the place was called?"

"Sisal Pond." Bet looked up and saw the sign that must have caught Mela's attention. "Yeah. That's it." Her heart skipped around in her chest and she had to focus on counting out slow, regular breaths. *No brown paper bag handy today.*

"You're sure about this?"

Bet nodded.

Mela turned right onto the dirt road and drove slowly on. "How far?"

"I'm not sure. About two minutes' driving and five minutes' walking in one shoe."

"Right." Mela shook her head but kept driving slowly. What seemed like a moment later, she said, "That's two minutes."

Bet studied the terrain, more marsh and swamp. Nothing looked terribly familiar. No trail cameras in sight. At the end of the slow drive, they came to a spot where there had clearly been a lot of traffic, tire tracks in the mud. "That's got to be it."

Mela parked the car, and both women got out.

The keening of the insects drilled into Bet's brain. She leaned against the fender of the car, her hands on the edge.

Mela put a hand on her shoulder. "Something?"

Bet just nodded. She closed her eyes and tried to think of that night. *This is just what it sounded like. Hang on to that.*

In her mind, she retraced her steps back to the car, pushing past her actions on the passenger side to checking the driver's side. *If I left the door open, why wasn't the light on?* She remembered opening the door—

I was choking on the smoke. It smelled awful. It had filled the car. I had to get out. No time to think why or how I was there. I had to get out. So I did.

Startled at the sudden recollection, she stiffened and opened her eyes. "I remember getting out of the car. Getting away from the smoke. I ran, and then I tripped and fell into the swamp over there." She waved a hand in the direction of where she'd first come to.

"Let's walk over there, then. Follow your memories."

Mela held her hand and they came to the end of the trail. One bit of the marsh looked much like the rest, the grasses waving in the hot breeze and muddy water at their roots. But Bet had a strong feeling about the exact location. She clearly remembered where she was in relation to the car when she counted her five things. She pointed.

"There."

While Mela waited, Bet waded gingerly into the warm water, then squatted down. *Yes, this was it.*

What happened afterward was clear in her mind. It was the 'before' that remained the issue. "I want to try something," she said. "Let's pretend your car is *the* car."

"You won't set it on fire, right?"

Bet rolled her eyes. "Of course not. I want you to shove me into the driver's seat. Let's see if that does anything."

"Bet, I—"

"Come on. I hereby verbally waive any liability. Just do it. And speak Spanish."

They walked back over to the car, and Mela set the seat as far back as it would go to accommodate their difference in height. "Okay, ready?"

Bet closed her eyes, willing her mind to think it was dusk or dark, not blazing midday. "Go."

Mela pushed hard on Bet's shoulder, yelling something about the Cubans in Miami. Bet landed hard in the seat and—

"Don't bang her up too much," a woman said in accented English. "We want her to remember this." She

handed the man a syringe. "That'll wake her up."

Bet screamed, then covered her mouth.

Mela knelt down, trying to comfort her. "What is it, Bet? Did I hurt you? I'm sorry!"

Bet counted through one of each sense, and fastened on her breaths, in, out…in, out…until she could speak.

"No, you didn't hurt me." She grabbed Mela's hand and squeezed it. "Fragments are coming back, though. I heard the woman this time." She told Mela what had recurred to her. "I don't know if I'll get more here. It seems like everything else happened after, and that I remember already." She turned and got out of the car. "We should go to Old Lisbon. See if I can piece together any of the missing conversation with the two abductors."

Her phone rang. She glanced at it curiously. "I didn't even know there was signal here."

Mela got out of her way, and Bet answered as she walked around to the passenger side. "Hello?"

"Hi, Miss March. Do you have a moment?"

No one else would call her that. *Ha.* "Dr. Rimon. Do you have news for me?" She leaned against the metal frame of the car, letting its reflected heat sear her back. It felt good.

"I do. Sahire Bhatti called to say she had a cancellation, but it's tomorrow morning at 7:30. Can you get there that early?"

Just my luck. The Jag would still be in the shop. "Oh, no. I don't have a car this week. Something…Um, it needed to be repaired." *And that was another involved, inexplicable story.*

He paused. "That's too bad. Well, I can take the evening shift tonight, switch with someone, if you'd like me to drive you."

A wave of excitement passed through her. "You wouldn't mind?"

"I'd like to see Sahire anyway. It's been too long. Sure. I'll pick you up about 5:30?" The thought of getting up that early nauseated her, but she agreed she could be ready, and gave him her address. "See you then."

She hung up and swung into the passenger seat. "The doctor from the ER is taking me to a specialist in Palm Beach tomorrow. Maybe he and I can do the Old Lisbon stop. Less suspicious."

"All right, if that's what you want." Mela studied her face. "That's an awful big smile for a doctor appointment."

Bet chuckled. "Yeah. Maybe I'll find out what's really wrong with me and get some treatment. And…"

"And?" Mela stared intensely.

"And the doctor isn't hard on the eyes, either. It should prove an interesting day."

"You do have a way of falling into hot soup and coming out with a spoonful of honey." Mela laughed and started the car.

Bet leaned out to reach the door handle. Her eye caught a large alligator watching from the marsh not ten feet away. It opened its mouth and let out a horrible growl, then lunged.

She yelped and slammed the door. "Let's get out of here!"

Chapter Twenty

June 11, 1996
Present Day

True to his word, Giamo was waiting in her driveway at 5:30 a.m. Bet staggered out to the older model Honda, wearing soft knit tunic and slacks in periwinkle, a thermos cup of coffee in hand. No makeup, even. She hadn't been up this early in months. Worry over the incident had kept her awake until after midnight. She'd taken her meds on an empty stomach; that and the lack of sleep left her queasy and in pain.

She slid into the passenger seat and laid her head back, eyes closed. "Hey."

"Wow. What a lack of enthusiasm." He chuckled. "Not an early bird, I take it?"

"No." She hunched in her seat and sipped the coffee.

"Hmm." He pulled out and headed for the nearest freeway. Palm Beach was a two-hour drive north, all on the interstate, and they were ahead of morning rush hour, so they should have smooth sailing.

"Thanks for driving," she murmured. The drugs were taking so long to work this morning. *What the hell...*

"What happened to your car? You didn't say."

She looked out the window, watching the chrome-and-glass urban sprawl of Miami roll by. "Yeah. I didn't." She sighed. "Someone shot it up. While I was with my kids."

"What?" His gaze was liquid and full of sympathy. "Are they all right? Are you?"

"We weren't in the car. We were at a festival and when we came back, we found it."

"That's horrific. I'll bet you were all terrified." He shrugged. "I would have been."

"It wasn't the best day ever, let's just say that."

"The police came?"

"Oh, yes. You know, the whole rigamarole, but of course they didn't find anything."

He drove for a while in silence. Bet was grateful for the pause, as her meds began to kick in, as well as the coffee. *Give me another hour, I might feel almost human. Right before they turn me into a pincushion.*

"Bet, that means you're being followed." His words carried an edge of darkness.

"I suppose so."

He glanced in the rearview mirror, but said nothing.

"I'm sure it's not something that would cause *you* a problem." She laid a hand on his arm, intending to comfort him. *How much can I say?* "We have reason to believe that this may be tied to my husband's financial practices, which is why they'd want to frighten the children. They've got no reason to bother you."

"Good Lord. What's he been doing that's worth killing for?"

Damn it. I shouldn't have brought that up. Too early in the morning. Brain fart!

"It's in the hands of the police now. I really shouldn't talk about it. I just wanted to make sure you knew you were safe."

He took a deep breath and slowly released it. "All right. I'd hate for anything to happen to you while you were riding with me."

She gave him a smile. "Thanks for caring. Now, tell me about your week instead. I'm sure it's got a happier vibe."

He turned to telling funny stories from the emergency room, and she learned for the first time about "GOMER." While doctors apparently didn't often tell people to Get Out of My Emergency Room, they certainly discussed patients that way behind the scenes. He shared other stories that let her see the doctors from a very human angle as well. The time passed quickly and before she knew it, they were pulling into a lot by the Atlantic Institute.

They went inside the average-looking glass-covered building, and sought out a directory. Dr. Bhatti was on the third floor. Bet felt some anxiety, now that they were actually here. What if she was fooling herself and she would participate in all the testing and find out nothing new? Wouldn't be the first time. Or the second. But she wanted real relief so badly that she was willing to do it once more. *Admit it, if someone offered up frog eyes as a cure for the pain, you'd be the first one in line to blind baby amphibians.*

The building inside looked like any other medical building she'd been in over the years—and she'd been in many. The doctor welcomed them into her office. From her name, Bet had expected Sahire Bhatti to have a strong accent, as many foreign-named physicians did, but Sahire was in fact from Indianapolis, and had a delightful sense of humor.

"I'm going to step outside," Giamo said. He winked

at Bet. "I'm sure the two of you will have plenty to discuss. I've already filled her in on my small part in all this."

The doctor grinned. "So, Giamo tells me you have been treating your symptoms, rather than discovering exactly what is causing your disease, is that correct?"

Bet studied the clean white office, its large southern-facing window lined with ferns and hanging baskets. It *felt* healthy, full of fresh air. Pristine. "Yes."

A discussion followed about her joint pain, morning stiffness or what she could and couldn't do at different times of the day. The doctor examined Bet's physical movement, and joints, noting which were tender or swollen. "What about fatigue?"

Bet shrugged. "If I get a good night's sleep, I can usually make it through until 10 p.m. or so. Otherwise, I feel ready for a nap about 4 p.m. Not just a nap," she clarified. "I mean, it's like an iron curtain descends over me."

"I've heard that described before, yes. Do you have any idea what testing you've already done? It would be good to have a baseline."

Bet handed the doctor a thick file of her relevant medical records. "They've tested pretty thoroughly, but haven't found anything specific to hang it on other than fibrositis."

The doctor smiled. "That's a nice catch-all. Well, not nice for you, but it gives the doctor something to prescribe for and pass on to the insurance company. Give me a minute here."

Sahire read through the paperwork, nodding every so often. "This looks fine, for what it is. Mostly what a GP would do. The specialists in Atlanta were a couple of years ago—we're just getting up to speed now on more exact testing and potential treatments. I'm assuming your doctors have talked to you about possibilities, since you're obviously an intelligent woman. What do you think about the chance you have rheumatoid arthritis?"

"All I know about that is that the tests said no."

"Any test is subject to false positives or negatives, especially if they're from a dated protocol. We'll do some more here today, if that's all right with you, and see what we can see."

"Sure. If the pain was at a manageable level, I would be so grateful. I'm not a fan of the opioids but right now that's all that keeps it in check. Otherwise I wouldn't be able to work."

"I understand. I do." The doctor came around and sat on the front of her wooden desk, facing Bet. "My mother suffers from the same disease, and I have watched what it's done to her. I don't want to see the same happen to you." She put out her hand and Bet shook it.

"A pleasure to meet you. I guess it's time for the vampires."

The doctor laughed. "The blood does give us so much information. I promise they'll leave enough for you to function. Then I'd like you to go downstairs for some X-rays."

Giamo walked Bet down the hall to the lab, which thoughtfully had blinds around its procedure room to protect privacy, then took a seat outside. Bet had hoped the doctor was kidding, but in fact the lab tech took twenty vials of varying amounts of blood, and racked them up in a row of test tube holders. Bet had to quit watching after a while—she felt dizzy, and a heavy buzz filled her ears. Her eyes closed and when they opened, Giamo was holding an ice pack to the back of her neck.

"Whoa," Bet said, her head spinning.

Giamo smiled. "Considering all that you've been through in the last month…what takes you down is a little needle?"

"Not so much the needle," Bet countered, hating the implication that she was weak. "I mean, loss of blood. Look at it!"

He did look at the rack. "It's a lot. But not enough to deplete you much."

"What's all that for, anyway?"

"Can I tell her?" he asked the tech.

"Doesn't matter to me." The scrub-dressed woman wrapped a bandage and some stretchy tape around Bet's arm. Bet was sure it wouldn't hold—the hole must have been a funnel's width at least to get that much blood. *Vampires, indeed.* Then she got a plastic bottle of orange juice and some saltine crackers.

Giamo scanned the vial labels. "Hmm. Complete blood count, sed rate, electrolytes, creatinine, some liver function tests. C-reactive proteins. Enzymes. Rheumatoid factors."

"Sounds like the laundry list they usually do."

"These will be top of the line tests, Bet. Better researched and developed than what's in a standard hospital lab. I think you'll be impressed with the results."

She took some deep belly breaths, feeling a lot more stable after drinking the juice. "All right. Radiology, yes?" He nodded.

"Why don't you spend some time with your friend? I can figure out how to get some pictures taken." She posed like a model from a zombie movie. "Gorgeous, right?"

"I can do that. Thanks." With a friendly pat on the shoulder, he left her at the stairs.

The X-rays were completed without a problem, and Bet met Giamo at the front door. "Ready?" She checked her watch, finding it was nearly eleven.

"If you're finished. Sahire seemed to think she can help you. I'm so glad."

"That sounds promising." *All the same, I'm glad we're done for today. A nap is definitely on my agenda. After the other things on my agenda.*

He opened her door, making sure she was seated comfortably before closing it, and then came around to the driver's side.

"Thanks," she said, unaccustomed to such manners of late.

"My mother would have insisted. You hungry? We could get something to eat. You really should, after that experience. Don't want you passing out driving us home."

"I feel okay, but sure. I have just the place in mind. It's down by the hospital. When do you have to be to work?" Bet asked.

"I don't, actually. I switched the whole day with another doctor. Testing sometimes runs late, depending on demand and… Why do you ask?" He glanced over at her.

"Let me take you to lunch," she said. "It's the least I can do after all you've done today."

"That wouldn't be very chivalrous of me. But as a starving ER staff doctor, I'll let you."

"Good. Let's go to Old Lisbon. Do you know where it is? On Sunset?"

Bet felt guilty for surreptitiously using her new friend to do her investigation, but she and Mela had agreed that with a man, Bet would seem just like any other woman out on a date. Less suspicious. *In case anyone was watching. I hope no one's watching.*

Bet provided him with directions, and they arrived before the dinner rush. They walked inside, and the hostess greeted them in English and Spanish. She picked up two menus and prepared to seat them in the dining room.

"No!" Bet said, more sharply than she intended. She studied the room where the bar was located, and saw that the table where the exchange had happened was empty. "That one. We need that one. Please." She added a winning smile.

Giamo turned to her. "Is everything all right?"

"Yes. I just… That table."

The hostess gave her an odd look, but held her hand out for them to precede her to be seated. She put the menus down at 9:00 and 3:00 positions. When she left, Giamo went to seat Bet at one of them, but she pulled out the chair between them and sat down quickly.

Just where I was that day. She closed her eyes a moment, then reopened them slowly. Giamo sat at her left hand, watching her.

"You going to tell me what you're up to?"

"It's a great table, isn't it? Away from all the little kids." She fussed with the colorful paper drink coasters lying in front of her.

"Mm-hmm. Very specific. Is this a memory for you and your ex, or something?" The look in his eyes seemed pained.

I should be honest with him. He deserves it. "This is

where that evening in the…the car started. I needed to come back here to see if it triggered any memories." She went on, "I feel stronger with you here. I hope you don't mind, too much."

"You don't suppose anyone will make note that you're here?"

She scanned the room, seeing no one particularly noticing her. "It's pretty random, us appearing here at this particular time, right?"

He finally nodded. "Agreed."

The tall, dark and handsome server stopped by to drop off some ice water and take drink orders. Bet asked for a Manhattan on the rocks. Giamo still had his eye on her, but he asked what beers were on tap, and chose one from the list.

The young man hurried off. Giamo settled into his seat and leaned back. "You stalled me off earlier about your ongoing tragedy, but I think now you've wrapped me up in it. Spill it, woman."

She raised an eyebrow at his casual demand. "I suppose you're right." She gave him the digest version of the video she'd seen at the police station, and then shared the success she'd had the day before at the crime scene. "I don't know what kind of drug they used, something like Rohypnol, obviously, because of the memory loss. But apparently the effects fade after some time. I was hoping if I really pushed it, I might be able to uncover the shadows."

He grinned. "So what's my part? I'm a veteran of community theatre—I even played Perchik in *Fiddler on the Roof.*"

"Is that good?" Bet set her bag on the next chair, intending to watch it every second.

He laughed. "Way to make me feel important. No, really, what do you need me to do?"

"I'm not sure. Let me get comfortablc, a little relaxed. I'll tell you if I think of it."

"Here comes your drink. That should help."

"Yep." When the waiter set the glass down, she seized it, startling him. The ice clinked against the sides of the glass.

"Uh—tough day, miss?" He half-smiled, but seemed fairly dubious. Bet pulled up her sleeve and showed him the wrapped bandage. He just nodded and backed away.

The doctor was shaking his head. "You're something, Bet Lenard."

"Let's hope it's 'free of all this crap' soon, right? A toast." She raised her glass and clinked it against his, then drank about half the drink at once. Closing her eyes, she tried to envision the scene from the security video.

Dark-haired woman sitting across from me, hair trailing into her face. On my left, the big, bulky man. Remember, you've just seen them again in the Glades. She's medium height, non-descript. His voice rumbles through his chest.

Which one of them is K?

In her mind, she looked from one to the other. Was either a client? A potential client? No paperwork was exchanged, not even a business card. What did they want? Or was it even them that wanted something?

That brought her eyes wide open.

"What?" Giamo asked.

"In the video, I came and spoke to them first. Several exchanges passed before I joined them. I must have asked them to come for some reason."

"So maybe the clue is in your office, not here."

She nodded slowly, assimilating her revelation. The waiter returned, ready to take an order. Bet had lost all interest in food, but as she'd promised to buy lunch for them both, she reluctantly ordered a wedge salad with blue cheese. Giamo chose a club sandwich with a side of steamed broccoli.

"Have to have something nutritious, after all," he said with a small shrug.

"Sure. Why not?" She was still wrapped in the mystery of what she could have desired from this team, something that didn't surface when she and Mela had sorted through all the paperwork on the top of her desk and the things she kept at hand, for quick access. *Maybe what I wanted had nothing to do with the office at all. Maybe it was personal.*

"I just don't know."

Giamo urged, "Tell me about the video again."

Bet recounted her memory of the security tape, her teeth gritting as she shared the quick work the man made of drugging her.

"Did he speak English or Spanish?" Giamo leaned forward, elbows on the table.

"We couldn't tell. The tape had no sound."

"I'm asking you to remember. Close your eyes again."

She closed her eyes, at first only aware of the mixed voices around them, conversations about the deep and the mundane. But then those faded. She fixated on the person sitting to her left. Muscular. Bald. Dark jacket.

And a red tie.

She snatched the clue with mental hands and pulled it toward her, like a cowboy roping a calf at the rodeo.

She could see his clothing from the front. *Now, his face…*

It remained fuzzy, but she recalled brown eyes, deep-set and shadowed by heavy brows. His lips were thick. Double chin. *What was he saying?*

She strained for it, perhaps too hard. The recollection dissolved into black-and-white video, all she could remember.

Opening her eyes, she shook her head. "Lost it. I almost had it, though. I almost did."

"It's a start. Maybe it'll come when you're sitting quietly, later." Giamo grinned. "But you let me down, my friend. I didn't get a chance to act at all."

Bet looked up, disappointed but glad for his encouragement. Her eyes caught those of a man across the room, who'd looked up at the same moment. *How did I not see him when we came in? Was he purposely hiding in the back corner?* She reached for Giamo's hand. "It's not too late. Act like you're my boyfriend." She turned to look deeply into his face. "Right now."

Without missing a beat, he leaned over to kiss her. It was no "pretend" kiss. She went right along with it. Maybe it was sudden, maybe it was even inappropriate in a public setting. But she prayed that whatever it was, it fooled John Lee. The kingpin had zeroed in on their table with all his attention once he'd recognized her. His cold regard had frozen her spine, and she couldn't stop trembling. Had he realized what she was doing?

Giamo pulled back slightly and kissed her on the forehead, retaining her hand in his. "Wish I had a jewelry box I could pop out of my pocket right now." He smiled, still leaning toward her. "I take it we're being watched? Something you hadn't anticipated?"

Bet still reeled from the kiss. *A long time since*

someone's kissed me like that. I miss it.

"Yeah," she whispered back, not daring to look away from his face. "But I think that Emmy-winning performance just might have hoodwinked him."

"I'll be sure to list you in my thank-you's from the stage," he said. "Should we leave?"

"No! That would be even more suspicious." Their meal was delivered by a runner, and she thanked them. From the corner of her eye, she noticed Lee and his crew getting up, preparing to leave. All of the four men with him looked like body builders, but none was bald. She applied herself to her salad, and changed the subject to the testing she'd had that morning. Giamo played along beautifully, and didn't take his eyes off her once.

Lee and his men left without saying anything to her, and she didn't give Giamo any indication that Lee had been the danger she'd stiffened over.

No sense in encouraging anyone else to get personally involved with the man. Don't know Giamo well, but something tells me he might be the type to jump in to play hero and get in trouble. I'll keep them from noticing each other, and that will keep my conscience clear.

Right now, my scorecard holds enough death.

Chapter Twenty-One

April 1995
A year earlier

Bet climbed into the queen-size bed she shared with Rich, her hip muscles aching. She'd spent a long day proofreading a brief for a divorce client whose case was going before the Florida Appeals Court the following week. *Sat too long. I always sit too long, damn it.* Stretching out her heels in alternate rhythm, she tried to alleviate the worst of it before Rich joined her.

The kids had retreated to their rooms to chat on the phone or their computer or whatever teenagers did at night these days. Rich had suggested it would be the perfect chance for the two of them to have some "alone time," a thing that seemed to come less and less often in the last several months. She'd like to think it had to do with the burgeoning files of their legal practice, the evenings one or both of them spent working on cases. But she knew they avoided each other more often than not because of her body issues.

The windows were open, and an occasional snatch of bird song or peeper frogs grounded the night. The shower off the master bedroom was running, and steam whispered through the cracked-open door, adding to the humidity of the April evening. Sweat beaded on Bet's face, and she wiped it with a tissue from the nightstand.

She missed their intimate moments, coupling like teenagers daily in the early days, even still an important bond between them after the children were born. Of course, they enjoyed other pursuits, fine food and drink, sporadic evenings dancing at clubs, an occasional weekend away. But their bodies had always fit together well. No matter what dirt and tragedy they dealt with during work hours, their reconnection in the dark restored equilibrium in Bet's well-being.

And certainly, this disintegrating body needs all the endorphins it can get.

As the water shut off, she spritzed a light air of perfume on her pillowcase, not wanting to taste like chemicals when Rich kissed her. She turned off the bedside light, opened the top two buttons on her silk nightshirt and lay back on the navy-blue sheets, envisioning a long hour pleasuring each other. It had been weeks coming. Now she waited.

Rubbing himself with a thick towel, Rich strolled out of the bathroom in a cloud of mist, looking like an apparition from a fantasy movie, backlit from the faint light over the mirror.

"It was a good idea putting in that new water heater."

Now that's romantic. Bet bit the words back before they escaped. She was still wrestling with a long muscle cramp in her thigh and trying like hell to ignore it. A few extra seconds wouldn't hurt. *Stay in the mood.* "Come here, lover."

"You don't have to ask me twice." He chuckled and dropped the towel, crawling right on top of her, his body signaling it was ready to go. "I like it when you command me."

She kissed him to avoid an answer, knowing he definitely hated when she tried to tell him what to do. He smelled of his aftershave-scented shower gel, a spicy rum-based aroma that always turned her on. Always, except when her muscles cramped like this. Cursing inwardly, she shifted her body weight slightly, hoping to loosen up her hip. *Stop, please…just stop…I need this…*

Rich slowly unbuttoned the rest of her nightshirt and nibbled down her neck, responding to her movement with a cool whisper. "Raring to go tonight, are you, darlin'?" He liked to affect a mild Irish brogue when they made love. Most of the time, it added to the magic and made their time special. With her anticipation and nerves twisted tight, it just irritated her.

She slipped her arms around him, holding him close, stroking his broad back muscles, hoping it distracted her body from its pain. He responded by moving between her legs, shoving her hip to the right.

And that was it.

The hip muscle tightened to a frenzied peak, sending hot nerve rushes down her right thigh. She jerked up right into his chin, knocking him aside.

"Damn it, Bettina, what now?" He growled and moved over.

Clapping her hand over her mouth to keep from screaming, she wiggled out from under him and fell forward, curling up in a fetal position as the twisting agony continued.

"What is it? Another cramp? Here, let me help," Rich said. His voice was tight, and he rubbed his chin with one hand, reaching the other out to massage her leg. He was rough, and the motions had the opposite effect intended.

"Rich, stop, please." Tears burned her eyes and she writhed on the bed, trying to cope with the stabbing pains. No matter which way she turned, she couldn't seem to relieve it.

"No, give me a minute. You know I can get it to relax. You'll just feel better if—"

But she couldn't hold still. Muscles cramped up her leg, across her belly, even in her upper arm. All at once, it seemed like an onslaught from some invisible army, determined to make her unable to be touched, to be comforted.

"Why does this happen?" she hissed through clenched teeth. "Why?"

It's not fair. It's not fair. All I want is a little cozy lovemaking with my husband. Why can't I even have that bit of relief?

"Beats the hell out of me, Bettina."

Rich pulled back, hands raised in surrender. "It was the perfect evening. Neither of us had a meeting, you weren't seeing your shrink, we even agreed to leave the dishes in the sink. And here we are again."

Bet couldn't stand the contempt in his voice. She angrily wiped the tears from her cheeks. "It's not like I'm doing it on purpose!"

"Oh, of course not. Never. Just every time we get ready to screw." He got up and slipped on a cotton bathrobe.

She turned around and managed to sit on the edge of the bed, pressing her feet into the floor, relieving at least the leg cramps momentarily. "I suppose you'd rather I were drunk."

After he'd complained about her drinking, she'd made the effort to avoid excessive alcohol on their nights together. But her disease, whatever the hell it was, didn't appreciate being uncontrolled by "self-medication."

"No, Bettina, I would not rather you were drunk. I would *rather* be able to have sex with my wife. It's one of the few things we can still do together that we don't argue all the way through." He snorted. "Or maybe subconsciously, your body is carrying on the argument for you. Either way, I end up with blue balls, you end up crying, and we both feel like hell. What's the point?"

"The point is—"

She broke off, unsure whether there really was one. "I love you, Rich, I miss you. I miss us. I know you don't understand this thing that's wrong with me. I'm trying to find out what it is. I'm trying to fix it. But I can't help what happens. I can't help it, and—"

"Shhh." Rich held up a hand, listening. He walked over to the bedroom door,

Bet realized the music that had been playing from the kids' rooms had stopped. When was that? Had they heard? She grabbed a handful of tissues and sponged off her face, pulling her nightshirt closed.

Rich opened the door and looked down the hallway. The lights were off. "They must just have gone to bed." He cleared his throat. "Be back in a minute." He disappeared down the hall.

Frustrated, she buttoned up and stood, walking in a circle, stretching out her legs and arms, feeling the tension retreat, protesting all the way. Maybe when Rich came back, they could try again.

But it felt more like the moment had passed.

When he returned with two cups of tea and some heated oil, she realized it had. They sat with their tea in silence, and then he invited her to lie face down on the bed for a hot oil massage. Saying yes felt like a betrayal, a capitulation. At the same time, such a massage would relieve tension that even now was ramping back up. She couldn't say no.

Trapped.

He flipped on the late-night news, half-heartedly working on the knobs and valleys of her tense muscles as he took in the weather report and sports scores. She tried to focus on the peepers outside, ignoring the drone of the late-night sportscaster.

Marlins' new pitcher? Damned exciting, right? Better get those box seats on credit, huh, Rich?

A lone tear trailed down her cheek. *At least we're alone together and he's touching me. It's not all we hoped for, but it's something. A very little something.*

Like always, the pain controlled her, reduced her, ending with both of them hurting, and tears in the darkness.

She wondered how long she could keep rationalizing the situation. It wasn't working. For her, or for Rich. Something would have to break, to change, or they wouldn't last. A man like Rich could be patient, but he was a man in need. Where else would that itch be scratched?

Chapter Twenty-Two

June 20, 1996
Present Day

The phone rang and Bet, concentrating on writing some overdue court pleadings, yelled, "Fuck! Not now."

But the phone kept ringing.

Mela was off, and for some reason the machine wouldn't pick up. "Fine." Bet threw her pen across the room. "Hello?" she barked.

"Geez, Bettina, what the hell? It's me."

"If I'd known that, Rich, I wouldn't have answered. What do you want?"

"It's not what I want, actually. John Lee has asked for a meeting. With both of us."

His answer raised goosebumps on her arms. "I don't have anything to say to that man."

"This time it's not up to you. What you want doesn't matter." Rich sounded defensive and unsure. *That wasn't his usual approach at all. This must be serious.*

"How can it not matter? What did you do now?"

"He's actually more concerned about what you did at this point." He quickly went on, "Not that I blame you. I know that you didn't want to deal with this from the get-go. If you don't want to rep his guys, I understand that—"

"I don't intend to be threatened into taking clients at

half pay. You sure as hell wouldn't take the financial hit. I don't care who John Lee is."

"Oh. He didn't mention the money."

"I bet."

"So can you meet?"

"Rich. Come on."

"Please. I need you to be here."

"Why are you so desperate? Especially if you think he had a hand in what happened to me, you have got to know that putting us in the same room…all THREE of us in the same room…could be a huge mistake."

"We…we'll meet in public. Denny's or something."

"Because no one gets murdered at Denny's?"

"I don't know. Do they?"

"The answer is no, Rich. I have no intention of being controlled by some punk drug lord. I've got work to do." She hung up.

The call troubled her. Rich's tone had changed quite a bit from the night at the 94th, when he confessed what he'd done as if it were just another business decision. Now, his voice was wound tight, in the frantic range. *And he was begging…*

She hated to admit it, but this situation was unraveling, slipping out of her control. She'd been able to ignore this, shove it away, cover it with mockery…but things were coming to a head. First, someone directly put her in danger, though her memories indicated they intended to frighten her, and for her to remember. Second, someone directly intended to scare her, and the children. Third, Rich sounded scared as hell.

Maybe I really am afraid. And afraid of looking at it.

But what the hell can I do against an enemy without

a face?

Then what happens to me, to the kids, to Rich…to whoever else…if I do nothing?

The nagging voice came back to her, wondering what she had to do with the other victim in this mess, Jackson Gutierrez, and what he had to do with her. Or what he had to do with John Lee. Gutierrez was obviously part of the fatal plan, somehow. She hadn't spoken to him in years. They hadn't had anything more than a professional relationship. He was just a guy who'd had too many whiskeys before driving home one night. That's all.

So why him?

I have no goddamned idea.

Too distracted now by her spiraling thoughts, she saved her work and got up to walk around the office. She rolled her shoulders, raised her arms up and down, anything to get the blood flowing, to wash these doubts from her head.

Taking a deep breath to reset her brain, she went to the cabinet of closed criminal case files and pulled out the architect's folder. She took it back to her desk and leafed through it, beginning to end. Nothing stood out to her. No injuries had occurred. He'd hurt no one else. The man had committed a first offense, and in Miami-Dade, a first DUI could be resolved by a 48-hour period of incarceration and taking a driving class. Gutierrez had completed his sentence quickly and the matter had been closed.

So, what had he done to John Lee?

If not John Lee, then who? Santos Silvina would hardly be in the same social group as Gutierrez— different neighborhood, different employment strata. He didn't know Mela, because Bet's representation had occurred before Mela came to work for her.

Maybe Detective Ortiz would have an answer.

Bet rang the detective's office number, and was put through quickly.

"Ms. Lenard? Another incident?" he asked.

"No, no. Not at all. I'm wondering if you have any theories about Jackson Gutierrez, and why he was in that car that night." She idly tapped a pen on her desk, rotating the instrument through her fingers like a twirling baton.

"Why the sudden interest?"

The question took her aback. She dropped the pen. "I'm sorry?"

"It's been over a month. Every time we've talked about the case, except that first day, you've only talked about your portion of it, as if the two are completely different incidents. You've never asked me about Gutierrez."

Was he right? I certainly don't remember. "I can see why you'd think that was odd. But there's no ulterior motive here. I'm trying to put pieces together, just like you are."

"Have you remembered anything else?"

If I want information, I'll likely have to give him something. Tit for tat, as it were. "I have, just quite recently." She told him about going to the site of the burning car, and what she remembered about the woman with the hypodermic.

"She had a Spanish accent? You're sure of it?"

"Yes. I don't know what was in the needle, but I'm guessing it counteracted what they'd put in my drink."

"I see." A long pause. Was he taking notes or

deciding if he believed her? "What else?"

"I was thinking about the video from Old Lisbon. I remembered that I spoke to the two people first, and led the discussion."

"Mmhmm? And that means what to you?"

"I think it means that I asked them to meet me there. That it was my meeting."

He scoffed. "If that's so, why did you get drugged and taken? That doesn't make sense."

The thought had also occurred to her. But her theory matched up with the video. So maybe somehow her meeting was sabotaged, and the two that showed up were not the two she'd arranged for. *And that meant someone switched up the program.*

She said this to Ortiz, who pooh-poohed the idea.

"Who would you have discussed the meeting with, besides your assistant?"

"I don't know. I can't remember what it was about."

"None of this really helps, Ms. Lenard. Frankly, it leans toward putting you back on the questionable list of suspects."

Irritated, she shoved her chair away from her desk. "Look, you wanted to know what I remembered, and I told you. So tell me about Gutierrez."

The detective sighed heavily. "All right, all right. We interviewed his family, his associates at work, people at his gym...no one had a negative thing to say about him, or could think of anyone with a grudge."

"Well, someone must have been a bit pissed off. His skull was bashed in." The smell came back to her like a whiff in the wind, and she shuddered.

"Would your husband—ex-husband—have believed you were having an affair?"

Why the hell were we back at that question? Didn't I clear that up at the beginning? "You think my ex did all this? Did you interview him?"

"Certainly, we did. He has an alibi for that evening."

"Oh yeah? What's that?"

"He claims he stayed late at the office. His office manager confirmed it. Delia Evans."

Bet made a face. Of course Delia would cover for Rich. *Suck-up.* "So then he's not a suspect."

"If he'd hired someone, he could have been anywhere. It wouldn't make a difference."

She sat back in her chair and considered it for a long minute. Could Rich have…? No. They'd shared a bed. They'd shared children. The divorce was six months past, and she'd surrendered everything, since she'd caused it all. Rich would have no reason to get rid of her, and even less to deal with the architect.

"It wasn't him. I'd know."

"I guess we'll find out, if we ever solve this." Ortiz cleared his throat. "Anything else?"

"No. Sorry to have bothered you." She hung up, a smoky band of disappointment swirling in her gut. Not only had she not found out anything of use, now she had more questions.

And Rich futzing around trying to deal with John Lee. Well, that is one I'm definitely staying out of.

And I have to wait another week to find out my damn test results.

She pulled her chair up and sat still for a moment, her hands on the edge of the desk. They trembled. The disquiet spread through her, and her heart rate crept up. *Things are not in my control.* Her breath caught. Before she knew it, she was in tears. Not just tears, sobs that ripped at her very being.

I'm in real trouble. We all are.

The realization added fuel to her meltdown. She cried until she had no tears left, no self-respect left, no sense of her own thoughts left. Sitting at her desk, frozen, she glanced up, startled to see someone walk across the grass outside her office window, close enough to touch it. She could swear it was the man she'd seen in her backyard a few weeks before. *What was he doing here? What did he want?*

The grief and anger bloomed like a hot mushroom cloud inside her. She grabbed her purse and ran outside, slamming the door closed behind her. Coming around the corner, she yelled at the man, "What do you want?"

He studied her, a lazy smile on his lips, and backed away until he hit the sidewalk. Then he walked off as if nothing had happened.

The heat inside her vanished as quickly as it had come. A chill set in. She got in her car and headed for the nearest pawn shop.

****

That night and the next morning, Bet was so knotted up with tension, she couldn't get out of bed. Perhaps it was the loaded pistol that now lay next to her on the nightstand. Perhaps not. She tried to sleep, but that burnt hulk with the blackened body inside kept appearing before her, demanding answers she didn't have. Lying in the bed, her nerves burned, keeping her from finding peace in any position. She called Mela and told her she wouldn't be in.

"And keep the office door locked," Bet added.

"Did something happen?"

"It doesn't matter. Keep the door locked."

"All right. Do you need anything?"

Bet gave a dry laugh. "Nothing you can give me, *chica.*" She hung up and rolled over onto her heating pad and soft blue comforter, closing her eyes. But it didn't help.

She'd already taken all the pain meds she was allowed, so that wasn't an option. Nine in the morning was no time to start drinking, even for her. *What else is there? I need something before I go mad.*

Wretched, she went to her bathroom and dug through the top right-hand drawer full of salves, liniments and all sorts of other things she'd tried over the years. *There. Lavender essential oil.* She leaned against the edge of the vanity and twisted open the lid, deeply inhaling the pungent aroma. It about knocked her off her feet.

Maybe not so close.

She took it back to bed, sniffing every so often. It definitely commandeered her attention, drawing it away from the pain. Seating herself on the bed, she assumed the position the kids had always called "criss-cross, applesauce."

I can't control all the things going on out there, but I am in charge of this body. The best way to get control is to let go.

Yes, Hyacinth, I'm trying the damned meditation.

Breathe in for eight, out for eight. In for eight, out for eight… The rhythm was easier to maintain than she would have expected. As she continued, she noticed how tight she held herself, almost defensively, as if protecting against an expected blow of some sort. She kept counting the breathing, but gradually let her shoulders drop, her rib cage fill, her leg muscles slowly release. It was a constant battle—every so often, she'd check and find herself all constricted once again. Back to the routine, letting go, letting go, letting go…

Some time later, she opened her eyes. It felt like she was returning from far away, another place altogether. She stretched out her legs and assessed her state of being. The pain had dialed down a notch, maybe two.

Well, I'll be damned. It actually works.

Feeling slightly more human, Bet meandered down the hall to the kitchen to make some coffee. Dishes were piled in the sink. She debated doing them, but decided to quit while she was ahead. Coffee cup in hand, she took a peek out the back window, half-expecting to see the mysterious man, but no one was there. She went back to bed, and tried to relax.

The phone ringing woke her. Forced out of the best sleep she'd had in days, she prepared to let loose on whoever had disturbed her.

"Bettina, it's me—please don't hang up!"

"Goddamn it, Rich." She pulled the covers over her head, cradling the phone receiver between her shoulder and ear.

"John Lee is here. I'm putting you on speaker."

Are you fucking kidding me?

A cheerful, mid-tenor voice sounded in the background. "Good afternoon, Bettina Lenard! So sorry you weren't able to join us in person."

She didn't respond. They could both burn in hell.

Afternoon? I guess I did get some sleep then. She pulled down the covers and glanced at the clock. Two p.m. Four hours in a row. And they'd been solid hours, too. She checked herself and thought she felt better.

Rich cleared his throat. "So, Bettina, John had some

questions about our future relationship. Since you're handling the criminal defense cases now, it seemed useful to include you in the discussion."

She grunted, still not willing to commit.

"Yes, I had sent a man who works for me to see you. He came back very disappointed," Lee said.

"Not as disappointed as I was that he expected me to rep him for next to nothing." She decided to be a grown-up and quit hiding. Exiting the covers, she sat on the edge of the bed and took a sip of her long-cold coffee.

Lee chuckled. "Come now, considering you've decided to break off our long-standing investing relationship, I'm starting to think you don't like me anymore."

Bet frowned, watching herself in the vanity mirror. "How 'long-standing' is that?" she asked point-blank.

"Now, Bettina—"

"Shut up, Rich. I want to know."

Lee must have leaned closer to the desk, because his voice came through loud and clear. "How long have I been paying you to save my money? Oh, about six years."

A sick wave washed through her. "That long."

"Bettina, we can talk about this—"

"Shut up, Rich!" She rubbed her forehead, breathing deeply and counting to ten.

Lee coughed. "I guess this is news? Interesting. Richard, you've been a naughty boy."

A silence set in. Bet felt the men waited on her to break it. Could she just come out and demand whether he'd tried to kill her? That seemed rather crass. Conversation-ending.

"So why is your man following me around town?"

she asked.

"I can't admit or deny that such a thing is happening," Lee replied in a smarmy tone. "Are you doing something you're ashamed to have eyes on?"

Rich interrupted. "We're getting off topic here. John, I think Bet and I are agreed that while we've had a good association—"

Like hell.

"--up until now, because of the divided situation in which we run the offices now, it's just not working out."

"So, what you're saying, Richard, is you want me to just walk away. To forget all we've done for each other. All the…favors." Lee spoke as casually as if he were being presented choices for dessert.

Bet bit her tongue to keep from blurting out her questions. *Favors? Rich has gotten favors? Hellfire, I don't even want to know.*

Rich answered, "Y-Yes. Exactly."

"And if I don't? Are you prepared for the consequences?"

"What consequences?" Bet growled. At the same time, a small part of her mind questioned why Lee was discussing this in terms of future actions. *As if he hadn't done anything yet. Was that true?*

"It would be a shame if your actions came to light, now, wouldn't it? Fine, upstanding members of the legal community tied to a drug cartel?"

Bet seethed. "You wouldn't do that. You'd have to admit your own complicity."

Lee laughed, but there was no amusement in it. "I'm afraid I have to agree. But I'm not interested in discontinuing our business relationship. As they say in the movies, you're not out until I say you're out."

Trembling, Bet found it hard to respond. "You've pressured Rich before, right? You have sent someone after me. Are you dogging Rich, too? Do you mean to kill him? Or me?"

The muscles in her hand contracted so tightly on the phone she thought they would pop.

"I'm sure she doesn't mean that—" Rich started.

"Oh, I think she does. Would I kill him? Why would I do that? Where else can I find such a golden goose? Anyone else, on the other hand…well, they seem expendable, don't they?"

Bet gasped and couldn't answer.

Rich finally pulled some gumption out of his ass. "Look, John, making threats is not necessary. You aren't going to hurt any of us. Now that all this is out in the open among us, if anything occurs, we know what's going to happen."

Lee replied, his voice dropping into a menacing tone. "Do we, Richard? Do we know?" The sounds of a chair scraping the floor came across the phone. "We'll find out, I guess."

Bet heard steps, and then the slam of a door.

Another long silence, broken finally by Rich's rattled breaths. "I'm sorry, Bettina. So sorry."

"What are you going to do to protect the children? To protect *me*?" she demanded. "You'd best do something, and soon."

"I-I just don't know. I need to think."

"You do that." She slammed down the receiver, then picked it up and slammed it down again. Part of the blue plastic split off and flew across the room. "Damn it!"

She sat there in disbelief for a while. *I have to admit, I don't have much more idea what to do than Rich does.*

But he got us into this mess, damn it. He should have to clean it up.

A knock at her front door grabbed her attention. She snuck to the bedroom window and peered out. Jeremy and Jane stood outside with backpacks, waving to someone in a blue truck that had dropped them off.

Now what?

As her tension ramped up, she seized another Vicodin and a muscle relaxer and choked them down dry on her way to the door.

She opened it and pulled the kids inside. "Get in here before someone sees you."

"Thanks, Mom. Nice to see you, too." Jane wore a tight T-shirt and cutoffs.

"Did you wear that to school? Doesn't your father even notice?"

"He. uh, he wasn't up when we left." Jane looked away.

Bet looked Jeremy up and down. Fortunately, fashion choices for boys weren't such an issue. He looked at her with wide deer-in-the-headlight eyes. He held out a piece of paper.

"Is it report card day already?"

She took the paper and read it. The dark block letters jumped out at her, dragging her into a deep pit of fear.

WE KNOW WHERE THE CHILDREN ARE, ALL THE TIME. THEY ARE THIS EASY TO APPROACH. IT COULD HAVE BEEN A KNIFE. IT COULD HAVE BEEN A GUN. REMEMBER.

"Who gave this to you?" she asked, clutching Jeremy's arm. "Where did it come from?"

"Some kid. I didn't know who he was," Jeremy said, his voice breaking. "What's happening, Mom?"

Could this be Lee? Did he know the timing of his meeting would coincide with when the kids got off school? What am I going to do?

"Okay. Okay. Let's all take a moment here. A moment." Her hand moved to cover her mouth, as if to keep her from blurting out the whole truth. Jane's gaze was hard, adult. She knew something life-changing was up. But she apparently decided to cut Bet a break.

"You got any snacks?" Jane's posture changed, and she ambled into the kitchen, more like the child she was.

"Mom?" Jeremy asked again.

Bet put her arms around him and held him tight. "Sorry, Jer, I don't have answers for you. We need to think. And talk with your dad." *But not until I cool off about that conversation with Lee.*

It suddenly occurred to her that Rich might have recorded that conversation. He did have equipment in his office to do so. Normally, it was used for client interviews, so they could have a secretary transcribe it. *But would he record something that could incriminate him?* That, she didn't know.

Jeremy disentangled himself. "Mom, we thought you could give this to your policeman friend. It's got to be the same people that shot up the car."

"I'll do that, babe. Come on and see if I've got cookies or something."

They followed Jane, where they found her already making a huge Dagwood-style sandwich on sprouted wheat bread.

"Make me one too, Janie," Jeremy said.

"Yeah. Me, too," Bet added, hungry for the first time in a while. "Use that good dark mustard."

"Sure." Jane grinned, happy as usual to be the center

of attention. She began putting the sandwiches together with a flair, as if she were working on a cooking competition. Bet was glad the activity seemed to distract the girl from the black cloud hanging over them.

They sat around the table and ate, Bet contributing her lone bag of rippled chips for a group nosh. No one said anything. What was there to say? It was all there on that paper.

And who knows how many people have handled that, if they were even able to get prints off it? I'll give it to Ortiz. Nothing'll come of it.

The real question? How long can I go without telling him about what Rich has done?

"Can we stay the night here, Mom?" Jane asked. 'It's Friday. No school tomorrow."

"Here? Um. Sure." It had been so long since they'd wanted to stay, the question caught her off guard. "Call your dad and tell him."

"Unless you have a date or something?" That Janie radar swiveled around and studied Bet. She even had a smirky little smile.

"No. Not a date." She sighed with relief. "It's just…it hasn't been a good day."

"Don't worry about us. We'll just watch TV and chill out. You can take a hot bath with your smelly salts," Jeremy said. He clearly wanted any excuse not to go home.

"Has someone been bothering you?" Bet asked. "I mean, besides this letter? At home, or on the way to school?"

Jane kept a focused gaze on Bet. "Like what?"

"Like anything! I mean it's not like the past month has been normal, right?"

215

"Right." Jane shrugged. "Nothing, really. We've been worried about you. But Jeremy was wrong. You really can't come stay at the house." An intense look shot between the siblings.

"I didn't want to," Bet said, wondering what that look meant.

"Yeah. So." Jane shrugged, and neither of them expanded on the discussion. *Another mystery for me to piece together. Damn.*

After they were finished, they piled the dishes on top of the rest of the dishes that had accumulated over the last few days. Bet took the letter back to her bedroom and called Ortiz. *He's going to think I'm trying to get on his bad side. But he needs to know about this.*

She got his answering machine, and left a message about the letter. "Please call me as soon as you can."

She went to the kitchen and pulled out a zip bag, slipping the letter inside. It might be too late, but she should preserve whatever evidence she could. She set the bag on top of the fridge. With a long sigh, she double-locked all the doors and went to join the kids in the living room.

The evening passed in denial. They sat together on the sofa and watched game shows and sit coms and pretended like everything was fine. Bet found it hard to keep her eyes open. Too long without good sleep, but she felt comfortable with her boy and girl there where she could see what they were doing.

She snapped awake when the eleven o'clock news theme music played. "I should get to bed for real," she said.

"Tonight, we have breaking news from the southwest side of the city. A one-fatality crash occurred on the Palmetto Expressway this evening. Our news team caught the action on camera."

The visual switched to a nighttime shot of flashing blue and red lights, multiple cars gathered around a car smashed into the median fencing. Shadowed emergency attendants in reflective vests bustled around the scene like starving ants.

"Isn't that…" Jeremy sat up straight.

"That's Dad's car!" Jane gasped.

Bet's eyes narrowed and she turned up the audio with the remote.

"The car is registered to local attorney Richard Lenard. The identity of the driver has been released as Delia Evans."

The broadcaster went on, but Bet didn't hear him.

"Fuck it all! He never *let me* drive the Ferrari!"

****

And then she remembered. About Rich. About Delia. About Kendrick.

Chapter Twenty-Three

June 21, 1996
Present Day

The impact of her memory returning hit her physically. Her heart raced. She couldn't move from her seat on the couch. Jane shook her by the shoulders, but Bet couldn't speak. Her thoughts spun in circles. Memories jockeyed for position, mental gears locked and finally, after what seemed an interminable time, everything came into focus.

"Mom!" Jane cried, tears in her eyes. "Are you having a stroke? What's happening?"

"I'm fine. I'm fine."

I'm not fine at all.

"Are you sure?" Jane leaned close and took Bet's wrist in hand, checking her pulse.

"Yes, Janie." She pulled her wrist loose and hugged her daughter. "I'm just…I mean, that's a shock." She gestured vaguely at the television, now blabbing about the weekend weather.

Jeremy pulled his knees up to his chest and sat in the corner of the sofa. "That could have been Dad."

"But it was Her. So." Jane sat down on the coffee table, facing them.

Bet studied her daughter, her shifting gaze, her uncomfortable body language. "So. It's been going on a while, hasn't it?"

Jane froze, then finally nodded.

"And your father told you not to tell me."

Jeremy spoke, his voice tight. "He said you'd start drinking again. That you'd hurt yourself."

Oh, did he? The bastard. How dare he put the kids in the middle of our differences?

I must have been close. Did he find out I'd hired a private detective named Kendrick? That I was meeting him at Old Lisbon on that date?

"So how long, Jane? I promise you that I'm not going to flip out or start drinking…not like I used to. I have medications now. And—I haven't told you yet, but I'm actually seeing a specialist who thinks she knows what's wrong and can help me. So please don't be worried about me. I'm an adult. I'll manage."

Her daughter's tears dripped down her face. "We *were* worried, though, Mom. He said…" She bit her lip. "But it doesn't really matter what he said, not anymore."

She sighed so deeply Bet thought Jane's lungs would pop. "Please. Tell me."

Jane cleared her throat and spoke again. "She moved in a couple months ago. She's not there every night, but a lot of them. They've been seeing each other longer than that, much longer. I remember even when you were still together, Dad would take us out on the weekends when you were sick. Delia would always show up wherever we went, and Dad wanted us to be nice to her. She was fun, sometimes. But I knew it was wrong."

"Yeah," Jeremy said, withdrawing even further into the corner of the sofa. "It's why we didn't come to visit you much, after you moved out and got this house. I was afraid I'd make a mistake. Dad would have been so mad."

Bet reached over and put her arm around him, pulling him close. "Jer, I'm so sorry."

"Yeah," Jane added. "What he said."

All the lost time...Rich put us all through the heartbreak just so he could screw his assistant. He deserves all the karma coming to him. I swear it.

"All right." Bet gave her son a last squeeze and stood up. "It's late, and we're all tired. If you want to call your dad, you can. He's probably wondering if you saw the news anyway. The guest room has twin beds. If you don't want to both sleep in there, someone can bring blankets out onto the couch. I'm getting some tea, and going to bed."

She didn't wait to see if they phoned Rich.

A steaming cup of chai accompanied her to the bedroom. Her room was down a hall, away from the guest room, so she couldn't hear if the kids had any further discussion. As far as she was concerned, they'd had a breakthrough as a family.

I will make sure those kids are never put in that spot again.

She climbed into bed, then took a minute to get herself centered. So much had happened in the last half hour. Finding out she'd been right about Delia, though, was really the least of it.

First, there was the wreck. Rich would be shattered. Maybe about the woman, but certainly about his precious Ferrari. And he'd know that Bet knew.

I wonder what he thinks I'll do.

A scene came up, unbidden, in her mind.

****

Rich was talking to her. It was spring a year ago.

They'd been on the back patio at the house in the Redlands, the kids off somewhere for the day. The trees had been in full bloom and it smelled like paradise.

"How much longer do you think this can go on, Bettina?" he said. He'd brought them both a coffee, but the mugs sat untouched on the black ironwork table.

The palm fronds overhead whispered in the wind, their fringe waving like tiny banners. "I don't know what you mean."

She did know what he meant. Ever since the Bar meeting where he'd asked her to get Hyacinth's card, he'd been more and more distant. She hated it. It made her even sicker. But he wouldn't stop, and made no effort to understand how his projected emotions impacted her health.

"You're ruining our lives, Bettina. The children are subjected to your alcohol and drug abuse every day. They cry about it, when they talk to me alone. It breaks their hearts. They worry about you, and it's tearing them up. It's tearing all of us up."

Bet's lip trembled, and she fought to keep the tears inside. *It's not my fault. It's not my fault! I'm just trying to get by, to fulfill these roles I've taken on…and no one is helping me…* "I don't want to leave, Rich. If I'm not here, I'll have no support at all. What will I do?"

"I think your behavior is what's controlling this decision. I hoped seeing a shrink might straighten you up, but it seems like the drinking has only gotten worse. It's ruining morale at the office, too."

"Who complained? Delia?" The red-haired administrative assistant had ruled the roost since she'd been hired six months before. Bet didn't recall being offensive to her, at least not on purpose. But the woman always gave off unpleasant vibes when Bet was around. *Jealous vibes.*

"It doesn't matter, in a place of business. One bad egg..." He trailed off and stared at her. "I'm not trying to be hurtful, Bettina. Truly. It just seems like it's for the best."

She wanted to scream, to shout, to curse him from one horizon to the next. But something in what he said rang true. She had been drinking to excess in an effort to manage her pain. She had spoiled many a family outing. She wasn't in control of her pain, or her body, or her life.

How could that be good for anyone else?

She'd just nodded, then got up and went for a walk in their fruit grove. When she'd come back, Rich had left a note that he'd gone to pick up the children. A week later, he presented her with divorce papers, and she'd signed everything away.

****

Back in her bed, she opened her eyes and saw that fiery crash replay in her mind. *And this is how it ended. I hope she was worth it, Rich.*

Was it possible that Rich had been the actual target? Of course.

But Rich drove the car all the time. It was assuredly not a coincidence that Delia happened to be driving this time.

That fucking burns me. All those years he tiptoed around that car, practically made love to it. I never drove it once. Not once.

But John Lee had said he didn't intend to kill Rich. What had he called him? The golden goose. Had he intended to kill Delia?

The new girlfriend would surely be more of a

consequence than the old ex-wife.

She wondered idly how soon the television crew had come on the scene. Was it possible they could have inadvertently caught the perpetrator on camera? Wouldn't that be an interesting break in the case?

And I wouldn't have to be the one that incriminated Rich. And myself.

Bet felt fairly confident that Lee was behind this. It seemed like a hit, something a drug lord would do to make a point. Similar to the burning of the car.

But some of the other things—the note, the Jag's windshield—were a different strain of threat. Lee didn't seem like the kind of man who'd tease. He'd *act.*

So where did that leave her?

And, most importantly, what had happened to Kendrick and their meeting at Old Lisbon? Someone had appeared in his place, perhaps knowing she hadn't met the man before, and turned the tables on her.

Who could it be?

Chapter Twenty-Four

June 23, 1996
Present Day

Monday morning, Bet drove the children out to the Redlands house to get clean clothes for school. They hadn't wanted to go. but because they'd never stayed with Bet, they kept no clothing at her place. They'd called Rich several times over the weekend, but never got an answer.

Oddly, none of them jumped to the conclusion that something had happened to him as well. Bet knew him; he was probably in mourning and couldn't drag himself to the phone.

When they arrived, Bet swallowed her usual reluctance to go inside. Confident now that she'd discovered how she'd been gaslighted, she didn't intend to let Rich be her master any longer.

"We only have a few minutes because *some* people couldn't be bothered to get out of bed on time." She eyed her daughter. "You kids go get changed, then find a suitcase, and pack what you'll need for a week. Whatever else happens, your father won't be in the mood to take care of you for a while. I can do that."

As they started inside, she added, "And no midriff shirts or cutoffs!"

They disappeared to grab their things. Bet set her

jaw and went looking for Rich.

She found him in the garage, sitting on the floor in front of the empty space where the Ferrari had been parked. The place smelled of old oil and dust. His rumpled T-shirt and khakis, his face smeared with dirt and shed tears made her believe he'd been sitting there perhaps all weekend.

"Rich?" she asked softly.

I won't feel sorry for him. I won't feel sorry for him…

He didn't look up. "The kids are all right?"

"They are. I'm taking them to school in a few minutes." She came over to hunker down beside him. He literally looked like hell. "What about you?"

He shrugged. "What's the point. What's the point of anything, anymore?"

She reached out and grabbed his chin, turning his face toward hers. "Don't you dare do this. Fuck, Rich, John Lee sat right in your office and told you he'd give you consequences. You are so damn lucky it wasn't Jeremy or Jane, or I'd take you out myself. Bad enough what you've done to them—"

His eyes opened wider, and he actually connected with her. "Them? What have I done to them?"

"They told me. How you peeled them away from me. Because of her." Bet's fingernails fastened on the skin of his face like a vice. "You lied to me, a year ago, and ever since. It's always been about Delia. I know that now. I don't intend to just let it slide."

She let go, leaving angry red marks along both sides of his chin.

"Delia…" The single, whispered word preceded tears, real, hot tears, that flooded his face, leaving streaks in the dirt.

Did he ever cry for me? Don't cry for me, Argentina... This is pathetic.

She stood, brushing dust from her pants. "The kids are going to live with me, until you get your damned act together."

"Bettina, you can't—"

"Oh, yes, I can. And I will." She started for the door back into the house. "You'd better find a way to deal with John Lee. If you don't, I'll have no choice but to tell the detectives what I know. He's openly killing people now. He's not going to get the children. Or me. You're on your own."

She slammed the door behind her. Heading for the kitchen, she grabbed a cloth shopping bag from the well-stocked pantry and tossed in some cereal and soup, then scoured the freezer, taking all the meat and vegetables and two of the three ice cream packages therein, the ones she knew her kids liked. *I wouldn't have picked Delia for a Rocky Road kind of person. I'll leave it for Rich to remember her by.*

Jeremy looked askance at the bag when she tossed it next to him in the back.

"Grocery shopping," she said with a shrug. She slid into the driver's seat.

Jane glanced over at her as they pulled out into the driveway. "Did you see Dad? Is he...okay?"

"I did, and he's not." She waited until she hit the main road to go on. "He's sitting in the garage, crying."

"I figured he'd miss the car more," Jane said.

Jeremy leaned forward, speaking between the two front seats. "It's like Cameron's dad's car in Ferris Bueller. You know, the sports car in the glassed-in room."

"Oh, honey, I know it." Bet smirked.

"What do you want us to do after school?" Jane propped her feet up on the dashboard.

Bet rolled her eyes and bit her tongue. "Can you get a friend to drop you off today? We can make some other arrangements, a bus or whatever, until school's out. But today I'm making a trip to North Miami to see the detective. He left a message to bring that paper up. I'll see what he can tell me about the accident, too."

Jane put her hand on Bet's arm. "You don't think it was an accident, do you?" Her tone indicated a foregone conclusion that it was not.

"Doesn't matter what I think in the long run. Let's see what the police think."

Jane's curiosity must have subsided. Instead, she shut up and fussed with her backpack the rest of the way to school. Jeremy, too, sank back and said nothing.

When she pulled up in front of the school, Bet turned in her seat to look at them. "I know a lot of people didn't see the note you got the other day, but I'm sure plenty saw or heard about the news, and your dad's car." She couldn't bring herself to mention that woman's name. "Sure you're up to dealing with whatever your fellow students have to say?"

Jane scoffed. "We dealt with you being almost dead and then a suspect for murder just a month ago. I think we can handle it."

"Yeah. It's hella cool to be half-famous. Even for bad things," Jeremy said. "Besides, we'll be done the end of the week."

"Oh, right." Bet hadn't thought about long-term consequences yet. What in heaven's name would she do with two teenagers all summer? *Not now, not now. Let's just try not to get killed.* "Okay then. See you after school. Maybe we'll get pizza."

"See ya. Come on, Jer, let's bounce."

The kids got out and walked up toward the front door. Several other students sidled up to them for animated conversations. Bet sighed. *Resilient. That's what I always tell parents when they're divorcing and worried, that their kids are more resilient than they think. I've got to keep believing that. Got to.*

She left the school and stopped by her house to drop off the groceries, then headed north.

****

When she got to the police station, she called Detective Ortiz rather than go in. "Hi, it's Bet Lenard," she said when he answered. "I'm out front with the note for you, sealed in plastic, like you asked."

"Good. Are you coming in?"

Surprised, she said, "Only if you want me to."

"Sure. I think we have something to talk about, in light of what happened over the weekend."

Crap. Was that good or bad? She couldn't decide. "All right. I'm coming in, then."

She entered the lobby, self-conscious that she hadn't dressed to be in public. The teal T-shirt and leggings were definitely from several years ago. She hadn't even put on earrings. But no one at the desk even looked up.

Ortiz came out the door to the offices and beckoned her in. They walked in silence past the conference room, back into the heart of the building. Men and women in worn clothing passed by them, deep in conversation. Ortiz took a sudden turn, and they were in a small cluttered office. He shut the door and cleared off a chair for her to sit down.

"I should feel honored, right? You've invited me into the Inner Sanctum. What's the occasion?" Bet was already uncomfortable with the change in procedure. "Where's Bill? Bob? Whatever?"

Her effort to inject a lighter note went by the wayside. Ortiz leaned against the front of his desk, inches from her. He held out his hand. She gave him the plastic bag. He examined both sides of the paper through the plastic.

"Who touched this at your house?" he asked.

"Jeremy. And me. Maybe Jane. I didn't ask her." She sat straight and crossed her legs to the side, giving the detective space. "Jer said a boy gave it to him. He didn't know the kid. Who knows who touched it before that?"

Ortiz nodded. "We'll take that into consideration. I'll get it to the lab when we're finished here." He reached behind him and dropped the bag on his piled-high desk, then turned back to stare at her. Several uneasy moments passed.

"What? You're scaring me, Detective. I swear. What is it you want to ask that's so frightening?"

"How do you know John Lee?"

She actually choked on her own breath. "John Lee?" She coughed and moved back a few inches. *Be careful, girl. That question was loaded like a medieval catapult.* "He was a client of Rich's, I think. Back when he had the criminal law cases. I never repped him." She looked up into the detective's serious brown eyes. "Does this have to do with the wreck?"

Ortiz got up from the desk and walked around to sit behind it. "You know who—and what—he is?"

Might as well go for it. She nodded. "But normal, law-abiding citizens usually don't need our services, obviously."

"Fair enough." He rubbed his forehead and fidgeted, stalling.

"Does this have to do with the wreck?" she asked again.

"Have you seen Mr. Lenard since Friday?"

I've got no reason to protect him any longer. Karma, she is a bitch. "Yes. I spoke to him this morning. He was in pretty rough emotional shape. I had to go to the house to get the kids some things. They'll be staying with me for the foreseeable future."

Ortiz raised an eyebrow. "I see. Actually, that sounds like a good idea." He fidgeted some more. "Bettina—"

"Bet, please. Only Rich calls me Bettina."

"Bet, then." He stared at her for a long moment, then nodded, as if coming to a decision. "If I tell you…I've got to be sure I can trust you. This has to stay between us for now. It'll all come out soon enough."

Bet was thoroughly intrigued. "You've been up front with me, Detective. I give you my word I'll be the same."

"Richard was involved with Delia Evans, then?"

"He has been for several years. But, between you and me—" She leaned closer. "I think he was more broken up about the Ferrari."

His eyes widened. "Oh. I see."

She smiled. "He did love that car."

"I…ah, okay then." He seemed to struggle to find the last place he was directing the conversation. "Anyway, did you see the news coverage of the scene?"

"I did. We did—me and the kids."

"It turns out the crew actually began filming several minutes earlier. They were coming back from a sports event of some kind and saw a black car dogging the Ferrari on the Palmetto. The cameraman started rolling, and caught images of this car trying to drive the Ferrari into the median. Eventually, as you saw, they were successful."

No way. Were they about to solve this whole mess? Bet's body flooded with adrenaline. "And?"

"The car's registered under Lee's corporation."

Yes! Yes! Finally!

She carefully composed herself before she spoke, despite the celebratory fireworks going off inside her head. "Oh, my God. He was trying to kill—Rich?"

"That's what we don't know. Can you think of a reason he'd want to?"

Ortiz studied her like she was on a slide under a microscope. It was all she could do not to burst out with the whole story. She resorted to a lawyer move: answer a question with a question. "Do you think he's the one who tried to kill me?"

"We haven't found anything that indicates that. What about your ex?"

Damn, that didn't last long. She sighed. "Not any more than the usual client who's dissatisfied with representation."

He continued to scrutinize her. "He's dissatisfied? Why?"

"You'd have to ask Rich," she said. "As I've told you before, we are barely on speaking terms. If the children hadn't needed their things, I wouldn't have seen him today, either."

"We're going to speak with him. I just hoped you might have insight that would help steer our conversation."

"All I can do is see if I can get access to the files in storage. If you find you need something after you speak to him, and you get the proper warrants, I may be able to help you."

Ortiz gave a tired laugh. "Well, that's fairly equivocal. About what I expected from a lawyer."

Even though she'd just used a lawyer trick, the detective branding her with the mild pejorative stung her. He seemed like a good guy, despite her opinion of cops in general. Hell, she'd even like him if they weren't involved in this mess.

Maybe even dating material?

No time for that. But she wanted him to like her, to see that she wasn't like all the other attorneys. *I can't just let all of Rich's confession out. Not yet.*

However, there was something she could share.

"You know, an odd thing happened during that news broadcast. When I heard that Delia had been driving Rich's car—which he'd never let me do, the whole time we were married—a layer of this fog peeled away. I remembered who K was."

Ortiz brightened. "Really? Who?"

"Roy Kendrick. He's a private investigator. I'd wanted to meet him to spy on Rich. And Delia. I had a pretty good idea that this might have been going on…" She waved a hand. "It's a divorce-related issue. Personal. Doesn't have anything to do with all this. But clearly whoever showed up was not him."

He scribbled furiously on a pad of paper in front of him. "Yeah. I've met the guy a couple of times. That was definitely not him. And who knew—"

"Right. That's the next issue, and I haven't pulled that one together yet. If it had been Mela, she would have known the calendar reference. So, I know it wasn't her."

"We'll get hold of him right away."

"That could be interesting. We'd never met before. I can't imagine why he wouldn't have shown up if we had an appointment." *Or why I didn't think to call him myself before I told Ortiz. Damn it. Oh, well. It's done now.*

"So, two new leads today. It may still be a great day after all."

He stood up. "Can I get you some coffee?"

"No, actually I'd better go. I've got a bunch of frozen food to take care of at home. But thanks for the offer." She got up and brushed imaginary lint from her clothing. "You know where to find me if you figure anything out."

Ortiz looked her over. "You sure you'll be all right? I might be able to swing protective custody for you and the children?"

Bet considered it for a minute, but knew the kids would hate it. "Maybe. I'll ask them about it. Just locate that guy and nail John Lee, would you?" She gave him a smile and waited by the door. "I didn't leave any bread crumbs. You'll have to show me out."

"Oh! Of course." With an embarrassed laugh, he came to open the door and led her back out to the front. "You know where to find me, too."

"I do."

"Call me if there's anything new. Or even if there isn't."

Bet went out to the car, feeling a little warmer about

Luis Ortiz. Adding that to her newfound confidence about Rich, it looked like it would indeed be a good day.

She broke the speed limit several times heading home, anxious to test out the new theory about Kendrick.

Now where did I put Kendrick's number? It must be here somewhere, since it wasn't in the office. She tore through her bedroom drawers and didn't find it. After half an hour, it finally occurred to her to look in the phone book.

Duh. Like the kids say.

She dialed the number listed, but the phone just rang and rang. Unlike many of the numbers in the book, Kendrick's had no address with his number. *Probably didn't want people he spied on coming after him. Can't blame him for that.*

Onward and upward. She took a deep breath. Time to empty out her storage room and get it ready for when the kids came home. They'd move one of the beds and start living as a family. *Now that I've got them back, I will never let them go again.* Would she also challenge the property distribution? Maybe. A judge probably wouldn't let her have the right, as she had signed the agreement with full knowledge of its contents.

But in his current state, maybe Rich would. I can get my own part of the practice back and he can deal with the crackheads and the murderers. Oh, yes, I'm done with all of them, that's for sure.

And Rich, too.

Chapter Twenty-Five

June 27, 1996
Present Day

Bet looked forward to her meeting with Hyacinth Martell this week. She wore a light green knit pantsuit, determined to feel comfortable and relaxed. When she arrived ten minutes early, she marched right up the stairs and knocked on the door.

Hyacinth welcomed her in as she had every two weeks for the last two years. "You're eager today," she said. "Coffee? Tea?"

"Just water, if you have it."

Bet wandered in and settled into the usual chair, her hands smoothing the brown leather. *I do love this chair. It's been a solid part of my life. Up until now. But since I've dug myself out of the lies—maybe I won't come much longer.*

Does it mean I'm cured?

Hyacinth joined her, plastic bottle of water in hand, and then pulled out her ubiquitous notebook.

"Do you really make notes of worthwhile stuff in there, or is it just a bunch of doodles?" Bet asked.

Hyacinth frowned. "I rather resent the implication that I'm not professional."

Bet grinned. "I'm just teasing. Sorry."

The psychiatrist pursed her lips and made a note.

"So, what's got you so fired up?"

"I had a bit of a breakthrough." Bet twisted open the lid of the water and took a gulp. "I remembered everything about Rich and Delia and the private eye."

Hyacinth cocked her head, with a curious expression. "You lost me. I know Rich. Delia is…?"

Bet frowned. "His 'assistant'? I know we've talked about her before. Delia. With whom he was apparently shacking up? Who died in a car wreck last weekend?"

"Hmm. I'm not sure I knew that."

"It was all over the news. Rich let her drive the damned Ferrari."

"Oh. I remember you had an obsession about that car." She made a note, and a calculating smile came to her lips. "You never got to drive it, did you?"

"No. Bastard." The reminder burned her all over again. *I'm not sure how my life would have changed if I'd ever driven the thing. Maybe I'd have crashed it on purpose. Would have served him right.* "And 'obsession' is a strong word, don't you think? That implies that it was inappropriate."

Hyacinth raised an eyebrow and didn't comment. "All right." She checked her notes. "And the private eye?"

"Didn't we ever talk about that?" Bet was sure they had, but it could have been conversations she'd argued out inside her own head. That happened more regularly than not. "I wanted to hire an investigator to check out whether they were having an affair. Well, I apparently *hired* one."

"I see. That's a big step. It seems a little ostentatious. Would it really matter if Rich moved on after your divorce? I mean, that's what is expected of most people."

Irritated, Bet set the water down on the table beside her, hard enough to knock the lid loose. *Come on, you're supposed to be on my side, dammit.* The sense of accomplishment she'd been feeling began to fade.

"No, not after. Before. Back when I first started seeing you. I was a bit impaired sometimes." *Okay, a lot impaired sometimes—whether by the pain or what I took to lessen it.* "I think when Rich asked for the divorce because of my situation, he used it as an excuse."

Hyacinth looked pensive. "Hmm. Let me review." She went to her file cabinet and searched out some other notebooks, bringing them back to sit in her chair. She flipped through the myriad pages in the notebooks, no doubt to the earliest ones. The process took several minutes. Bet's irritation grew, but she contained it to a tapping finger on the soft chair. Quiet.

"You seemed to be in a lot of pain at the time. Agreed, there were times you were here under the influence. We talked about that, too, how that could impact your home life and work, as well." She leafed through a few more. "The children probably suffered through some days they didn't deserve."

Bet stiffened. "Yes, but—"

Hyacinth looked up, her expression innocently puzzled. "But I'm not sure how that relates to Delia."

"I wasn't either. Until the accident. Somehow that slapped me into the recognition that Rich wanted the divorce *because* of Delia. Maybe he was also unhappy with the fact I had pain and alcohol issues, but he convinced me it was all my fault." She paused and savored the discomfort of realization, both sharp and sweet. "When he wanted out all the time. He waited long enough that he knew I wouldn't fight him, the bastard."

"Ah." Hyacinth's face lit up. "Do you intend to confront him about this?" She studied Bet for a long moment, then laughed. "No. You already have. Probably couldn't wait to rub it in his face. Am I right?"

Damn. She is right.

Bet's face flushed. "Okay, so I did. After he lost her—well, the car—he was essentially curled in a fetal position, so I challenged him."

"Mmhmm. And how did that make you feel?"

"Powerful." Her pride in her accomplishment began to rekindle.

"I can understand that." More notes. "But doesn't it say something about your worth that you came in third behind a piece of metal and rubber and a flirtatious secretary?"

Bet sat up, stricken.

Hyacinth shifted forward. "In his eyes, I mean."

Is that what she meant? I don't understand.

"No, now, don't get all twisted up. I can see it coming," Hyacinth said, meeting Bet's gaze firmly. "Really. You're taking huge strides and making good progress. I'm very proud of you."

"Oh. All right. Ah…thank you."

Silence passed between them, until Hyacinth finally asked, "Did anything else come of this revelation? What did the children think of the situation?"

That was a more comfortable topic. Bet seized on it. "I ended up moving the children into my house. It took some physical rearranging, but it seems to be working out."

"I'm surprised." Hyacinth's pen hung midair, and she stared blankly. "Over the last year, you've expressed some pretty negative feelings about them and their behavior around you. What possessed you to bring them home?"

"The night of the accident, we had an honest talk. Rich had told them lies about me. He'd warned them not to reveal his relationship with Delia, which they'd known about since before the divorce. Long before, apparently. They felt guilty and tried to avoid me because of it. Because of Rich. Not because of me."

Hyacinth still seemed a little shaken by the disclosure. "Well. That's big news. Still, taking on full-time responsibility for two teens is fairly challenging, even when things have been friendly all along. Do you think you're up to it?"

Bet chewed her lip. "I have to be, don't I? We're in a serious situation. Threats are coming from all sides. I've got less ties to the evildoers…" She trailed off. The conversation was getting dangerously close to confessing what she knew about John Lee, and she had no intention of sharing that with anyone, confidentially or otherwise.

"Evildoers? Now that's an interesting word. What does it mean to you?"

"Clearly, whoever is shooting up my car, wrecking the Ferrari, trying to set me on fire? Sounds evil to me. Doesn't it to you?"

"But you believe that this person or persons have ties to you? That they are targeting you? Or is it because of Rich?"

Bet just shrugged, and chugged some water to avoid answering.

"So Rich is the source of your threat, is what you're saying."

Hyacinth studied her, the blue eyes piercing Bet's

hoped-for shield.

She just nodded.

"Then you're doing the right thing by removing the children. He does seem to care about them, whatever else he's mixed up in." Hyacinth closed her notebook. "And don't forget, it's my job to challenge you. Like I said, I'm proud of what you have accomplished. Seems like you've nearly reached the pinnacle of your life."

Bet smiled tentatively. This was more what she had expected when she'd planned to reveal her successes to Hyacinth. "Thank you. And I mean that—thank *you*. You've really been a great sounding board all along. Even when I must have sounded crazy."

Hyacinth pursed her lips again. "Well, you know, we don't like to use that word. Let's say that you were experiencing some rough times. Therapists don't expect people to be at their shiny clean best. Those who don't reveal their depths often can't make progress, so the credit is yours."

Feeling like a Chip and Dale act, Bet sipped more water. *We can agree to agree. We're both magnificent.* "So does that mean I'm…cured?"

"I'm not sure you ever get 'well,' in the usual meaning. You have handled your life the best way you knew how, yet you still fell into some pits through your depression and grief. The similarities of the mother-child relationship, of course. And there's the excessive use of alcohol. You'll have to work through that. But people have issues they must deal with. Life isn't always what we wish it would be. But I do think you've moved through the worst of it, especially now that you've learned the truth about what caused your pain and confusion."

"Oh, I forgot to tell you. I may have found a solution for the physical issues." Bet told Hyacinth about the clinic in Palm Beach, and what she hoped to find there. "So, maybe I can get properly treated and my life will turn around." She grinned. "I'm actually looking forward to the next part of my existence."

Hyacinth broke into a genuine smile. "Well, isn't that great. Bet, I am so happy for you. Having such a sunny outlook—it must be life-changing indeed." She set the notebooks aside. "I'd like you to schedule one more meeting, not for the purpose of therapy, necessarily, but for closing forms and paperwork. A proper farewell, if you will." She leaned closer. "No charge."

Bet was thrilled. She could really be done with the time commitment and bother of checking her sanity bi-weekly, and just concentrate on her family. *Delightful.* "Of course, I'd be glad to. Let me give you a call when I have my calendar. In a week or two?"

"Perfect." She got up and warmly shook Bet's hand. "Now, this doesn't mean I don't want to hear from you. I expect you'll have problems adapting to the children living with you, so please feel free to call sooner. Otherwise, I'll see you then."

Bet grabbed her purse and headed out to the car, a spring in her step. If the cops caught John Lee and left her family alone, 1996 could become a banner year for Bet Lenard.

Chapter Twenty-Six

July 1, 1996
Present Day

Bet was both excited and terrified to be back on the road to Palm Beach to see Dr. Bhatti. She drove this time, but Giamo had volunteered to go with her, to be her medical "translator" if there was something she didn't understand. It seemed like imposing on him, as far as Bet was concerned, but he insisted he didn't mind.

"I like talking with you," he said. "It's refreshing. Not everyone speaks their mind like you."

"Ha! Now that's a backhanded compliment if I ever heard one." She switched lanes and headed north on I-95.

He chuckled. "Besides, it's nice to have a friend."

"It must be hard to find time for friends as an ER doc."

"Exactly. I work odd shifts, doubles more often than not. I can never be sure I can keep an engagement after I set one up." He shrugged, looking out the side window.

"Good thing I'm self-employed. I can still get free for a coffee now and then."

She'd enjoyed the few times they'd met, talking about the case, their days, family and craziness. *But the whole debacle with Rich is still too fresh. Trust isn't coming with anyone any time soon. No serious relationships for me. I'm still figuring out who I am. Who I'm going to be.*

And hopefully this meeting today will help define that.

Dr. Bhatti had left her a message the day Bet had brought the children home, asking her to make an appointment to discuss the test results. She'd had to wait a whole week, which in the usual scheme of doctors' offices wasn't a lot—but Bet didn't like to wait. She'd imagined a hundred different diagnoses from a bloody nose to imminent death from some rare cancer. Better to have actual information, right?

Unless I won't like that any better.

They arrived without much fanfare, parked the Jaguar in the lot, and went up to the doctor's office. Bhatti welcomed them both with a cup of green tea, and an invitation to have a seat.

Bet eyed the cup. "Hmm." *Something tells me, since this isn't coffee, I might be about to hear something I don't like.*

Sahire wasted no time getting to the point. "Well, Bet, I'm afraid your instincts were right. It is rheumatoid arthritis." She discussed the technical test results and what they meant, and how it was that her new testing showed a positive when the others had produced a negative result.

"The good news is, we can get you on proper medications, some of which have only just been approved. These will assure that your body will stop damaging itself, and will hopefully provide you some pain relief as well. The best thing you can do for yourself now is to follow an autoimmune protocol, which will involve some changes in your diet."

Bet frowned in protest. "Let me guess. Nothing good. No sugar, no salt, no meat, no…" She sighed.

"No pastries," Giamo added helpfully. Bet shot him a look.

Sahire laughed. "Well, not quite. No sugar, no gluten—that would be wheat products—no dairy at first. Preferably no coffee. We can work back into that if you do well. But you can have any meat that's not processed, all sorts of vegetables, some fruits, and you can use spices to flavor them well. The less processed anything you eat is, the better."

Bet's mind whirled. *How am I going to keep track of that, too? Especially if I have to feed two teenagers at the same time? So much to remember…*

The doctor slid a thick folder of papers across to her. "It's all in here so you can review it when you have plenty of time. Basically, you want to eat like our ancestors did—vegetables in their most natural form, and meat to supplement."

"You know what I remember about our ancestors?" Bet asked. "They're dead."

Giamo elbowed her.

The doctor leaned forward and looked her in the eye. "You said you wanted to cut your pain. The medication won't do it all for you, but this diet, if followed to the letter, will halve your inflammation. I guarantee that. But it's tough, I know. No gluten means none. Any bit you have undoes all the rest of your sacrifice."

Internally spiraling down, Bet grimaced. "I'll give it my best try." She picked up the folder and leafed through it. *I bet I'll lose ten pounds, anyway. That can't hurt. I can wear that Versace dress again.*

"Here's your preliminary prescriptions. I'll need

you to keep in touch with the office and let us know how you're feeling. We can adjust them up or down as needed. I'll also expect to see you in person once a month for a while. They won't be long appointments. Like most rheumatologists, I'm busy. But I want you to feel better as soon as we can make it happen."

"Sounds like a deal to me." Bet stood up and shook hands with the doctor. "Thanks for giving me some real answers for the first time."

"It's my pleasure. I put a printed copy of your test results in the folder, if Giamo wants to look them over." She winked. "It's nice to have your own pet doctor."

Both Bet and Giamo sputtered responses. "It's not like that," Giamo said. Bet couldn't come up with a coherent answer.

Sahire just nodded and smiled. "Nice to see you both." She walked them to the door. "Remember, call if you've got any questions."

"Will do."

Giamo opened the door for Bet, and they walked out into a light shower. "Wasn't the sky perfectly blue when we got here?" Bet said. "It's like the weather got my diagnosis."

He pointed out the darker clouds to the west. "Looks like it might be an all-day event."

"Great." She let them into the car, and they sat in silence, listening to raindrops bouncing off the roof.

"Should we get lunch?" he asked. "I don't have to be back until three."

"I wouldn't mind. And I know just the place." She put the car in gear and drove to a Southern-style restaurant, where she ordered chicken-fried steak and sopped up a plateful of gravy with hot biscuits. "The condemned's last meal," she groused.

"You've got a healthy appetite, that's for sure," Giamo observed. "Imagine if that had been roasted vegetables and a boneless chicken breast."

"I'd rather not. Ugh." But she knew he was teasing her. She also knew that if she wanted to get better—which she did—that she should follow the doctor's orders to the letter. *Just as well I'm finishing with Hyacinth. I can't stand letting too many other people be the boss of me...*

"But it's good to finally have a diagnosis, right?" he asked.

"It is. All these years, I... Rich made me believe it was in my head, and I couldn't refute him. I had no evidence, no proof. But now I know. I really went through this. The alcohol wasn't an irresponsible habit. I was in pain. And this is why." She patted the envelope beside her.

"I'm glad you have answers."

"I'm glad you helped me find them."

The route home was soaked with more downpours. The front moved in, just as Giamo had predicted. Bet didn't mind driving in pouring rain, with lightning and thunder overhead. She'd lived and worked in Florida long enough to manage the roads in most any condition. But tourists, who were thick in June just after school let out, didn't always understand that torrents of rain wouldn't slow the locals to twenty miles an hour. It made driving tricky.

They'd nearly reached the Miami city limits, when the car riding Bet's bumper flashed its lights at her. Driving in the left-most lane next to the concrete divider, she glanced right but had no way to get over. She tapped her brakes. The driver behind her flashed their lights again.

"Where do you think I'm going to go, you idiot?" she muttered under her breath.

"Drivers here are rude compared to Ohio," Giamo said. Bet noticed he clung to the armrest on the door.

"If you want to drive in Miami, you've got to be fairly aggressive. Natives can be deadly."

As if in response to her comment, the car behind pulled forward and bumped into the back end of the Jaguar.

"What the fuck!" she yelled, glaring into the rearview mirror.

Giamo opened his mouth to say something, and just closed it.

The car bumped her a second time. Traffic was steady at sixty miles an hour, and there was no way she could even pull ahead or into a different lane. They were trapped.

"I don't know what's wrong with this *pendejo*, but if I get my hands on him, I'll let him know what's what." Bet concentrated on moving the car forward, as fast as she could go.

The car to her right suddenly pulled away, and Bet went to take its place. The car behind sped up into the lane on her right. Bet was already halfway into the lane, so the front left fender of the big black SUV plowed right into the passenger side of the Jaguar. Bet had hit the brakes, but too late. The impact flipped her car upward and over the median.

Bet had time to see the bright lights of oncoming traffic, and to grab Giamo's hand for luck before the Jaguar landed hard. It was hit again and spun horizontally. She smacked her forehead on the steering wheel before the airbag went off, shoving her into the seat, then her neck snapped backwards, and her head slammed into the side window. Everything went black.

Chapter Twenty-Seven

July 5, 1996
Present Day

She woke up under glaring fluorescent lights. Machines beeped. Her arms were heavy; she couldn't lift them. The smell of bleach was in the air, strong enough to tickle her nose. Her eyelids fought to close again. She tried to force them open.

Where am I? What the hell happened?

A hospital room.

Bet, you've got to quit waking up like this. It's getting repetitive.

Her fingers twitched around, searching for a call button. None found. She couldn't move, or sit up, without pain shooting one place or another. "Help!" she yelled. "Someone help me!"

Thirty long seconds later, that brought a passing nurse to her bedside. "You're awake, finally. I'll call the doctor."

"Doctor….doctor…" Startled, she asked, "Where is the doctor? Giamo Rimon, he was riding with me. Where is he? Is he all right?"

A solemn look came over the woman's face. "Dr. Rimon is in intensive care. He was quite badly injured." Biting her lip, she added, "I really can't tell you more than that. Maybe the doctor will." She checked the readouts on the machines, then left the room.

How long have I been here since the accident? Hours? Days? No way to tell. I should have asked her.

The kids! Where are they? They were supposed to be with me. Did someone get them? Where's my phone? I should call them right away.

But she couldn't move to reach the bedside table, much less figure out where the staff had hidden her phone. If it was even here.

As she came to full consciousness, she realized her arms and legs were fastened down. That was why she couldn't move them. She wriggled against the itchy white sheets, trying to loosen the ties, but got nowhere.

"Whoa," the doctor said, as he walked in the door. He pulled the curtain closed. But it was only a curtain. She remained vulnerable until she could be behind a locked door.

The doctor put a hand on her wrist. "I'm Dr. Allen. You're in Baptist Hospital. You've been in a car accident." He studied her with serious gray eyes. "Look, you kept trying to rip out your IVs while you were half-awake, so we had to restrain you. If you're awake now and will leave them alone…?"

"Whatever, anything. I need to call my kids."

He stepped back and studied her. "I'm sure someone contacted your family. I'll check with the nurses."

"When can I go home?" She fidgeted in the bed, swirling thoughts attacking her like an angry flock of crows.

"Not for another few days. You—"

"My kids can't be home alone. They can't! I need a phone."

What is wrong with this man… I mean, who is this?

What am I... Thinking is difficult.

"Ms. Lenard, please. Calm down." His eyes narrowed. "If you're having some difficulty with cognition, it's because you've had a serious concussion. You'll be sore from a lot of bruising, and I expect your neck will need heat packs for some time to come."

"I have RA," she said, the fact just appearing on her tongue. *Where did that come from?* "I-I don't know why I said that."

He nodded as he released the restraints. "Good to know. We can add that to your chart. I'd like you to rest now. If you must call, you've got a phone there on the bedside table. The nurse will come in and see about getting you a tray for…" He glanced at his watch. "Lunch, I guess it is."

Panic gnawed at her courage. "What time is it? What day is it?"

"It's just after noon on July 5. You've been out a few days."

Four days she'd been in the hospital? What had happened on the outside? Has someone gone after the kids? Overwhelmed, she just nodded.

The doctor smiled. "Don't worry. Your progress is good. We'll let you go home as soon as it's medically feasible, all right? Just rest now. That's what will help you the most."

He left before she could generate a snappy comeback.

Just rest. As if the world isn't coming to an end.

She gingerly lifted her hands, worried she would dislodge the needles embedded therein. When she was comfortable that they were well-secured, she twisted, among many groans of pain, reaching for the phone.

Dialing was difficult with the bandages and tubes, but she managed to input her home number. *One ring. Two. Three....Ten. Eleven. Twelve....* She hung up and dialed again. Still no answer.

She called Rich's house. No answer there, either.

Where the hell were the kids? She tried in vain to remember their individual phone numbers. That was a bit of memory that escaped her. Who else had some idea what was happening?

Mela.

She dialed Mela's cell number. It rang eight times. But she answered. "Hello?"

"Mela." Relief flooded through her.

"Bet? Oh, *Dios mio.* Where are you? Are you still in the hospital?"

"Yes. You know I'm here? Do you know where the kids are?"

"Don't worry, *chica.* I've got them with me. We took a little...vacation."

Bet's brow furrowed—and that hurt like the devil. "What do you mean? Why are they with you? What the fuck is going on?"

"Okay, okay, honey, calm down, please. After the accident, your detective called the office. He was very concerned and asked if I could get the children. So, I did."

"What about Rich? Why didn't he come?"

"Bet, Rich has been arrested. So has John Lee."

Bet blinked, letting that information sink in. She couldn't make words come out.

Mela went on. "I hope you don't mind, but I took the credit card from the office. Jane, Jeremy and I went—"

"Shh. Don't say it." Different facts flashed, one after another, in her mind. She had a hard time holding on to any of them. But she wanted the children to be safe. "We don't know who's listening."

"Well, no one here. Oh, you mean on the phone. Okay. Do you really think they are? Listening, I mean?"

"I don't know but—someone ran us into that barrier. Just like the Ferrari."

"What? Who would have—"

"Mela, not now, please. I've got one hell of a headache."

"Okay, okay, I got it. Listen, we're safe, and eating good food and trying to have some fun. Well, considering. The kids will be glad to hear you're awake, though. They've been really worried."

Bet took in all that Mela had said. It was overwhelming. She had to get out of here. "All right. Thank you, Mela. Thank you. I'll call you when I'm ready to go home."

"Honey, take your time. We're good. No sense in going off half-cocked. Even if that is your usual operating mode."

"Eh." A wave of fatigue passed through her. "We'll talk."

She plopped the receiver back in the cradle. Determined, she used that hand to grip the bedrail, trying to pull herself up. Dizziness flooded her. She laid back down as the door opened.

"Where do you think you're going?" the dark-skinned nurse asked. She set a tray on the overbed table with wheels, and rolled it up where Bet could reach it. "If you need to sit, please use the bed controls." She handed the controller to Bet, who dutifully—and much more slowly—raised the head of the bed. Although when she got a look at what was on the tray, Bet regretted the effort. *Is that chicken? Something green. And white bread wrapped in plastic? Maybe I'm actually glad gluten's off the menu.*

A knock at the door distracted her from the so-called food. The nurse left quietly. Luis Ortiz walked in.

"What are you doing here?" Bet asked.

"I thought you could use a boost." He pulled up a chair. He carefully removed a covered white Styrofoam cup from his jacket pocket. He set it on the table and reached for two tiny plastic cups, then he poured them each half a shot of what had to be Cuban coffee.

She smiled, then winced as it hurt the bandaged area on her face. "You're an angel."

He glanced over his shoulder, then to her. "I'm not sure it's good for you. So go slow. And if you get caught, you never saw me." He winked.

She raised her cup to him and sipped the bittersweet drink, not even caring that it was lukewarm. Or if she wasn't supposed to have it. "So why are you really here?"

Ortiz made a wry face. "What do you think? I'd left the hospital staff a message to call me when you were coherent. Fortunately, I'd gone back to your South Miami restaurant to ask some questions about Kendrick, so I was in the neighborhood." He took a notebook from his inside jacket pocket and clicked a pen into action. "So, what happened the other day? I understand the person in the passenger seat got the worst of it again."

Bet glared at the callous dismissal of Giamo's condition. "Are you kidding me?"

"No. I thought it was a joke." He shrugged, with a

sheepish smile. "It's just an unusual coincidence. Sorry. Not funny. I get it. Do you remember what happened?"

She hadn't really thought about it yet; she'd been more concerned with the wellbeing of her offspring. "Have you seen Giamo? They wouldn't tell me how he was, just that he was in ICU."

"I've spoken to the doctors. He's expected to live, but his right thigh and arm took a hard impact in the accident. They've needed reconstruction."

Bet's eyes burned with tears. *He was just helping me. Just being my friend. That's no way to treat a friend. Damn.*

"So, have you figured out who it was? Just some bastard trying to gain thirty seconds on the way home?" She closed her eyes, trying to reconstruct her past.

"What do *you* remember? Let's start there?" Ortiz seemed to be begging. What was it he needed to hear?

"We went to my doctor appointment in Palm Beach." She took a deep breath, moving her memories forward in time. "Then we stopped for lunch. Then…" What had happened next? Was that the day it was raining, or was that a different day? "Raining, I think. Heavy rain."

He nodded and made notes. "Okay. Definitely raining that afternoon. Good. What next?"

Nothing came to her.

"Do you remember where you were, driving? What road?"

"I don't remember, actually. Something with a concrete divider in the middle. If it was from Palm Beach to Coral Gables, it would have been I-95."

"You don't remember that for sure, though?"

She shook her head, and immediately wished she

hadn't. "Ow. That's what he meant by needing a heat pack. Damn, that hurts."

"Don't injure yourself. Take your time. What's the next thing you remember? Think, Bet. It's important."

"I held his hand...we were flying." Even as she spoke, she thought it sounded ridiculous.

Ortiz raised an eyebrow. "Oo-kay."

"I'm not sure what that means. Sorry."

"Let me ask you a different question. Have you heard from your children? They aren't at your home."

"They're safe," she said.

"You're sure?"

"Yes."

"You've also heard about your ex-husband?"

"Not all of the story. Just that he was... unavailable...for the kids." She studied him. "Why don't you fill me in?"

He sighed and leaned back in the chair. "Well. John Lee was charged with the wreck that killed Delia Evans. We had strong evidence that we believed would survive the arraignment. He owned the car, even though it was in his man's possession. So, we could infer his culpability."

"Okay." Anxious and needing to do something with her hands, she poked at the cold food on the tray with a plastic fork, thinking it really couldn't be any more dead.

"Want me to move that?"

"Would you?"

"Sure." He pulled the table away from her bed, then poured them each another half shot of the Cuban.

"I'm surprised I lived for the past three days without my standard *colada.*"

"They probably don't do IV coffee here." He cleared

his throat. "Apparently Lee's attorney offered a deal—to flip on your firm, accusing you of money laundering."

Bet's hand shook, spilling the little bit of coffcc all over the white sheets. "What?"

He just looked at her thoughtfully, then took her hand and set it on the table with her little cup, pouring her another tablespoon. Finally, he went on. "Yes. He said that Richard had proposed the initial plan, and had threatened him to make him continue the arrangement when Lee had wanted to end it."

Bet was glad she could look genuinely surprised. *Lee was a bigger asshole than I thought.* "I don't know about anything like that." *See, the truth does set you free.*

Ortiz nodded. "Richard said as much when he was arrested. He gave a full confession as to his part in the transactions, though his version was different. But he insisted that this was done without your knowledge or complicity."

Stunned, she let her scrambled brain work through the ramifications. "And he's in jail?"

"Richard? He bailed out. He's got a court date coming up, but I don't know when it is, off the top of my head. It'll wait until you're recovered. You'll have to be a state's witness."

"Of course," she said without enthusiasm. A wave of fatigue came over her, and her eyes closed without her volition. She yawned. "But if Lee's locked up—"

"No, he's bonded out, also."

"Oh." That fact made her feel unsafe, even here in a public building surrounded by professionals. *I've seen that movie, too.* "Do you have a guard outside? Someone watching?"

"Do you think Lee came after you the other day?"

His voice held a challenge, but her mind was swimming again and she couldn't seem to grasp its point.

"Lee is dangerous. He may not be satisfied with the destruction he's caused to date."

"Fair enough. We can have someone keep an eye on the floor, certainly." He flipped through several pages of his notes. "Witnesses at the scene of your accident say that your car was hit by a large black vehicle. Very similar to the one that caused Delia Evans' death."

Was it? I can't picture what happened. I just remember pain. Bet tried again to put the pieces together. "It was raining, really hard. Traffic moved fast. We were just heading home."

"Why was this doctor riding with you?" He glanced up, studying her over the top of the notebook. "Someone you're seeing?"

"No." She scowled. "Why does everyone keep asking that? He referred me to the doctor I saw in Palm Beach. They went to school together. He helps me understand the medical stuff."

"Why were you seeing a doctor in Palm Beach?"

"None of your business." Bet's reluctance came automatically. She normally didn't share details about her life. She knew that. People had gained too much access to her personal information in the last month. But snapping at the investigating detective wasn't necessarily a great idea, either. "Just medical treatment. Nothing to do with this case."

"Mmm." He made some notes. "Did anyone know you were going there? Anyone who might be suspicious?"

She shrugged gently. "No idea. The kids. Mela. Dr. Rimon. I don't think I told Rich, not after I chewed him out about his secretary."

"If it was Lee, he had you tailed there and back, one assumes. It's certainly possible."

"I'll let you follow up on that, then." A fleeting thought touched her mind. She asked about it before it could vanish, like so many others were doing. "Kendrick? The investigator?"

"Haven't been able to locate him. No one's seen or heard from him in weeks. Since just about the time you contacted him." He raised an eyebrow.

"Huh." *That won't do much for his business, I suppose*. The initial burst of adrenaline she'd experienced after waking up seemed to be slowly fading. She closed her eyes, just for a moment.

"Ms. Lenard? Bet? Bet?"

"Hmm?" She opened her eyes again to find Ortiz on his feet, looking at her with a worried expression. "Sorry. What were you saying?"

"I asked whether you'd spoken to your ex-husband since you've been here."

"No. I just woke up, what, half an hour ago? An hour? I checked on the children. Everyone else can take care of themselves." She fidgeted and rubbed her itchy nose. "Can you get them to take me up to ICU to see him?"

"See who? Oh, the doctor. You're giving me powers I'm sure I don't have. You'll have to work that one out with the medical staff." He stepped closer to the bed and lowered his voice. "By the way, Lee completely denies having anything to do with the car fire in the Glades."

She looked up at him. "Oh, really? Do a lot of murderers volunteer their culpability? Of course, he denied it."

Ortiz nodded. "Yeah. I guess you're right. Ah…are they letting you out soon?"

"As soon as I can. He wouldn't tell me when."

"All right. I'll come back to see you when you've recovered a little more." He let out a deep breath. "Really, I'm glad to see you're doing this well. I mean…" He gestured at her bandages. "Could have been a lot worse."

"Sure. It's bad enough as it is. How about we get this phase of my life over with? Throw the book at whoever you have to. I want to feel safe in my own skin again, Luis. Please." She reached out and he gingerly took her hand in his.

"We will. I promise you, we will." He smiled. "And if—"

"Yeah, yeah, if you remember anything else, please let me know. I got you."

"No. If you need anything, I want you to call. Really. Even another fix of Cuban coffee."

Now he was being silly. But kinda nice at the same time. It made her smile. "Fine. I will. Go on, now."

Ortiz pulled his chair back to the wall, then left the room. Bet listened for several long seconds to see if anyone else intended to disturb her, but she heard nothing.

Rest, they said. It'll make you better, they said. She sighed. *Whatever it takes to get me out of here, I guess I'm on board.* She closed her eyes and let herself slip back into sleep.

Chapter Twenty-Eight

October 16, 1995
Nine months earlier

Bet carried a cardboard box loaded with kitchen utensils to the back of Mela's car, which was parked in front of the Redlands home. It was moving day.

Rich had taken the kids to Metrozoo for the afternoon, out of courtesy to Bet. *Or was it to soothe his conscience?* She didn't know. She didn't care. She'd agreed she'd move out, so once she'd bought a house with her payout from the divorce, she picked a Saturday, and this was it.

Mela came hurrying out the door behind her. "What did you decide about the cuckoo clock?"

Bet cocked her head and frowned. "I don't know. It's valuable. But it annoys the hell out of me." She forced a smile. "Let's move it to Rich's bedroom."

Mela's mouth opened in surprise. "Really? That seems inordinately cruel."

"We're talking about Rich. It seems to fit."

Though she'd signed all the legal documents without argument, Bet had found herself resisting the split with all her heart. She dragged her feet on finding a house. She passive-aggressively denied Rich's requests to take necessary steps. She discussed the situation with Hyacinth, but couldn't find a way to get joint counseling for her and Rich back on the table. Hoping the children would protest her leaving as a last resort, she was disappointed as Jane went on yet another long rant about Bet's use of alcohol for self-medication.

Inevitable.

She shoved the box in the cargo area and went back for another. She'd left Rich the great majority of the furnishings and accessories in the house. Her new place was smaller. It would be only her living there. *No need for all the fancy crockpots and cookware in that little kitchen.*

Most of the furniture she'd had moved by professionals earlier in the week, as well as the wardrobe boxes that held her clothing, shoes, and other personal items. Her jewelry she'd taken to the office as soon as she'd signed the papers; something told her Rich might believe he was solely entitled to the valuable gold and diamond pieces he'd bought for her.

Mela passed her in the kitchen with several large department store bags hanging from her wrists and a hat in each hand. "This is the last from the bedroom."

Bet nodded. "All right. I'll do a sweep." She checked the time. "We'd better be gone before Rich comes back."

Mela muttered something about letting Rich see how much pain he was causing, but Bet let it roll off. To be honest, she wasn't all that sad about leaving Rich. Other than his infrequent attempts to make her feel better with massage or running a hot bath, he was much more invested in the business, making money and putting it away, recruiting new clients, being the man of the hour at every gathering.

He doesn't need me anymore, either.

Bet walked through the house one last time, little stabs of pain melting her when she passed décor she'd installed, furniture she'd chosen, the bedrooms of Jeremy and Jane, which she'd decorated while they'd been away at their grandparents' house on vacation. Family pictures of all of them together in happier times. The pit sofa that exactly held all of them cuddled up to watch a movie together…

The aching increased as she finished the survey, ending in the kitchen. Wanting it to go away, she stopped at the cabinet where the family liquor was stored, only to find it empty except for a note: *Why don't you buy your own?*

The odd thing was, the note was typed and printed. She had no way of knowing who'd written it. The written slap was the last drop of water into a tank of sadness that now overflowed. She got as far as the outside steps before her knees simply gave way. She landed on the concrete, bent double, tears pouring from her eyes, sobbing until she could no longer catch her breath.

"Oh, honey." Mela sank down next to her, putting an arm around her shoulders. "Come on, now. You'll be fine. We'll work things out."

Bet couldn't listen. Even though she'd known this was coming, she'd put off dealing with it. Now that the final steps were here, she thought they'd kill her.

Rich pulled up in the BMW, parking on the drive past the house. He gave the two cars and Bet herself a long once-over stare as he passed by. The children both sat in the back seat, which seemed odd to Bet. When she took them somewhere, they jockeyed for shotgun fairly vigorously. *Really? That's what's important about this scene? Who's in front? Who's on first? Who…cares?*

Mela urged Bet to get in her car, but Bet's grief spurred an electric wave of anger that she knew had to be released somewhere. *Might as well direct it where it's deserved.* "You go on. I'll follow you out."

Mela studied her a moment. "Don't..." She trailed off. Bet imagined half a dozen places that phrase was headed. But nothing Mela said would change her mind, and they both knew it. Mela got up, went to her car and headed out of the driveway.

Bet stood up slowly and wiped her face, irritated they'd caught her crying.

Rich got out of the car and hesitated. "Are you going now?"

"I'm in your way, is that it?"

"Bettina, you promised—"

She snapped, "Well, I'm sorry, Rich. It took longer than I expected because I'm physically impaired, right? Not like you didn't know. You could have stayed around and offered to help, but that was too much. So, I'm *sorry.*"

His face rippled through several emotions, but he ended by setting his jaw and crossing his arms. He gestured to her car.

Too bad the divorce is already entered. I might have come out ahead if I accidentally ran over him with my car...

"Let the kids say goodbye, at least."

He rolled his eyes, but he loosened up and knocked on the car window. "You kids, come say goodbye to your mom."

Jane and Jeremy clambered out of the car, dragging as only reluctant teenagers could. Rich put his hand on Jeremy's shoulder, stopping him for just a moment. They exchanged glances.

What was that about?

Bet didn't have time to ask. Jane slouched over and gave Bet a perfunctory hug. "We'll see you soon, Mom. Take care of yourself."

"Yes. That's all I get to do now." Bet regretted the words as soon as they came out. *This wasn't Janie's fault. Don't take it out on her.*

Jane's bottom lip quivered and she hurried into the house, slamming the door.

Jeremy came over and put his arms around Bet, holding on tightly. "Mom," was all he said.

She hugged him back, feeling like it was the last time. Surely, it wouldn't be. He would visit. Jane would visit. Maybe someday they could have a civil conversation over a huge ice cream sundae and three spoons.

I hope so.

Rich cleared his throat loudly and Jeremy slowly released her, then went inside. He watched her out the screen door.

She wanted to toss something up in Rich's concrete face, get a reaction out of him. Somehow, she wanted to know he still cared, even a little. But he'd give her nothing. He just stared.

Her heart breaking, she forced herself to walk to the car and get in it like it was just another day and she was headed to work. In her head, she heard Mela's voice, warning her to behave. She didn't care.

"Fuck you, Rich!" she yelled as she gunned the engine. She flipped him off, then sped away.

Chapter Twenty-Nine

July 7, 1996
Present Day

I always did get A's in moot court for my argument skills.

Bet managed to talk herself out of the hospital a full two days before the doctor had expected to release her. She promised him that she'd have around-the-clock observation, and that she'd be much more likely to rest in her own bed.

They probably just wanted me to stay because I'm a lawyer. In order to avoid a lawsuit, they'll order every test and provide every overreaching bit of care. But I can't stay here. It's not safe.

She called a taxi to drive her home. "I'll just be five minutes inside," she said. "I've got to go downtown after this."

"Your dime, lady." The cab driver turned off the car and sat back in the seat, eyes closed, to wait.

Dizzy as she walked up to the front door, she paused, leaning against its familiar panels. Inside her head, she put together a list of her immediate needs. When she felt more stable, she opened the door and went in.

Her first order of business was to check all the windows and doors to see if anyone had attempted—or succeeded—at getting inside while she was gone. To her relief, everything looked all right. She went to her bedroom and pulled a suitcase from the closet, filling it with assorted clothing, nothing fancy, all practical. Her makeup bag sat on the bathroom vanity; she grabbed it and tossed some earrings and bracelets in, then added it to the suitcase. Finally, she got the pistol from the bedside table drawer and tucked it in her purse.

I'm not going anywhere without this sucker until the whole mess is over.

Satisfied she'd brought enough to manage for several days, she went back out the front door, locking it behind her. No strange passersby on the street, which maybe meant she'd thrown whoever was dogging her off the trail with her unexpected release.

The cabbie saw her coming and climbed out to stash her bag in the trunk. "Where to?"

"The nearest convenience store."

He shrugged and opened the door for her, then got in and started driving. "Any one in particular? Quick-Mart? Stop-N-Go?"

"I don't care. Just pick one." Bet turned sideways in the seat, watching behind to see if anyone was following. *Doesn't seem to be.*

The cab pulled into the parking lot of a nearby store, and she directed him to park by the pay phone. She dropped several coins into the slot and dialed Mela's number. *I hope she'll answer even if she doesn't recognize the number.*

The phone rang multiple times, and finally it was answered. But not by Mela. The big, deep voice sounded like a man. "Yeah?"

"Who's this?" Bet demanded.

"Mom?"

"Jeremy?" Her nervous relief rolled over into a giggle. "How funny. Okay. Listen. Write down this number." She gave him the number of the pay phone. "Tell Mela to go to a pay phone somewhere nearby and call me back."

"Are you okay? Are you at home? Are—"

"Now, Jer. Call from an unknown number." She hung up.

It was the safest plan she could think of. As long as they weren't using their own phones, and no one was following her, she should be able to join them, wherever they were. She definitely did not want to be at home.

She waited for what seemed like interminable minutes for them to call back. Sweat dripped between her shoulder blades, and her legs hurt. For just a moment she wished she was back in the hospital with its regulated temperatures and regularly distributed drugs. The cabbie eyed her sharply through the windshield but didn't protest. *He was in nice air-conditioned comfort. What did he care? It was her money.*

Finally, the phone rang. She jumped, having been distracted by her train of thought. "Mela?" Bet asked.

"Yes. Where are you? Do you want us to come back?"

"No. I'm coming to you."

"Okay. We're at the airport Hilton. I'll leave a key for you at the front desk."

"See you soon."

The Hilton, was it? She hoped her credit card could take the hit. She returned to the car, and within half an hour, she was deposited at the front entrance of the hotel, less a substantial fare and an even more substantial tip.

She hurried inside.

When she came to the room, her reunion with the children was tender and tear-filled. The two sat with her on the bed, refusing to leave her side. *We missed so much. I'm not going to let this go, ever again. If Rich thinks he's getting them back, he's slipped a gear.*

"Okay, okay," she said aloud. "Give me a little room here, will you? You're setting off my bruises, kid."

Jane mock-scowled at her mother. "We can't let you out of our sight without you getting banged up. What do you expect us to do?"

Bet leaned over and kissed the girl on the forehead. "We're sorting it out, piece by piece. Believe me, when I come to a part that's your size, I'll invite you to it." She gave Jeremy a similar kiss, and sent them off to the video game room so she could get a nap. Even if she'd been in bed for days, she hadn't gotten any restorative sleep. No telling who'd walk into that hospital room. Mela was a trusted guard, and the four hours' rest Bet got that day was the best she'd had in weeks.

They spent another five days at the hotel, soaking up the sun on the pool deck, dining on whatever Mela went out to pick up. During that time, Bet located her car, which had been towed and apparently totaled by the insurance company. She checked on Giamo, who remained in intensive care. She did *not* contact Luis Ortiz. This would no doubt lead to some frantic moments on his end, but she didn't care. Her priority was staying safe until she knew where all the pieces had landed on her deadly chessboard.

Mela checked the office answering machine daily. She'd left an outgoing message saying that the practice would be closed for an indefinite period of time. It would, of course, leave some of the clients stranded, but since the initial incident, Bet had slowly disentangled herself from a number of her cases. Those clients would be free to retain new counsel. Some were glad enough to distance themselves from someone who clearly had a target on her back.

On the fifth day, while the kids were at the pool, Mela listened to the messages with a frown. "Bet, I think you need to hear this yourself."

"Is it John Lee?" she asked.

"No, it's Rich."

"Took him long enough." She swallowed some harsher things she wanted to say and took the phone.

"Bettina. I hope this message will reach you. I wasn't sure of your plans. I wanted you to know that I've installed a new security system at the Redlands house, so it will be safe to take the children…take Janie and Jeremy back there. I've made certain other arrangements…"

His voice sounded strained. Could it be he was crying?

"Well, you'll find out if you go back. I kept my word about holding you harmless from any of Lee's accusations. The children need a parent. The house is yours again. Hopefully you can move on."

The message ended abruptly.

She handed the phone back to Mela. "What the hell was that?"

"I was wondering the same. He says the house is yours."

"He sure did." She sat down on the bed. "What's he up to?"

"Maybe he's not up to anything. If he was a man,

he'd own up to all the crap he's put you through. This could be his way of doing that. Of saying he's sorry." Mela came and sat near her. "You don't really think it's a trap, do you?"

Bet considered what she heard. "I don't think so. He sounded genuinely upset. And if he was giving up that house, he sure as hell would be."

"Could you ask that Detective Ortiz to have the place checked out before you go in?"

"I probably could. But I won't. There might be evidence there. Who knows what kind of evidence— against Rich, or against us both, or maybe he's grown a stash of pot in the back forty. Even if some of the police are nice to us, we can still never trust them. Including Luis."

"Mmm." Mela nodded and checked her watch. "It's almost dinner time. You don't want to go out there at night, do you?"

Bet walked over to the little balcony overlooking the courtyard, watching the kids splash happily in the clear water. "No. Let's wait until morning. Even Scarlett O'Hara thought everything would be better tomorrow, right?"

****

Bet pulled into the drive, parking just where she'd parked the day she'd moved out. She remembered this because the revisiting of that awful day had kept her awake most of the night. She had worked so hard through therapy to ameliorate that memory, to force the closure she didn't feel she'd gotten, to integrate the pain into her life in a way that didn't flash hot red neon whenever she approached it.

But it still haunted her.

Can I ever live here again? Certainly not if Rich is going to be here. Why did he say the house was mine? And why didn't he leave me a number?

She'd tried to call Rich back; his cell phone and house phone were both disconnected. The staff at the office said they had no way to contact him.

Pam, who ran the front desk, had asked if Bet was going to sign paychecks. "No one's been paid since Rich was…ah, arrested. We all want to be team players here, and we know you've had a bad time. But…"

"Right. I'll see what I can do," Bet said.

Another fine mess you've left for me to clean up, Richard.

The kids climbed out of Bet's rental sedan. "Is it safe, Mom?" Jane asked.

Bet chewed her lip, then got out of the car, too. "I think so. Your father didn't say the locks were changed. Your keys should work."

Jane nodded. "All right." She went up the flat concrete steps and put her key in the lock. It turned, the door opened, and then all hell broke loose. The porch light started strobing and an alarm pierced the air. "What do I do now?"

Bet shook her head. Rich had to have considered this situation. "See if there's instructions inside!" she yelled, to be heard over the cacophony. She followed Jane in. A slip of paper was taped just to the right of the door frame next to a small keypad. Bet pointed, and Jane read it quickly and entered the code. The instant silence reverberated.

Mela and Jeremy inched inside as if they were afraid to start the clamor all over again. When it became apparent they would not, both relaxed. The teens went to their rooms. Mela put on a pot of coffee.

"So. Welcome home," she said.

Bet wasn't sure she felt either a welcome or like it was home, not after all the time it had taken to separate her from it. Maybe it would take just as long to work her way back in.

A white envelope lay in the middle of the kitchen table, contrasting against its red-and-white gingham cloth. "Bettina" was written on the front in stark black marker.

Bet picked it up. She showed Mela, who made a face. "I'm going to sit and read this," she said, nodding her head toward the back door.

"I'll bring you a cup when it's brewed."

"Thanks." Bet went through the kitchen door onto the back patio. She let herself down into the seat of the Adirondack chair with the soft red cushions, and closed her eyes, breathing a moment before she opened it.

This is where Rich and I agreed we'd divorce. Right here. When he lied. Remember, he lied.

Removing the single sheet inside, she opened her eyes and read it.

Bettina:

I hope you'll bring the children home. They deserve to grow up here. You and I worked very hard to build this place for us all. Maybe you and I didn't get the happy ever after we hoped for, but life has its ways, doesn't it?

I can't face the thought of 15 years behind bars, and so I've moved on. I've had Eddie Weiner draw up a new deed for the house, and a trust document that will pay you money enough to make the mortgage and care for the kids' needs every month. You won't hear from me again.

It's my understanding that John Lee is satisfied with the deal I made with the police, and he'll walk away. I left a written confession with the detectives detailing everything I did, and some things I didn't, but that I had to admit to get the deal. I made it very clear that you had no knowledge or part in it whatsoever. Hopefully they will accept that and leave you alone.

In the days since Delia's passing, it's become clear to me that I was the one who failed this marriage. When you had such trouble, and such pain, I should have tried harder to help you. Turning outside the marriage for respite didn't bring me the relief I hoped it would. It certainly didn't serve the spirit of our vows. I can't excuse what I did. But I have caused you enough pain, and I am sorry. All I want is for you and the children to live in peace from here on out.

Be strong, take care of the children, and carry on with your lives. Have fun once in a while, will you? And try not to think of me forever as the bad guy.

Rich

"Well."

Bet sat still as she could, listening to the insects in the trees. All the techniques Hyacinth had taught her to be "in the moment," to experience all she felt at once, went through her mind. She sensed the hard plastic under her relaxed arms, the lumpy padding of the cushions beneath her. She fixed her gaze on a passing cloud. First, it resembled a dragon, then a horse, and finally it dissipated into something unrecognizable.

Like Rich.

She had imagined many outcomes for this course of criminal action, but she would never have guessed he would take the coward's way out.

How could we have been married so long, and I still did not know this man?

She reread the letter. Rich seemed to believe that giving her the house and the children in retrospect, would make up for the pain and disappointment of the last several years. *I need so much more now. Will the house make me feel safe? Will the additional burden of the children just give me more to protect than I can handle? I'm not that woman any more, either.*

"No, I'm not," she said aloud. She sat up straight.

I'm a woman finally on the right path, who's discovered her "cure," who's survived some pretty heavy trauma, who's been gifted another chance to move forward. Who has her children back in her world. I did not become my mother.

She stood up. *A woman who's finally free of the man controlling her life.*

Letter still in hand, Bet walked into the house, past Mela's outstretched hand holding a cup of coffee, and into the living room. She climbed up on the sofa and pulled the cuckoo clock off the wall. Holding it in her hands for a few seconds, she wished all her anger and pain into it. Then she smashed it on the floor with a loud scream.

"Mom!" Jeremy burst into the living room, holding a tennis racket as his weapon. "What's… Are you all right?"

Mela and Jane followed on his heels, their faces pale and drawn.

"I'm fine," Bet said. "I need a broom, though."

They all stared at her. Finally, Jane said, "I always hated that thing."

"Me, too." Jeremy looked at his sister.

Mela shrugged. "Me, too."

They all looked at the mess on the floor. Someone started to giggle, Bet didn't know who. Pretty soon, they were all laughing. And crying. And laughing again. She stepped over the debris and walked over to wrap them in a group hug.

"We're going to be all right," she promised.

Chapter Thirty

July 27, 1996
Present Day

It was unusual to have an appointment on a Saturday morning, but that's the soonest Hyacinth had available, and Bet just wanted to get the business over with. So she took it.

She knocked several times before Hyacinth answered the door.

"I'm so sorry," the psychiatrist said. "I was on the phone, making some arrangements. Come in. We'll see what we can do to get you out of here quickly, so you and the children can enjoy this beautiful day."

"Sounds good." Bet came in and looked out the window at the blue sky above, the heavy traffic below. *The last time.*

Hyacinth met her at their usual seats with two short cups. "I brought a special new brew for our meeting," the doctor said. "Green tea, which as you know is best for your condition. It also has ginger, honey, turmeric—it's a little bitter. But it should help cleanse your system."

Bet took the warm cup and sniffed it. "Whoa. Strong."

"That's the ginger, I bet." Hyacinth smiled. "It's an acquired taste. But like I said, suited to your condition." She drank about half of what was in her cup and set it on the table. A clipboard lay next to it with a couple of pens and a stack of typed sheets. *The beginning of the end.*

Bet took a deep breath. "To you, my friend," she said, holding the cup in the air, honoring her companion. She drained the cup in three gulps, finding it bitter enough that she shuddered deeply, almost gagging. "Something tells me I won't acquire that taste any time soon."

Hyacinth continued to smile, loading the white sheets of paper into the clip. "All right. There are several of these to sign, so we should get started, right?"

Something troubled Bet about their conversation, but she couldn't identify it. It wasn't the tea. It was... "I'm sorry, did you say you knew about what was good for my 'condition'? What did you mean by that?"

"Your rheumatoid arthritis, of course." She held the clipboard out to Bet.

"Did I tell you about that when I called for this appointment?"

"Oh, no. Your doctor in Palm Beach told me. Dr. Bhatti." She continued to hold the clipboard.

Bet slowly took it, but her brain raced ahead. "I didn't tell you to contact her. What—"

"Bet, you signed consents for me to speak with your doctors the first time we met. Do you remember, to coordinate your care? She had much to say, and seemed very positive she could give you the good life you deserve." Hyacinth gestured. "So, if you sign those..."

"Right." Bet glanced over the top sheet, which seemed to be permission for the doctor to keep the file open for three years and then destroy it if no further action was taken by either of them. She signed it, then hesitated, something nagging at her mind. "When did I give you that doctor's name?"

"I'm sorry?" Hyacinth seemed confused. "You told me, last time you were here. You said you'd found a doctor to look into your diagnosis, and you thought she'd do you some good."

Did I tell her? I can't remember exactly. Especially after the accident. Details are hard to recall. Maybe I did.

But in her heart of hearts, she didn't think so. *I certainly didn't expect Hyacinth to call her.*

Puzzled, she flipped the first sheet over and went on to the next one. It was another form document absolving Dr. Hyacinth Martell of responsibility for any actions Bet might take now or in the future. "Do you think I'm dangerous?" She tried to laugh. "What's this about?"

"Well, Bet, you must admit that people around you seem to end up in terrible situations. I mean, that poor doctor from the ER, injured practically beyond recognition. Rich, arrested, and looking at a long jail sentence. Not to mention that incident in the Everglades. Horrible. At some point, if it was learned that I was counseling you during this time, someone might feel that suing me for their pain would be the thing to do. I just want to make sure I'm protected." She studied Bet, her eyes hard. "You know how lawyers are."

Neither of them had mentioned the burnt car for weeks. *Why now?*

"That's ridiculous. I'm not signing that. It's essentially an admission that I'm unstable. You've said yourself that I'm making great progress. We're here to close the case, right? You wouldn't do that if you thought I was a danger to myself or others. You'd Baker Act me."

"Commit you involuntarily?" Hyacinth shrugged

delicately and held out her hand. "Fine. Give me that paper and move on to the next."

Bet pulled the offending document from the stack and gave it back. The next paper addressed financial responsibilities, saying that she'd paid in full. Bet affixed her signature and moved on.

As she read the next several documents, her eyelids grew heavy. She rubbed them, wondering if she'd passed some blooming plant she might be allergic to on the way in.

"Is something wrong?" Hyacinth asked.

"No. Just the usual." She signed a couple more papers that seemed innocuous, but the feeling like heavy syrup pouring over and through her continued to grow. Her "condition" made her tired from time to time, and in a manner similar to this, but not in the mornings. *And certainly not on exciting occasions like finishing therapy…*

"It's a shame you had to take Richard down with you. He could have been just fine."

Bet blinked. "What?"

"But I have to admit, his troubles with John Lee opened so many doors. So many opportunities."

Bet put down the clipboard. Was her fatigue disguising what Hyacinth said? She'd missed conversations before, certainly. But she thought she was hearing this one. *It just didn't make any sense.*

"Rich? Is he involved with you, too?"

"Good heavens, no. This is between you and me, my *friend.*" She mockingly echoed Bet's toast.

Bet's breath caught, and she struggled a moment. "Then what are you talking about?"

"Just that knowing you were 'under the gun,' so to

speak, made it easy to join in. To puncture your windshield. To ruin your child's school day with a note. To copycat poor Delia's death."

Bet tried to right the suddenly spinning room, and failed. Her stomach roiled. She blinked her eyes a couple of times, but they kept closing, her eyelids weighted. "What…?"

Hyacinth sat perfectly straight, across from her, ankles crossed, ladylike. "Is something the matter?"

Bet forced her head to turn left, to see the mug on the table. Everything seemed to move in slow motion. "You. Did. Something."

"Actually, Bet, you're the one who did something. You killed my mother."

Bet struggled to focus. Her tongue felt thick as she spoke. "I don't even…know your mother."

"That's the sad part. She was a wonderful, loving, caring person. Much better than your mother. Much better mother than you were to your children. It's a crime, what happened to her."

"She was in an accident, right?" Bet pushed herself up, out of the chair, forcing herself to move around the room, to get her blood flowing. A wastebasket sat behind Hyacinth's desk, and Bet bent over it, her stomach rejecting whatever she'd drunk in a splattering mess. That didn't relieve her nausea, though.

"That's what the police said. It was an accident. But she was killed by a drunk driver. Do you know who that drunk driver was?"

Bet turned slowly to face the psychiatrist, her brain very belatedly piecing in the answer. "Jackson Gutierrez."

"Very good, Bet. Jackson Gutierrez."

"He didn't come to me…not after your mother was killed. I…" She pinched her arm, hard, hoping the pain would let her gain control of her slipping thoughts. "I hadn't seen him in years."

"But you got him off the first time. He could have been in jail, he could have gone to rehab, but you just got him a slap on the wrist. Then he was out in the world, free to destroy anyone he chose. And it was my mother!" Her voice had risen steadily until the last words were screamed. Hyacinth came to her feet.

Bet lurched toward the chair for her purse. Her phone. She had to call 911. Her heart raced. *Five things… Oh, screw that. Just…*

Hyacinth moved left to easily block her. "You know what the best part is? They'll think it was a suicide. All this Vicodin in your system. Eighteen pills, that's all it takes to kill someone. They say the acetaminophen gets you before the hydrocodone—weird, right?" Her blue eyes glittered with hatred. "Same outcome. I don't really care."

"But—"

"My brother's coming. He'll help me take you away. The kids will find you lying in the back yard…and they'll probably believe it was their fault, now that their father is out of the picture. Sharing trauma down through the generations." She yelled, "Georgie!"

Bet growled and groggily shoved her out of the way. "Like hell they will." She grabbed for the purse, stumbling into her favorite chair, bruising her knees. She hardly felt it. Picking up her bag, she stuck her right hand in but couldn't remember what she was going after.

The door opened and a big, burly bald man stepped in, then closed the door behind him. Through her blurring vision, Bet managed to recognize him. *The man from Old Lisbon.*

"I…I thought he was Kendrick," Bet mumbled.

"Kendrick? I'm afraid he's alligator food. Don't worry, I paid him your retainer first."

"You…what?" Bet's thoughts spun madly in circles. *Hyacinth? Hyacinth had killed Kendrick? And Gutierrez…*

And me?

The big man loomed closer, her slanted vision skewing him into an even more menacing monster. He came toward her, making her scrabble even harder in the cluttered bag. Her hand closed around the pistol grip. She let the purse slide to the floor, then forced her arm upward, pointing the weapon at him.

The man grinned and kept coming. "Now you be a good girl. I think I like you better when you're sleeping." He reached for the gun.

Through her fading awareness, Bet just knew she had to squeeze. *Squeeze. Squeeze. The instructor said squeeze.* She squeezed the grip but instinctively knew that was wrong. She shifted her finger to the trigger as Georgie's hand closed on the barrel.

SQUEEZE!

The pistol went off with a bang that reverberated in the room and through Bet's head. She lurched into the coffee table between the two chairs and fell, still holding the gun tightly. Pain registered, but at a distance. The next thing she noticed was Hyacinth screaming. The doctor ran to the big man, who'd fallen on the floor. He didn't move.

Bet didn't want to get up. A nice warm, comfortable sensation deeply entrenched itself in her body. She could finally relax after all the trouble of the past weeks…

But you can't, Bet.

Get your ass up, Bet.

BET!

Unhappy that someone inside wouldn't leave her alone, Bet grabbed the arm of the chair and painfully pulled herself upright. Hyacinth turned to her.

"You bitch! Not enough you took my mother? Now you kill my brother with your own hands? I was trying to be kind, but a drugged death isn't painful enough for you." She came running at Bet, her long nails curved like claws, reaching for Bet's face. She caught Bet leaning to the right, trying to keep her balance, and pushed her toward the windows.

Can I get killed falling from the second floor? Or will I get rabies from those claws first?

It didn't matter. When her head hit the glass, it hurt like hell. She tried to fight back, and found the gun still in her hand. As Hyacinth reached for it, Bet pulled the trigger. The barrel was pointed at the floor, and the bullet vanished.

Pick it up.

She jerked her arm upward and pulled the trigger again. A gush of blood spurted from Hyacinth's knee. Both women screamed.

Move. Phone. Move.

Bet had to fight to focus her eyes. *It won't be long now. I've got to make it happen. Right. This. Minute.* She kicked Hyacinth in the wounded knee and shoved past her, staggering and falling to the ground, her left hand almost on her purse.

Hyacinth came after her, and Bet barely rolled over to her back in time. Hyacinth landed flat on her, raising her fist in the air. Bet pointed the gun upward and fired. Hyacinth's hand fell, hitting Bet in the eye. Then her body just stilled, on top of Bet's.

Using her last bit of will, Bet pushed the dead weight off her. Her left hand grabbed the end of her purse's strap and yanked it close. She glanced over and saw Hyacinth, perfectly still, watching her. Her lips moved, but she made no sound. Perhaps two feet lay between them. Bet had to release the pistol to use the phone. Could she do it?

Not in front. Too close to Hyacinth. Not behind. In case brother wakes… Back in purse. Yeah. Back in purse.

She reached into her purse with her right hand and dropped the gun, picking up the phone instead. Pulling it close to her face, she dialed 911.

When the operator answered, Bet gave the address of the office, adding, "Send ambulance, maybe coroner. Gunshot victims. Intruder. Poisoned. Women lying…on floor…"

The operator asked her to stay on the line, but Bet's diminishing attention focused on something else. She hung up and speed-dialed her daughter, grateful she'd added that number at the hotel.

"Hello?"

"Janie. L-love you. And Jer. Be good."

"Mom? What the hell. Where are you? Are you all right?"

"L-love you. Baby."

"Mom?" Jane's voice register climbed. "No! Mom?"

The warm feeling sank in again, and this time Bet was too tired to fight it. Her hand dropped to the floor, and the phone slid from her limp fingers. Hyacinth's blue stare burned a path into Bet's consciousness as it faded into the shadows.

****

Bet woke up in the emergency room. Again. "God damn it."

She closed her eyes against the light, her bed enclosed by a blue curtain. She felt like she'd been roto-rootered. Her throat hurt, she had IVs stuck in her arm, and oxygen blowing full tilt up her nose.

"Dammit!" she said again.

The curtain flipped open and Jane's head popped in. "Mom? Oh, my God. Mom." She leaned out and yelled, "She's awake!"

Footsteps sounded, headed her way, and the curtain was opened. Jeremy and Jane, Mela and…was that Giamo? In a wheelchair?

I must be hallucinating.

A nurse wheeled her way through the group, fussing with the machinery and checking Bet's pulse. She smiled at Bet and left again, and a tech came in with a vampire tray. Bet eyed her with hostility.

The tech smiled, too.

All these people were too fucking happy.

"I just have to draw a little blood to test your blood gases." The woman went for her wrist, and Bet pulled her arm back.

"Wait, what? Why there?"

Giamo—for it was indeed he—leaned forward to intercede. He was bandaged and had a cast on both his arm and his leg. "They need arterial blood for that, Bet. The wrist is the best place for someone in the ER."

"What are you doing here?" She relaxed the best she

could, still anxious, and focused on her doctor friend while the painful draw was done.

"The question is, what are you doing here? I, at least, have an excuse."

"I'm so sorry about what happened to you. It was my psychiatrist. She's a lunatic. She and her brother…tried to kill me? You? Us?" Bet frowned as the pieces started fitting together. "Everyone? For real this time?"

The sound of a clearing throat sounded by the curtain's edge and she looked over to see Luis Ortiz, jacketless, in his shirt sleeves, but with a tie.

"Oh, hail, hail, the gang's all here," she muttered.

He chuckled. "Come on, Bet, what would the police have to do all day if you didn't keep getting in trouble?"

Mela told the kids they'd better step aside and let the detective speak to Bet.

"But you come right back, will you?" Bet demanded.

"Of course, Mom," Jeremy said. "We're a team, remember?"

They slipped out.

Ortiz stepped close to the bed. "I had no idea you carried."

"Hell, yes, I carry. People are trying to…" She eyed him. "Are they dead?"

He shook his head. "If you really want to be able to protect yourself, you'd better come to the range with me. I'll whip your aim into shape."

"So, what now?"

"The big man—that's apparently the man from the video."

"Yes. Hyacinth's brother George. And that's her in

the video. In a wig." Even if the doctor hadn't confessed it, in her gut Bet knew it to be true. "They must have spoken Spanish to throw me off. And it worked." She scowled, thinking how she'd been duped by the siblings.

She shared what Hyacinth had confessed in her office. "I was sure...I mean, enough Vicodin will do someone in..."

Giamo interjected, "Apparently your tolerance is higher than average, after your years of use. You got rid of some of it. Add in a dose of an opioid antagonist, and a stomach lavage..."

So that's why I feel like that. Ugh.

"So, you're going to be okay?" she asked Giamo. "If my insurance doesn't cover your treatment—"

Ortiz said, "I expect that will be part of the restitution expenses assigned to Dr. Martell and her brother. That one's going to be a long list."

Giamo nodded. "And I got a bonus of sorts."

"What's that?" Bet asked.

"I asked my physical therapist to go out. She said yes." He grinned.

"You meet the nicest people in the hospital, yeah?" Bet relaxed her shoulders and looked up at the ceiling.

"Sure. Well, I should head back up to my room. They only gave me a short pass because the detective said you were here."

"Thanks for coming. And I'm happy about your new date." Bet squeezed his hand, then an orderly appeared to roll him away.

"Nice guy," Ortiz said.

"He is. He deserves a nice girl. I'm glad he met one."

"You're a nice girl. Woman. Um, lawyer."

Bet studied him. "Thanks. I think." She yawned.

"So, is this over? They're going to be charged? I can finally relax a little?"

"Seems so. And I meant that about teaching you to shoot better. I mean, you're not going to continue the criminal law practice, right? So, there wouldn't be any conflict of interest if…"

She realized his not-so-subtle intention and snorted. "I won't be continuing the criminal law practice. Right. Not my crowd."

"Glad to hear it." He practically wriggled like an excited puppy. "All right. I'd better go file this report. I'll send your kids back in." He paused. "They seem like good, solid citizens. I like 'em."

"So do I. I'll see you later, Luis."

He smiled and left. The children came in with the doctor, who said she'd have to stay another few hours to make sure her system had cleared the medication, but that she'd be all right and could go home then.

"Perfect," Bet said. "Thank you."

After the doctor left, Jane sat on the edge of the bed. "Hey, Mom, Jer and I have been talking, and we think you should sell the house. Sell both houses."

"What?"

"Yeah," Jeremy chimed in. "Let's get a new house, that's just for us."

"And a dog," Jane added. "Maybe horses?"

"Horses! Geez, girl, do I look like Annie Oakley? Maybe you can have a goldfish."

"Mom!" they whined in stereo.

Yes, it was going to be a new life altogether. A new family, a new house, a new…firearms instructor? She smiled. She didn't have to feel inadequate as a mother or anything else any more. First day of the rest of her life and all that bad motivation calendar crap. But it could be great. It would. She'd make it that way.

"Okay. Maybe a hamster."

A word about the author…

Alana Lorens dreamed for many years of finding her very own knight on a white steed, or perhaps being one herself. Instead she settles for flights of fancy, inspired excursions into fictional places with fascinating companions from her imagination that she likes to share with others. She has been a published writer for over forty years, including seven years as a reporter and editor at a newspaper in Homestead, Florida. Her list of publications is eclectic, from science fiction to romance to horror, from tech reporting to television reviews, and a blog about autism, a journey she shares with other parents of special needs children. Alana has retired from her life as a family law attorney, and now lives as a post-modern hippie in Asheville, North Carolina. www.alana-lorens.com